# Bedside Manner

By

Writers Anonymous

Published 2008 by arima publishing

www.arimapublishing.com

ISBN 978 1 84549 307 3

© Writers Anonymous 2008

All rights reserved

This book is copyright. Subject to statutory exception and to provisions of relevant collective licensing agreements, no part of this publication may be reproduced, stored in a retrieval system, or transmitted in any form or by any means, without the prior written permission of the author.

Printed and bound in the United Kingdom

Typeset in Perpetua 12/14

This book is sold subject to the conditions that it shall not, by way of trade or otherwise, be lent, re-sold, hired out, or otherwise circulated without the publisher's prior consent in any form of binding or cover other than that which it is published and without a similar condition including this condition being imposed on the subsequent purchaser.

In this work of fiction, the characters, places and events are either the product of the author's imagination or they are used entirely fictitiously. Any resemblance to actual persons, living or dead, is purely coincidental.

Swirl is an imprint of arima publishing.

arima publishing
ASK House, Northgate Avenue
Bury St Edmunds, Suffolk IP32 6BB
t: (+44) 01284 700321

www.arimapublishing.com

Cover photography by Terry Withers
Cover design by Simon Woodward

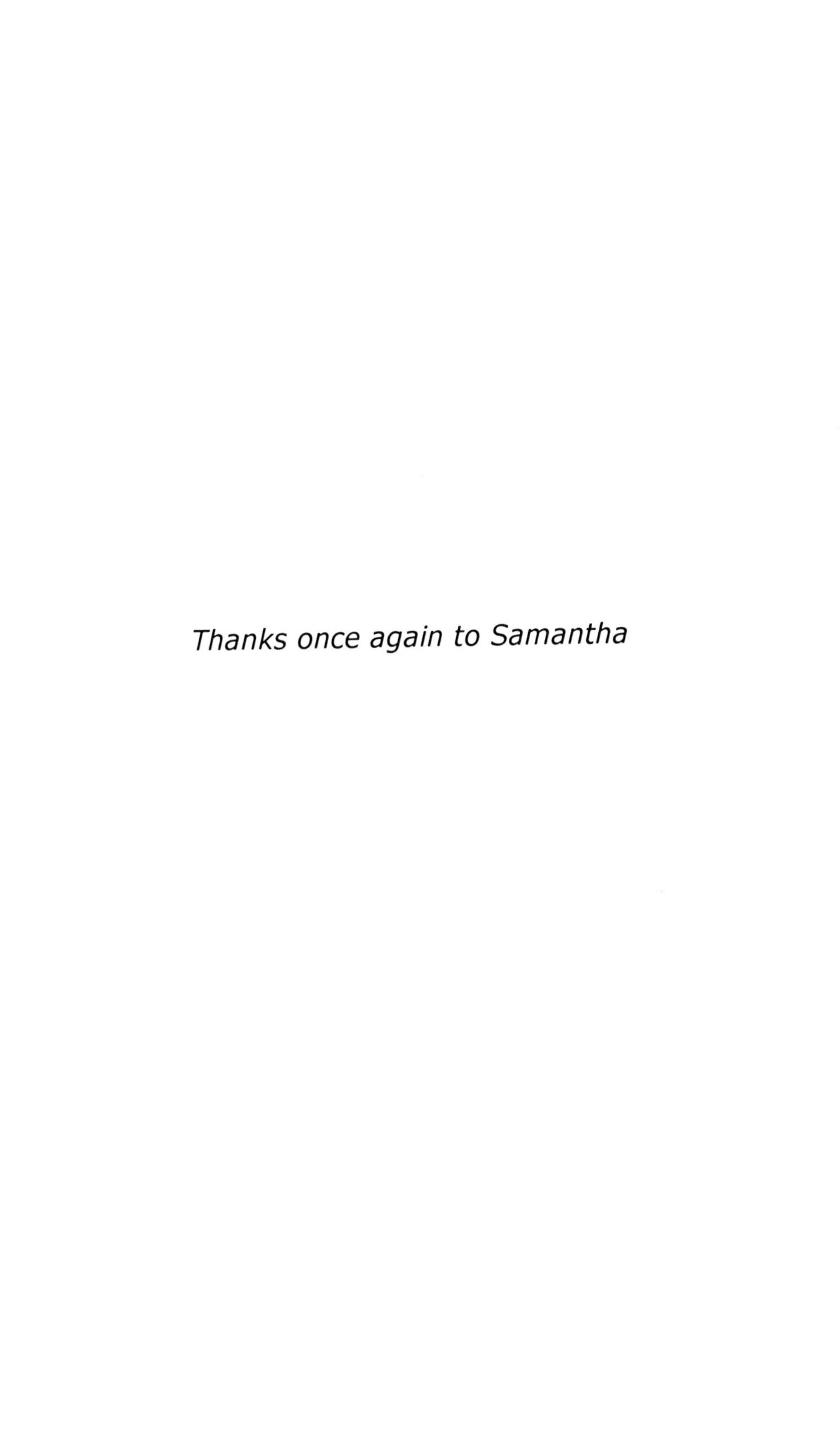

*Thanks once again to Samantha*

## Contents

# Bedside Manner

By Colin Butler

The doctor has a bedside manner
To treat all his patients, young and old
To hold aloft the Hippocratic banner
Even in the red-tape ridden NHS

A lover must soon learn to acquire
A bedside manner, to woo his love
Cajoling, seducing, inspiring desire
With words and songs and many gifts

The Bluebeard has a special manner
By the bedside to seduce his prey
To acquire money, jewellery and a manor
Sometimes killing to gain his goals

The hospital visitor by the bedside
Bringing the patient grapes and flowers
Trying to maintain a calm outside
Whilst making small talk to pass the time

At the last the doctor and the priest
Employ their special bedside manner
Pronouncing the last rites as the deceased
Departs for a far-off unknown shore

# Baffled in Brighton

By Nicolette Coleman

The train rattled its way past the backs of houses. Peering into back gardens, wondering how other people lived their lives, I smiled at Lawrence as the motion of the train made him fall against me for a moment, and he reached over and squeezed my hand. I was pleased. He did not normally go in for public displays of affection, although I would have been happy for him to hug and kiss me in public. We had been married for 10 years that weekend, and I loved him as much as ever. We rarely got a chance to be together without the children, so when my mother had surprised us with an offer to have the children while we went away to celebrate our anniversary I had been thrilled. Two and a half days of just the two of us! It was almost as good as another honeymoon. Our honeymoon had been 5 days in Margate, two weeks after VE day. Lawrence had been on leave when the war ended, so we celebrated by getting married on a special licence. Margate had been rainy and cool, but we didn't mind, spending hours huddled under the blankets in the room of our guest house, forgetting to go and eat breakfast so often that the landlady offered us a discount at the end of our stay. I wondered if this holiday would be at all like that one. At least the weather was shaping up to be a bit warmer. May was the kind of month when you could expect any kind of weather, from hot sunshine to snow or sleet.

I had never been to Brighton before, and was looking forward to visiting the pier and exploring the town and shops. I had treated myself to a new costume for the journey, and was feeling very chic in my dove grey suit and hat. I had pinned a silk flower to the lapel of my jacket, and it was almost the same shade of pink as my blouse. With Lawrence in his best suit, I felt we made a handsome couple, befitting our room in a hotel, rather than a guest-house.

On arrival in Brighton, Lawrence splashed out and hired a taxi to take us to the hotel, rather than the bus I had been expecting. The taxi took us through the town and down towards the seafront, where we could see the sun shimmering on the green sea. I felt as excited as a small child at the sight of the pier and the sand. The hotel we were visiting was right on the seafront, its frontage looking out over the water. In the reception area I felt slightly out of place, almost as if I had no right to be here with this handsome man. Lawrence took charge of booking us in, and we were shown to our room. Unfortunately we were not given a room overlooking the sea, but it was lovely nonetheless, with a large bed with a pretty blue coverlet, which matched the curtains. I looked around me, opening wardrobes to peer inside at the padded coat hangers.

"Are you ready for lunch?" Lawrence asked, once we had unpacked, "There is a restaurant downstairs. Perhaps we could eat there then go for a walk?"

"Oh yes! I'm famished!" I replied.

In the restaurant we ate a lovely luncheon and drank a cup of tea before setting out for our walk. As we left the restaurant a large sign caught my eye.

> *'Tonight, for one night only, Miss Amelia Lytton-Gore, hypnotist to the stars.'*

Fascinated I walked closer. The sign was hung on a door with 'Theatre' marked on it. Miss Lytton-Gore was appearing here at 7:30 this evening. I felt an irrational urge to attend and see this hypnotist. I smiled at Lawrence.

"Shall we come here tonight to see her?"

"It is hardly our kind of thing, Jane," he replied, his brow crinkled. "Why on earth would you want to see such a performance? Neither of us believes in such nonsense."

"I know. Isn't that half the fun of it though? It might be amusing for a while."

By the time we had reached the promenade, Lawrence had agreed to give it a go. I slipped my arm through his and we commenced our walk. The weather was bright and breezy, and we had to hold on to our hats as we went. Lawrence took my hand in his and began running down the pebbled beach, pulling me, laughing, in his wake. He ran full pelt towards the water, and I was concerned that he might pull me in, ruining my best shoes in the process, but he pulled to a halt just before the water's edge. He stood there laughing down at me, and my heart skipped a beat. He looked just like the young soldier I had fallen in love with such a long while ago. Impulsively I threw my arms around him, resting my head on his shoulder. He held me tightly to him, kissing the top of my head, and I was unable to look up for a moment, as my eyes brimmed with tears. We stood like that for some minutes, and my heart thrilled with love for this husband of mine.

Eventually Lawrence pulled away, and headed up the beach, my hand tucked cosily inside his.

We spent a lovely, lazy afternoon roaming the town and the lanes of Brighton, stopping for a cup of tea in a charming little tea room and returning to the hotel late in the afternoon, laden with parcels.

We ate our dinner in the formal dining room, returning to our room in time to change before the evening's big event. I ran myself a bath, throwing in a large handful of the bath salts the hotel had provided. I wallowed in the hot fragrant water until I found myself becoming drowsy, at which point I decided I ought to start getting dressed, otherwise I would never make it to the theatre downstairs. Back in the bedroom I chose my outfit carefully, wanting to look smart for the occasion, although I was not sure why it mattered. Walking around in my slip I became aware of Lawrence's eyes on me. Turning around I smiled at him, asking; "What? Why are you looking at me like that?"

He walked towards me, reaching out to touch my arms. Gooseflesh bumped along my flesh as he ran his fingers lightly up and down my arm. He pulled me to him, kissing my neck, sending shivers up and down my spine.

We were, therefore, somewhat late to the theatre and missed the hotel manager's announcement of Miss Lytton-Gore. As we were seating ourselves at the back of the hall a very short lady appeared out of the wings of the stage, paused for a moment, then descended the steps to stand in front of the audience, but on our level. I looked at her with some surprise. She was not at all what I had expected; being squat and plump, and not dressed in the outrageous garb I had imagined she would wear. She wore a calf-length tweed skirt, a rather ghastly green twin-set, and of all things a clerical collar. I stared, amazed, at this vision of unloveliness. Tension was coming from Lawrence's arm, close to my side, in fluttering waves.

Miss Lytton-Gore raised her arms, looking straight at her audience. "Good evening Ladies and gentlemen" she began, "Tonight I wish to teach you about the powers of the mind." She looked around the room, nodding a little before continuing; "May I ask you all to look straight at me for a few moments." And she stood, terribly still, looking back at us all. The room was hushed, with hardly a murmur or a rustle from anybody. I am not terribly tall myself, although slightly loftier than Miss Lytton-Gore, and I was having trouble seeing her through the surprisingly large number of people in front of me. I craned my neck for a better view, twisting to see around the wide shoulders of the man in front of me. As I caught a glimpse of the lady, a man at the very front of the room rose up and walked towards the theatre door, closely followed by a lady two seats to his right. "How very rude,"

I thought to myself, and turned to say as much to Lawrence. I felt a tightening in my throat to see that Lawrence was looking down at me with a stricken expression, tears swimming in his eyes.

"Whatever is it, my dear?" I asked him, reaching out to touch his trembling arm.

"I don't want to leave you Jane," he said, his voice hoarse and wobbly.

"Leave me? Well don't then," I replied, unsure as to what he meant. But Lawrence began to walk towards the door, one arm stretched out towards me, tears coursing down his cheeks. As I watched him go I realised that most of the audience were also leaving the room, and I was unable to get to Lawrence for the crush of people between us.

Feeling shaken I turned my attention to the front of the auditorium, I blinked. There were only three other people remaining in the room, apart from Miss Lytton-Gore, who now smiled and raised her arms again. "There you have it. The powers of the mind have caused your friends to leave the auditorium. Just by looking into my face they have been compelled to leave the room and go to the bar." She continued in this vein for a few moments more, before asking if somebody would go to the bar and ask the others to return.

A tall and exceedingly ugly man stood up and made his way to the door. I hurried after him, anxious to find Lawrence. The theatre was housed in the basement of the hotel, and to reach to upper floors we had to go along a rather bizarre corridor, lined with some kind of bronzed metal. We quickly headed to the bar, where the tall man pushed open the door. Inside the bar was empty – even the barkeeper had disappeared. The tall man turned to me; "Where the devil are they all?" he asked. I shook my head. I was beginning to feel afraid. "I shall check our bedroom, to see if my husband has returned there," I said, and hurried towards the stairs, the man following closely behind me.

At the door to our bedroom I paused for a moment, my hand to my chest to try and still the palpitating of my heart, before opening the door. I was terrified about what I might see in the chamber, but all I discovered was another empty room. As I turned back towards the stairs, the tall man reappeared, a frown creasing his brow. "I must admit, dear lady, that I am beginning to feel a little perturbed."

We walked slowly back down towards the auditorium, musing on the whereabouts of the others. On re-entering the theatre, we discovered that Miss Lytton-Gore and the two remaining members of the audience had now disappeared as well. The tall man hallooed a little, but, on receiving no response, we hurried back to the hotel foyer. The tall man pushed open the door to the promenade and leaned out for a moment, before turning back to me.

"Do have a look at this, my dear," he said, ushering me towards the door. I looked outside, turning my head to left and right. The whole seafront was deserted, the only movement a leaf blowing along the path. Even the birds were silent.
Coldness crept over me. Where had everybody gone? How was I to find my Lawrence again? I turned to look at the tall man, to find that his eyes were brimming with unshed tears, his chin wobbling.

I opened my mouth, preparing to ask a question, but he shook his head at me, taking a deep breath and steadying himself before speaking.

"My wife," he managed at last. "My dear wife, Pauline, went out with the others. I truly don't think I can bear to be without her, not to know where she is. It is so unlike her to have left me behind. Usually she would not go anywhere without me. A very shy lady, don't you know."

I found myself nodding as he spoke. Lawrence was also not in the habit of leaving me in strange places, and I felt cold panic inching its way through my stomach. I wanted to run outside and find Lawrence, but had no idea of where to begin.

"What should we do?" I asked, "Where could they be? Shall we telephone for the police?" I realised that I was prattling on, in what was probably an annoying way, and took a hold of myself.

"Perhaps we should first of all introduce ourselves," the tall man said. "I am William Barnes. And you?"

"Jane Elliott. My husband is Lawrence. Lawrence Elliott."

"Pleased to meet you. May I call you Jane? It seems we may be in a predicament here, and Mrs. Elliott seems a trifle severe in the circumstances."

"Yes, of course you may, if I may call you William." We smiled at each other cautiously. "Umm, William? Do you think we should telephone for the police? Perhaps they might be able to shed some light on what has happened."

"Good idea." William looked around the foyer until he found the public telephone on the wall next to the restaurant. We walked towards it, William all the while searching in his pockets for change. He lifted the handset of the telephone, then jiggled the button, looking perplexed.

"This telephone does not seem to be working," he said, replacing the receiver. "One would have thought they would have placed a notice explaining it is out of order. I wonder where we can telephone from." We looked around the foyer, then the bar, but could see no other public telephone. William began to walk towards the door of the manager's office. He knocked on the door twice, but when there was no reply, he turned the handle and entered the room. I found myself wondering what we would have done had the manager answered the door. It would seem such a natural thing to happen, but in the circumstances so peculiar.

Inside the office there was a large walnut desk, on the top of which stood a telephone. William strode towards it and lifted the receiver, only to find that this telephone was also out of order. I began to feel very afraid now. Had all the town telephonists disappeared, along with everybody from the hotel?

"I do believe that the local police station is not far away, in the town itself," William said. "But I do think it is too late to go there tonight. We cannot telephone for a taxi to take us there, and I don't feel it is wise to walk there in the dark." He looked at his watch. "My goodness! It is almost midnight! I know it is difficult, but perhaps we ought to try to get some sleep, and we can go to the police station in the morning." He looked at my face, which I could feel was beginning to crumple. "Of course, I am sure our dear ones will have returned before then. Why! I am sure they will return from wherever they are hiding while we are in our bedrooms." He smiled kindly at me, and I appreciated the sentiment. We walked slowly towards the stairs.

"Which floor is your room on?" I asked.

"Fourth. And yours?"

"Oh! Fourth also! Thank goodness, I didn't fancy being the only person on the floor. Our room number is 425."

"Ours is 430, so we are not too far away. If anything untoward should frighten you during the night, do feel free to knock on my door."

"Thank you William. Shall we meet downstairs in the foyer at, say, 8:30? We can find something to have for breakfast if the staff have not reappeared by then."

"Good idea." We had by now reached my room. "Goodnight Jane. Do try to get some rest."

"Goodnight William." I opened the door to my room slowly, hoping, oh hoping, that Lawrence would be there, sitting in the blue chair by the window, smiling at me and asking where I thought I had been for so long. But the lights were off in the room, and when I reached out and switched them on, the room was empty of Lawrence. He was not in the chair, nor in the bed, and the room was colder for it.

I sat down on the bed, tears welling in my eyes, my throat constricting. "Where are you Lawrence?" I whispered into the emptiness. I lifted Lawrence's jumper from the chair where he had left it earlier, hugging it to me where I could smell his dear, familiar smell. Tears poured from my eyes, wetting the wool, and I pressed the jumper to my mouth so that no sound would come out.

Eventually the tears began to slow, and I dared to get undressed and slip into bed. There was a cold space next to me, where Lawrence would have slept. Unable to relax enough to sleep I sat up in the bed, switching on the light on the bedside table. I had brought a book with me, in case of quiet moments, and I now opened it, trying to find something to busy my mind. This was a book of poetry my mother had given me for my last birthday, and I had read a few of the poems already. Leafing through the book my eye was caught by a passage:

*Just one step back outside my skin*
*I look down on my life within,*
*I breathe a sigh and all release,*
*At bedside now I rest in peace*

My eyes stung, and I clasped the book to my chest. Oh, where was Lawrence? And where were all the other people in this town? If only I could rest in peace. I longed to sleep, to wake in the bright morning light to find Lawrence asleep beside me. I lay down again, Lawrence's jumper next to me on the pillow, and tried every trick I knew to make my mind relax. Counting sheep was no good, as I found myself looking past them to see if Lawrence was in the field. Eventually, however, physical exhaustion must have overtaken me, and I fell into a restless sleep, where I dreamed of Lawrence opening the bedroom door and asking me where I had been all evening.

The dream was beautifully real, and I awoke to find sunlight streaming through the gap in the curtains. I could smell Lawrence's clean linen smell next to me in the bed, and I turned to him, ready to laugh off the experiences of the previous night. But the pillow beside me was empty, save for Lawrence's jumper. I looked around me, dread stealing upon me once more, as I realised that last night had been real.

Slowly I dressed and descended the stairs to the foyer, hoping against hope that there would be people around, milling about as they do in busy hotels. But the foyer was as empty as it had been the preceding evening. I walked to the front door, stepping quietly over the parquet flooring, and peered out into the street. All was as bare as yesterday, the only change the strength of the sun.

"Good morning," a voice said quietly, making me start. I turned around to find William Barnes looking down at me, his strained face looking as mine felt. "No change then?" He asked, and I shook my head mutely.

Without speaking we made our way to the dining room, with its un-set tables, and from there through a green baize door into a large, clean kitchen. I opened the gleaming refrigerator and located a carton of eggs and a pack of bacon. By the time I had closed the fridge door William had lit the gas under a large frying pan. We set about making breakfast, and carried it through to the dining room, where we sat and made a show of trying to eat. The food stuck in my throat, catching on some lump which had appeared overnight. The only thing I felt able to swallow was the tea, of which I drank two cups. I gave up the struggle and laid down my cutlery, just as William did the same. Looking at his plate, I could see that he was having the same difficulty as me. I smiled sadly at him.

"What should we do now, William?" I asked. "Should we try to find the police station?"

William nodded, and we took our plates to the kitchen, washed them and left them to drain, before collecting our coats and meeting again in the foyer. I couldn't believe that nobody else had emerged during this time. I had been expecting somebody to materialise while we were cooking and ask what we were doing in the hotel kitchen.

William and I walked along the front, heading towards the town. The day was beautiful, bright and sunny, and much warmer than yesterday. I wished so much that I was walking there with Lawrence, as I should, by rights, be doing today. I took a deep breath, to steady myself.

The nearer we got to the town the worse my trepidation became. The whole area was silent, apart from the washing of the waves on the shore. We did not see one person on our walk, and as we came closer to the police station, moving past empty, hushed shops, I slowed my steps. William stopped and turned to look at me.

"Is there a problem?" he asked.

I started to laugh, a little wildly. "Apart from the fact that we appear to be the only people left in the world you mean?"

William smiled a little at that. "I wondered why you had stopped walking."

"I'm afraid. There is nobody here in town. We have seen not a soul on our walk. What if there is nobody in the police station?"

"Oh, I'm sure there will be. British Bobbies are the best you know. They will know what is going on and will help to get things sorted out."

I envied him his simplistic view, but followed him up the path to the police station. The blue light was lit over the double doors, and it gave me a small lift of hope. William opened the right-hand door and entered the building, holding the door open for me to follow. Inside was the usual counter, with a few chairs against the wall. The lift-up part of the counter was raised, but there was nobody in sight. We stood by the desk for a moment, then

William rapped his knuckles on the counter, calling out; "Hello?" Silence greeted us. We waited a few moments more, and William again called; "Hello? Anybody here?" The silence echoed around us, and I shivered, despite the close warmth of the day.

After a few moments more, William walked through the raised counter, calling still as he went. He disappeared through the doorway to the back of the station, where I imagined there to be cells full of murderers and bank robbers. I rubbed my arms, hoping that William would not now disappear too, but too afraid to follow him into the silent rooms beyond. I could still hear his voice from time to time, and then he reappeared, shaking his head.

"No idea what's going on Jane. I would have thought there would be people here at least, but there's no one at all. Even the cells are empty."

I shuddered at the thought of those cells. My heart had become a heavy rock in my chest, and I wanted, more than anything, to sit down and cry. I realised that I had been holding out a great hope that we would find a jolly policeman to tell us not to worry, that he would put everything straight for us. Looking at William's strained face I knew he had had the same hope. I went and sat down on one of the chairs, and William came and joined me.

"What now?" He asked, looking down at the floor. "What the heck do we do now?"

I shook my head. I had absolutely no idea what we could do, but we couldn't sit here in the police station and do nothing.

"Let's head back to the hotel," I suggested. At least we know that, if our loved ones reappear, that is where they will head for.

We began our dejected walk back towards the seafront, not talking. I kept an eye out for any signs of life, constantly thinking that I could see movement out of the corners of my eyes, and turning my head quickly in order to see what always turned out to be nothing more than bunting flapping in the wind, or an abandoned newspaper fluttering along the pavement.

We had almost reached the promenade when William stopped, his head cocked as though listening. I stopped too, looking at him with raised eyebrows. When he said nothing, but continued to stand like that I asked; "What is it? Have you heard something?"

William nodded. "Listen. Can you hear that strange humming sound? I think it is coming from the direction of those hills to the right."

I listened, and became aware of a low humming, and that the ground was vibrating slightly below my feet. The electricity to the town was still working, and I wondered if it was a large generator running somewhere behind the town. When I suggested this to William he shook his head.

"It is too loud and deep for that. I don't know. Shall we walk in that direction and see if we can work out what it is?"

My mouth felt suddenly too dry, and I swallowed, rather loudly, but nodded all the same. What else was there for us to do? We began to walk towards the hills. The ground became steeper as we went and I found it harder to keep up with William and his long legs. I was soon quite out of puff, and called to William, asking him to slow down a bit.

"I am sorry," he said, stopping and waiting for me. "I tend to forget how much longer my legs are than other people's. Shall we have a rest for a moment?"

I nodded, conserving my breath. There was a bench to our left and we made our way over to it and sat down. I longed for a cup of tea or a glass of water, but could see nowhere we could get one, so felt there was no point in mentioning it. We sat for a while as I got my breath back. I took my shoes off and rubbed my feet. I had rather foolishly worn my new brown court shoes for this expedition. I think I had hoped to look smart for the police, although of course that had turned out to be a pointless exercise.

While I rubbed my feet I gazed into the distance, out towards the sea, which glimmered in the sunshine. There were no boats on the water. The clouds in the sky sat still above the waves, and we could have been the only people left in the world. I fought down panic at the thought, concentrating on the way the sea moved up and down and the waves moved against the pier. Suddenly I stood up, shading my eyes with my hand.

"William!" I called, "Look at the sea. Do you see anything odd about it?"

"Apart from the fact that there are no boats, on it, no." he said after a pause, but then; "Oh! Jane! The tide appears to be washing sideways, rather than in to shore!"

"Yes. That's what I noticed too. What on earth could have caused it to do that?"

"I have no idea. The tide is to do with the moon I believe. Could there have been a strange lunar eclipse of some kind? Which would somehow explain our spouse's disappearances?"

"And everyone else's? Oh, I don't know! I don't understand anything any more. I feel so scared and confused, and I so wish Lawrence was here!"

William reached over and rather awkwardly patted my hand. I took a deep breath, determined not to embarrass us both by crying.

"Come on," I said, falsely hearty, "might as well keep on slogging on up the hill and see what's at the top!"

We walked on, trudging our way upwards and onwards. The hill became steeper for a time, but thankfully began to level out before we reached the top. We walked in silence, and I was reminded that I really did not know this man striding along with me. At the thought I began to feel shy. I hoped we would soon find other people so that William and I were not left alone together in a false kind of intimacy.

Finally we reached the summit, and paused to look around. The humming was louder up here, and, as if pulled magnetically, we walked in the direction of the vibration. There were many trees up here, and it was impossible to see what we were walking towards. William strode ahead, every so often pausing for me to catch up. The path led between the trees, shading us from the sun, and as we rounded a bend in the path we saw before us a large squat concrete building. We stopped in our tracks and stared at the ugly structure. The humming was most definitely coming from there. The very air seemed to vibrate and buzz around us. As we neared the building, I found myself reaching for William's arm, slipping my hand through his elbow as surreptitiously as possible. We moved towards this strange edifice, saying nothing, progressing slowly, our steps hesitant and quiet. We reached the corner of the building, and I tentatively reached out my hand to touch the wall. It looked like concrete, grey and nubbly, but to my fingers it had the texture of something not quite solid, damp, but dusty at the same time. I don't think there is a word to describe the feel of it, and I gave a little cry, pulling my hand quickly away. William watched me, then reached his own large hand out to touch, but promptly removed it, a look of horror on his face.

We continued around the place, searching for a door. I noticed a complete lack of windows, although the humming seemed stronger in some places than others. As we arrived at the next corner, William hesitated before cautiously peering around, then pulling his head back.

"There's something, a kind of door, at the far end," he said. "Shall we go and knock?" I nodded, too afraid to speak. I really did not want to knock on the door of this strange structure, but it seemed the only option open to us.

We walked slowly towards the end of the building. William was right; it was a kind of door, unlike any I had previously seen. To my mind, a door should be wooden, painted blue or green, with a window at the top. Or, perhaps in a very modern hotel, it would be all glass. But this was, well, it is hard to describe.

Imagine, if you will, a metal gate, with something resembling plastic between the pieces of metal. It was a curious pink colour, and appeared to shimmer with the vibrations. As we drew level with it, William reached out and knocked on the door. Or that is what he intended to do. As he rapped at it, the door seemed to absorb his hand for a moment, and he quickly drew back. My knees had completely turned to jelly, and I was afraid they would not hold my weight for much longer. I gripped tighter to William's elbow, and he, absent-mindedly, patted my hand.

We stood looking at the door for a moment. I felt that if we had no luck here we had no recourse to any other help. For I was sure there was somebody here. All around us, in the town and at the seafront, there was silence, as if the whole world had fallen asleep. No motor cars went by. No music issued from the coffee bars. Nothing. But here, something buzzed with life. There had to be help here. There simply had to.

William looked around, then leant forwards, feeling around the door with his fingertips.

"Aha!" he said, "Perhaps this is a doorbell?" and when I looked I saw a tiny depression in the wall of the building. William pressed his finger into it, and, all at once, a ringing sound filled the air, as if dozens of tiny bells were ringing. I was enchanted, and, for just a moment, felt happy and peaceful. Until the door slid open, and we were face-to-face with the strangest looking man I think I had ever seen. His hair stood on end, rather like a mad professor, but it was an unusual shade of bluish-grey. His eyes were huge and boggled at us, above a large bulbous nose. His mouth did not look as though it was used to smiling.

We looked at him, and he looked at us. Finally William spoke;

"Hello. We are so pleased to find somebody here. We have been staying in the Willows Hotel on the seafront, but last night a strange thing occurred, and everybody in the hotel disappeared. We came out today and there is nobody at all in the town. We thought we must be the last people left alive." He gave an embarrassed laugh as he finished speaking. We waited for the man to speak, but he continued to observe us silently.

"Can you help?" I tried. "We don't know where everybody has gone, and we are really quite frightened. I really wish to find my husband again, and Mr Barnes here needs to find his wife."

I had begun to think that the man was unable to speak as he looked us up and down, but at length he cleared his throat and said; "You do not belong here." His voice was rusty as though from disuse, and I could not place his accent.

"I know," I said, "We are very sorry to disturb you, but you seem to be the only person around. We won't bother you longer than necessary, but we do need help. Do you by any chance have a working telephone we could use?"

The man looked startled. "A telephone? I do not think that would be any use to you. You do not belong here. You cannot telephone from here to there. No good."

William and I exchanged glances, puzzled. Was the man sane, I wondered?

"You must go back where you from. Same time, same place. Do not linger here, will be no good for you."

I was truly mystified now, and more than a little nervous. William coughed.

"Yes. Thank you. Come Jane, perhaps we had better go." And he turned to walk away. The man called after us;

"Do not forget what I say. You do not belong here. Go back where you from. Same time, same place. Find right time and place and you return where you from. Not good for you stay here. Go quick."

We walked away, although I wanted to run down the hill as fast as possible. The man had undoubtedly put the wind up me, and I hurried after William. We went some way before William spoke, and he turned to me and slowed down as he did so.

"I don't suppose you have any idea what he meant, do you?"

I almost laughed. "Well, no. Did you? It made no sense to me at all. Do you think he was perhaps a bit mad?"

William was silent for such a long time that I began to wonder if I had really spoken. He continued to walk down the hill, but slower than at first. At last he spoke;

"I am not sure. Certainly he was not your usual run-of-the-mill fellow. But he seemed to know something we don't." Again there was a long silence. "Jane? Where do you think we are?"

I was baffled. "Up the hill above Brighton seafront," I replied, hoping I did not sound rude.

"That is what I thought until a short while ago." He stopped dead and put his hand on my arm, his brow crinkled in consternation. "Suppose we are not? What if your Lawrence and my Pauline and Miss Lytton-Gore and everybody else are right where we left them? What if it is we who have disappeared, not them?"

I was truly worried now, and not a little afraid. Whatever did he mean? We had not gone anywhere. William seemed to read my thoughts in my face.

"We went through that passageway, didn't we?" I nodded. "I know this will sound very odd, but what if we passed through…." He was obviously racking his brain for the right words; "I don't know what to call it. An anomaly in the universe or some such. So that we passed through into a parallel world of some kind. Something that looks like Brighton but isn't. Remember how the sea was washing the wrong way? And how that man's hair was not a normal colour? Jane, I think it possible that we are not in Brighton, but somewhere else."

I tried to speak, but the words were lodged somewhere beneath my throat. Was William mad? Was I, for starting to think he might be right?

"Where did you get such an idea?" were the words I finally managed to splutter.

"I'm not too sure. I began to think something was amiss when we looked at the sea earlier. It feels as though we are in the normal world, but with a few things slightly off-kilter. Wouldn't you agree?" I nodded, in spite of myself.

"William? Just suppose what you say is true, and that we are somewhere – different. How will we get back? Lawrence will be wondering where I am. If it is we who have disappeared, then we need to find a way to get back."

"Yes. I think perhaps that is what that man was trying to tell us. The right time and the right place. Maybe what we need to do is to go through that passageway again at a particular time. Retrace our steps so to speak. We just need to find the right time to do it."

"We must have walked through at around 8 o'clock last night. Perhaps the same time tonight might do it?" In spite of myself, I began to feel a little excited at the prospect of working out the problem and finding our way back.

William nodded and began to walk again. I followed him, my mind whirling with the possibilities of all he had said. If we were not in our normal world, then where were we? If we were on another planet I would not expect to be able to breathe the atmosphere, but there were no problems with that (although I found myself short of breath at the thought). It was true that the sea was not flowing in its normal manner, and I had noticed that the sky was a different shade from that to which I was used. Was there such a thing as a parallel universe? I remembered that Lawrence had gone through a phase of reading science fiction novels a year or so back and had talked about these things to me as though they were real.

I had a sudden shocking thought, which stopped me in my tracks. What if this was a terrible, complicated dream? Would I awaken suddenly to find myself cosily in bed beside Lawrence? Oh, if only that could be so.

William had stopped farther down the hill, having noticed that I was no longer walking. He came back to my side, concern etched on his now-familiar face. I no longer thought him so ugly.

"What is wrong, Jane?" he asked.

I looked at him, then around, to the sea that was wrong, and the clouds which were somehow off-beam. "How do I know this is happening?" I asked, hoping I did not sound as silly as I felt. "What if I am having a complicated dream and none of this is real? How would I know? How would I make myself wake up?"

"I believe one is supposed to ask somebody to pinch them to prove their wakefulness," William replied, looking amused.

"Go on then – pinch me." He looked a bit shocked, then leant forwards, took hold of the flesh above my elbow and pinched me. Hard.

"Ow! William that really hurt." He was smiling now as I rubbed my arm. "You didn't have to do it so hard!"

"I think I did, if only to prove that you really are awake. Sadly, my dear, I think we are awake, and this is really happening to us. The questions we should be asking ourselves are how did we get into this mess? And how are we going to get out of it?"

We continued to walk in silence. I listened to the world around us. The sounds were all wrong too, I realised. Where were the seagulls which should be screeching as they had been on our arrival in Brighton yesterday? Was it really only yesterday? I felt as though I had been here for weeks, months even. My usual life seemed as though it was part of another far-off time, somewhere deep in the past. I had not thought of my dear children all day, so caught up had I been in what was going on around me. As I had this thought we came upon a red telephone box, standing at the side of the road, the sun glinting hotly off its roof.

"Wait," I said to William. "I need to try to telephone to my mother and see if the children are all right. I really ought to speak to them."

William looked a little non-plussed, but stopped obediently by the side of the telephone box, his hands deep in his pockets.

Inside the box I searched in my purse for some change, and laid it out along the shelf, before picking up the receiver. I put the telephone to my ear, but there was no sound. Jiggling the button I called "Operator? Operator?" but there was no response, only the lonely sound of my pulse beating in my ear.

I stood for a few moments before replacing the receiver and rejoining William outside. The air felt fresh and cool after the stuffy inside of the telephone box. William looked at me, his eyebrows raised.

"Any luck?"

I shook my head. "The telephone seems not to be working."

"Like the one at the hotel?"

I nodded, unwilling to speak.

"In a way, I am a little relieved you had no luck," William said, surprising me. "It only goes to prove that we are not where we ought to be."

"Well, where are we then?" I knew that my voice was sounding petulant, but I was too upset to care very much.

"That is the question, isn't it?" William put his hand on my shoulder. "Now come along, my dear, I do believe that everything will work out in the end. We will find our way back eventually. But first we must make our way back to the hotel."

William cupped my elbow with his large hand, and I stumbled along next to him, down the hill and back towards the town.

As we reached the town I looked around, hoping against hope that things would have changed, and that the world would miraculously have returned to normal. Imagine if I were to look up towards the seafront, and see Lawrence walking along towards us, searching for me as I searched for him! But, of course, no such thing happened; the town was as bleak and deserted as it had been when we passed by earlier. A small whimper escaped from me, and I faltered, nearly falling. William's hand held me steady, and prevented me from tripping over.

"Steady on, old girl," he said, leading me towards a bench which looked out towards the sea. He sat down beside me for a moment, before lurching to his feet again.

"Stay there, Jane, I won't be a moment," and with that he was gone, loping off towards the shops. I was bereft, alone in this strange land. I put my head in my hands, letting the tears fall through my fingers, splashing onto the light blue of my skirt, where they spread into dark patterns. I wondered if William had decided to leave me too, fed up with my despairing attitude and tears. And of course these thoughts caused my tears to fall faster. Searching in my handbag for a handkerchief I didn't hear William's return, so was surprised to look up and see him standing in front of me, with a glass of water in each hand.

"I thought we could do with something to drink. I can't remember when we last drank. Tea is off the menu I'm afraid, but water will do you good."

I nodded, unable to speak, and terribly grateful to see his funny face again. William had not left me to fend for myself in this strange land, but had been thinking of me all the time. I smiled a tremulous smile, and managed a whispered "thank you."

When we had finished our water William placed the glasses underneath the bench. I was surprised, thinking he would return them to wherever he had got them, but he smiled at me.

"I don't think anybody will be missing them for a while." He held his arm out, and I slipped my hand through his elbow. We continued through the town, approaching the seafront, and ultimately our hotel. As we neared the promenade my heart thudded faster in my chest. I had no idea what to expect when we reached the hotel. I longed to find things back as they had been last night, but knew this was just fantasy. What else could possibly go wrong? I wondered. My legs were shaky, and I realised we had not eaten since breakfast so many hours and heartaches ago.

We both hesitated as we reached the front door of the hotel, then William took a deep breath and pushed it open. Inside the lobby was just as we had left it. Silent. Empty. So very, very quiet. I swallowed hard on the lump in my throat, and squared my shoulders. Looking up at William I saw that his eyes were also suspiciously bright, and I patted his arm. He cleared his throat and looked down at me.

"I think we ought to get something to eat, don't you?" he asked, his voice much quieter than usual. I nodded, and we headed towards the kitchen, where I managed to rustle up a fairly reasonable dinner from what was left in the cupboards.

As we ate, we mulled over the problem of deciding what time to try walking back through the corridor. Should we go through at 7:30 p.m., which was when the meeting with Miss Lytton-Gore had begun? Or at around 8:00 p.m., which must have been when William and I walked through? And should we approach from this side, retracing our steps? Or start again from the ballroom? It was such a worrying puzzle – one wrong turn and we would be stuck here for at least another 24 hours. I could hardly bear the thought of another day without Lawrence. I was minded of the years when he was away at war, and how I longed for his letters and his occasional visits home. Then I had worried for his safety on the battle front, but now I had no idea where he was or what dangers he might be facing.

Eventually, after batting the problem back and forth, we agreed to approach the corridor from this side just before 8:00 p.m. Looking at my watch I saw that it was now 7:15 p.m., and I had no idea how we would occupy ourselves for the next 45 minutes. William took things in hand however, steering me towards the bar and pouring us each a large sherry.

"Here's to an end to these adventures," he said, raising his glass.

I clinked my glass against his. "Hear, hear!"

At last the time did pass, and the small hand on my watch crept around to 7:55 p.m. We walked towards the corridor, creeping along as if afraid somebody might hear us. At the entrance to the corridor William looked at his watch, took a big breath and said "Here goes." He took hold of my elbow and steered me along the corridor. There was a faint, sharp ringing in my ears, although I couldn't be sure if it was inside or outside my head.

It seemed to take an age to reach the doors to the ballroom. We stopped just outside the doors, looking at each other in trepidation, and then William reached out and pushed the doors open. A sudden wall of noise hit me, and I looked up to a glorious sight. The ballroom was filled with people – Miss Lytton-Gore was once again at the front of the room, her arms raised – and I was sure I recognised people from the night before in the audience. Craning my neck I looked around for Lawrence. Was he there? Suddenly he stood up from the back of the room, and hurried towards me, his face full of anxiety.

"Jane! Wherever have you been? We came back into the room and you and this lady's husband had disappeared! I've been so worried!"

I took his dear face in my hands and smiled up at him through my tears. "Lawrence, it is a long, peculiar story. I'm not sure I even believe it myself, but I will tell you all about it later. This is William Barnes, and he has helped to keep me sane through the past 24 hours of trying to get back to you."

I motioned towards William who was busy hugging his wife, and pulling her towards us.

"What do you mean?"

I turned towards Lawrence, who was looking at me in disbelief.

"24 hours? We only arrived here this afternoon. Jane, what are you talking about?"

"How long have I been gone, Lawrence?" I asked.

He looked at his watch. "About an hour I think."

I looked at William and he began to laugh. I also started to giggle, and before we knew it all four of us were hooting away, although I am sure that Lawrence and Pauline had no real idea why.

Two years have now passed and I still have no real explanation for what happened to William and me that strange day in Brighton. Lawrence and Pauline still insist that we were gone no more than an hour, although William and I insist on 24 hours. Lawrence, after much deliberation and research, thinks there may have been what he calls an anomaly in that unusual, bronze-lined tunnel. A portal through to another world, so similar to this one that we thought nothing had changed, but so different that there were no people around, save for the strange man in the building at the top of the hill.

We will never know of course, but I do know that I never want to go to that hotel in Brighton again.

But we have kept in touch with William and Pauline Barnes, having shared such a strange adventure together that spring, and I do believe we shall be friends forever.

## Nighty Nighty

By Jessie Hobson

"Charlie, go to bed", said she
"I won't. I won't" said he.
"You naughty boy," his mum replied.
"You'll be the death of me."

"I want to watch the telly now".
Said Charlie in a huff.
"It's far too late", his mother said.
"It's all the grown-up stuff."

That wasn't true, of course, because
The TV watershed
Is after nine, when Charlie's gone,
Long bathed and into bed.

It doesn't do to tell them lies
Because you want your peace.
They sense you mean to have your way
So arguments can cease.

This makes them worse and crosser still
Until they drive you mad.
You give in then, or even more,
You sink to something bad.

You bribe the little fiends right then
With promises of treats,
Of outings and designer clothes,
Of comics and of sweets.

They go at last, so pleased and smug
All sweetness and all light,
While you, exhausted, just about
Can kiss and say goodnight.

# The Stalker

By David Shaer

## Chapter 1 – The Stalker

I had known her for years. We had never met but I knew her intimately. I suppose it would be called stalking but I thought I was subtle. She worked somewhere in the West End of London because I had travelled on the same train. Not every day but as often as I could.

She had a smile. It was infectious and whenever she smiled, without even knowing I existed, she made me smile. Her blue eyes sparkled, complimenting her long, soft, fluffy hair and some mornings she joined the Central Line already smiling. She was happy and so beautiful that, unwittingly, she made the people around her happy.

Every morning, I started to look out for her and, if I failed to see her, my day was miserable. She was slightly younger than I and obviously an educated lady, who played sport and kept fit. On Mondays, whenever I saw her, I could tell that she was bruised from a weekend of strenuous exercise. She probably played netball or hockey, because sometimes she limped a little on the Monday. So did I but my battering was from playing rugby, albeit not very well.

By Tuesday mornings, she was somewhat less stressed and walked slightly faster. Like me, she got off at Oxford Circus and walked up the escalator to the street level, just to maintain the movement. As she walked up to street level, I tried to keep up but sometimes my bruising was more debilitating and I lost her.

As she turned onto Regent's Street heading towards The Beeb, I was never far behind. In fact, I followed so often that I knew every last ripple in her body and, if she had been injured, I could tell by her different stance. But, of course, I could say nothing. We didn't even know of each other's existence. Well she knew not of mine.

My job was regular, because I was being trained and I left from the surgery in Cavendish Square at 5:27 p.m. every evening, in order to be able to catch the six o'clock from Fenchurch Street. But she never travelled at that time and I had never seen her set off for home.

Until one day, just before Christmas, I was late and had had a couple of pints before shuffling down onto the Central Line. And there she was – standing alone on the platform at just before 7:00 p.m. I tried to hide but the platform was relatively empty. She turned towards me, and smiled. Not a big, beaming, glowing smile but just a cursory acknowledgement. I smiled back but she turned away. She didn't know me, after all.

Ashamed, I also turned away but not for long. As the train finally rolled in, I turned back and looked for her again, but she was not to be seen. My shame had turned to disappointment but only momentarily. There she was, down towards the front of the train and I broke into a rapid walk in that direction.

With the platform relatively clear, I had only seconds before I heard the doors being closed and had to leap onto the train only a carriage or so nearer. I had lost her again and was reduced to walking between the cars towards the front of the train. By the time I had reached Bank, my normal station for leaving, I still hadn't found her and was only two cars from the front. And there she was – seated and not getting off. But her head was buried in a paperback book and she wasn't paying attention to anything, except its content.

Hiding discretely, I stayed on the train at Liverpool Street but moved slightly so that I could keep an eye on her from behind a pillar. She carried on reading but did look up to see Bethnal Green, then carried on reading.

By now, my aim was to get off at Mile End and switch to the District Line to Barking, where I could pick up the slow 7:40 p.m. from Fenchurch Street. The lengths to which I had gone were coming to nought, because I hadn't a clue to where she would stay on and I was now going to have to get off and never see her again.

As the train pulled into Mile End, there was a District train standing on the next platform, but looking distinctly ready to pull away. As the doors of the Central Line train opened, I jumped off and, with four giant steps, leapt across the platform and into the District train, just as the doors hissed and started to close. I had just landed and steadied myself when I received an almighty thump in the middle of the back and went down onto my face.

With wounded pride, I rolled onto my side to prepare for a good kicking from someone and was confronted with a body lying next to me on the floor. It turned and there, facing me, albeit on her side and on the floor, was mystery girl, still smiling.

Blessed with a good accent, she started to apologise embarrassedly and would have continued the profuse apology all the way to Bow Road had I not intervened.

"I'm Mike," I said, "and would have preferred to meet you some other way than a drop kick in the middle of my back."

"I'm so, so sorry, Mike and I'm Veronica. Normally, I put the boot in first and ask names afterwards...... which is, I suppose, exactly what I have done tonight. Would you please let me make up for it by buying you a drink? Where do you normally get off?"

Wanting to answer something coarse and vulgar, I hesitated and Veronica realised what she had asked and duly went red.

"I have a much better idea," I responded, trying to change the subject but going red myself. "Let me take you for a drink. Where would you like to get off?"

We smiled tenuously as we skirted around the issue until I said Chalkwell, to which Veronica replied with a grin, "Well I get off at Thorpe Bay. Which means, I suppose, that you get off first." We both went even redder.

## Chapter 2 – The Stalkee

My name is Veronica, a huge and disappointing error of choice by my parents, who didn't want it to be shortened. As soon as any of my friends could talk, they called me Ronnie.

I don't consider myself to have an exciting life but I do play rugby for a ladies' team and I work as a stills photographer for a small film making company in the West End of London. Apart from that, I own a motorbike, a Kawasaki 650 ER6f, which is big, powerful and, I suppose, quite exciting in its self.

My job can be interesting because, in a small company, one does many jobs and, since I have been there for nearly four years, I do a great deal of production but also do some directing, which can be both exciting and scary. And I also make the tea because nobody else has ever got the time.

We do a great deal of work in the advertising sections of the BBC, who sell many of their productions abroad after they have been seen on UK television. That is my specialist area and I have to go to Chandos Place first thing every morning to deliver and pick up the latest jobs. I then walk round to Soho Square, which is good to walk off the bruising at the beginning of the week.

I find the walk from Oxford Circus to the BBC and to Soho Square exhilarating and inspirational, because many of my productions are based upon the people I watch in that small journey. I love watching people because they can, without realising it, convey feelings and sentiment totally unwittingly and, for the creative mind, that can launch many great ideas.

People in a hurry, grumpy people, stressed people, secretive people and furtive people have often given me great scope for my day's creations and they don't have a clue how useful they are.

There are little cafés with steamed up windows where husbands and wives sit huddled and holding hands first thing in the morning. They whisper and gaze into each other's eyes with love and affection. Of course, none of them is married to each other, and they all think they're "getting away with it."

Then there are much less common sights, like the two guys who don't ever talk to each other, except for grunting goodbye as one gets off the Tube. They sit in silence reading their papers and obviously have travelled for miles being "early morning unsociable," because people, even best buddies, just don't talk to each on public transport. Until something goes wrong. One morning, the guy who normally got off first, stayed on at Tottenham Court Road, and his buddy was totally thrown. At Oxford Circus, the one who always got off there, waited until the doors were about to shut, then suddenly leapt up, leaned over to the buddy who had normally gone by now and said, "Ill see you tonight, then, Love," and kissed his buddy on the forehead and jumped off as the doors shut. His poor buddy was left sitting there so red-faced and trying to clear his throat with a very deep tone. They don't travel together anymore now. I made up my own story about what happened afterwards but what a super wheeze to pull.

In looking for this sort of inspiration, I used to travel from Thorpe Bay to Fenchurch Street and walk down to the Central Line at Bank, but nobody in the City gives out that sort of glow. Everybody is pushing and shoving and just has to get to an early morning meeting or that first cup of coffee. The City is full of dead people all on autopilot. Only once did I witness anything unusual and that was on a wet, miserable morning when yet another of those pompous, arrogant, pin-striped know-it-alls was walking through the tunnels at Bank, reading his Financial Times but with his dripping, wet umbrella pointing out in front of him to ward off plebs in his way. I had seen him do this every day and was amazed how nobody had challenged his arrogance. And then, on this one particular day, his umbrella stabbed a young lady in the leg, ripping a hole in her tights. Her reaction was brilliant – she just opened her bag, took out a cigarette lighter and set fire to his paper – in about two or three different places. She then strode off with a look of smug satisfaction on her face, leaving the arrogant one, screaming and wrestling with his flaming paper. I actually stood in awe and amazement watching the guy in serious trouble as the fire spread to one arm of his striped suit. Nobody stopped, of course, they assumed it was a fire-eating busker performing for money. Sadly, I have never seen either of them since but I would have loved to have been there when they met again.

My life, then, involves voyeurism but one day I was shocked to learn that I had never seen a guy who had been watching me for months. Our encounter was, as ever, by chance. A soft landing, literally.

## Chapter 3 – The Soft Landing

As we lay there on the floor talking, which, I would think, was not normal after a first encounter on a train, we realised that everybody was looking at us and making up their own stories. Mike, very chivalrously, clambered to his feet and offered me an extended arm to help me up. We didn't even hold hands. Either he had no sentimentality or was even more chivalrous than was reasonable.

There were, of course, no seats available anywhere, so we stood in the middle of the carriage where everybody could continue to watch us.

"Leigh Old Town, then?" I offered, to which Mike graciously nodded, with a smile, and we then stood there in silence until we reached Barking, some fifteen minutes later. As the doors of the tube train opened, Mike stepped forward but held his arm out to let me off first. Our c2c train was already standing at the platform in front of us and this time it was my turn to take four enormous leaps across the platform and through the doors before they shut us out. Mike followed but a pace behind and we landed in the entrance to a carriage. Of course, the doors didn't shut immediately and we both looked pretty stupid for the performance of hop, step and jump with all of the related sound effects.

There were only two seats available, neither next to nor opposite each other but at diagonally opposite corners in a bank of six. Mike offered me the window seat and took my bags to place on the overhead rack. I always carry a rucksack or kitbag and a less-than-ladylike handbag which holds my entire life, apart from my kitchen sink – although that might well be in there – it's just that I haven't found it yet. As he stretched upwards towards the rack, I saw him wince and wondered which part of me had caused that – the weight of the bags or the force with which I had landed on him earlier.

After he stacked the bags, including his small, flat briefcase, he sat down and winked at me, thereby catching me staring at him throughout his stowage routine. Can you believe it, I went red again? I never go red but in the last twenty five minutes had done virtually nothing else.

My offering to take Mike for a drink was purely a knee-jerk reaction. I had never seen the guy before and knew absolutely nothing about him, other than he might have been a stalking pervert or even a gentleman. I hoped that he may have been something in between. Buying him a drink was the least I could do, for felling him so publicly.

As fate would have it, nobody got off our block of six seats until Benfleet, by which time it seemed inappropriate to start shuffling seats purely for the last stop.

So the stretching process started again and this time I averted my gaze, lest I might be deemed lustful; apart from the odd glimpse.

## Chapter 4 – Getting to Know You

By the time we were approaching Leigh-on-Sea, I had spent most of the train journey discretely examining Veronica from head to toe, more or less in the same way that I had done for many months, but this time with at least a chance of finding out about some of the things that I was thinking. She certainly seemed nice enough but the question was nice enough for what? At least I had attracted her attention, albeit in a strange sort of way. If she were to buy me a drink, the very least I could do was to offer to buy her one back and, on that basis, there was the prospect of getting to talk to, and find out about, her for about an hour.

Being somewhat of an introvert, I was relieved that no seats had appeared around us until Benfleet, because starting to chat someone up on a train is far too public and everybody around you wants to know more, especially how it all ends. So we sat in silence and then, as the train started to draw into Leigh, I leapt into action and dragged Veronica's bags down. Oh, Boy – talk about heavy. It wasn't just about wondering what was inside them, it was also worrying about how she carried them when I wasn't there. This girl must have been pretty strong. I reckon this hockey thing, or whatever it was, kept her very fit.

The arrival in Leigh was unspectacular, although I couldn't really imagine it being anything else. We left the train and climbed the stairs with dozens of other ordinary people and then swung right through the automatic barriers and out through the side door to cross the bridge and climb down the steps to the road past the cockle sheds. Without discussion, we were heading for the Crooked Billet, a pub that was a great receiver of City types, some tired, some pompous, but many already the worse for wear. We were none of these and were just lining ourselves up for a couple of drinks and a quiet chat. A quick "pick-me-up" drink, in more ways than one, possibly.

Conversation along the road to the pub was not easy as the tide was in and high and it was quite noisily windy. Every so often, spray from the sea would blow across the road and, by the time we reached the car park under the flyover, we were both wet and cold. It was, after all, December and a dark and stormy night. I suggested that the Crooked Billet was closest and that there might even be a fire burning in the public bar. It was unlikely that there would be many customers, mainly because of the uninviting weather.

So we climbed the steps up to the entrance and, holding the door open for Veronica, I also pushed open the door into the public bar on the left. She smiled as sweetly as ever and stepped inside.

The bar was heaving. It was noisy, smelly and, although warm through the log fire, totally not what we wanted. To make matters much worse, there were about four or five guys I knew from my rugby club and they fitted very clearly into the category of City workers who were much the worse for wear. Oh dear.

"Jones," came a screech from about three different people, "what bloody time do you call this?" One of them then added, "And who's the totty? Great puppies!" Who on earth needs enemies when you have friends like that?

Veronica was very good and handled herself brilliantly. She walked straight over to the main offender, a barrister and picked up his full pint of beer. She then emptied it completely over his head and into his lap.

"Thanks, Jonathan," she said, "I love you too," and then turned and walked straight back out of the door, into the other bar. "Mike Jones, what do you want to drink?" she called from the other bar and I had no choice but to walk through there, humiliated.

## Chapter 5 – This is fun

What a complete bastard. That Jonathan used to be my fiancé. And now he has humiliated me in public in front of this new guy, whose biggest crime to date is knowing my ex-fiancé. But I am not going to be beaten by this. OK, so maybe I was still a bit angry but not with Mike Jones. In fact, if we stand strategically, we can look through the serving hatch into the other bar and I can, from time to time, wave and smile at Jonathan bloody Duffy to get the last word in. And if I'm seen to flirt with his mate Mike Jones, even better.

"So, Mike, what is your pleasure?" I'm not sure but I think he might be terrified of what just happened, not sure whose side to take.

His response came as no surprise. "My pleasure would be to take you from here and have a drink in any other pub in the world."

I smiled but knew that I was going to stay here and beat that ex-fiancé into total submission. Poor Mike would have to work out whether I was a nice person from another source and on another day. He could see that I wasn't going to be leaving for some time, so he acquiesced and said, "A pint of IPA would be nice, please?"

Without hesitation, I blew it by saying, "The question was "What is your pleasure?" I shall dictate what the volume will be," and knew instantly that I had handled that very badly.

Mike recoiled and almost threw a verbal punch. "I'm sorry – that just slipped out," I said. "It was an old quip used by a very old and dear friend of mine and I just thought it was very funny. OK, so I've been waiting nearly ten years to use it and I'm sorry it had to be on you. Perhaps it might be better if we had our drink on another occasion." His answer was mortifying.

"I've been waiting over seven years for this evening and if you think I am going to give it up for the price of a half of bitter, you're not the person I've been dreaming about all this time."

You could have knocked me down with a feather. What was all that about?

Well, I had to ask.

"What do you mean, seven years? I've known you for less than three hours. Seven years ago, I was working in the City. I was a Hooray Henrietta who worked in a dreadful insurance company. I was in my mid-twenties, an insurance broker with the gab and I've never seen you before I felled you in Mile End today."

"Ah, but I've known you for almost ever," came his reply.

I walked to the bar, forgot Jonathan Duffy and simply ordered our drinks. I was shell-shocked. By the time I had been served and came back to our small round table onto which I spilt a large proportion of our drinks, Mike was sitting there looking much more confident than before. We toasted each other and wished ourselves Happy Christmas.

"So, what did you mean about waiting seven years for this evening?" I blurted out, not really very sure about where this was going.

Mike was beginning to relax a little but was still nervous about the direction in which we were going.

## Chapter 6 – Holding it in for 7 years

I wasn't sure how to broach this subject with Veronica without sounding like a serial stalker, which, to an extent, I was. Sure I had known her for seven years and yes, I had been in love with her all that time, even though I had never spoken to her and she didn't even know I existed. Worse than that, when I started to tell her, it all fell out awkwardly and my explanation was, to an extreme, perverse.

"It was almost seven years to the day when I fell in love with you."

Her eyebrows shot up and her eyes stared at me in disbelief.

"Friday, 3rd December (I know because it was my sister's birthday and she was three years older than I and exactly thirty). I remember the evening so well and have written about it in a diary with so much detail. In fact, I have re-written it about ten times to try to capture the moment. I do apologize profusely because you probably won't remember the incident at all but, I can assure you, it is emblazoned on my mind."

I could see her looking at me with incredulity and an element of suspicion.

"In fact, in my briefcase here, I have the complete works and would like to read it to you. May I, please?"

I could tell that she was flattered but I could also sense that she thought she was dealing with a complete nutter.

"Look," I said, "it's not very long – in fact only 340 words long."

"Is that all I'm worth?" she enquired, looking somewhat put out.

"It is the quality, not the size," I said, touching her hand, with instant regret. She recoiled slightly and any progress was cast aside.

"I'm sorry," we both said and smiled instantly.

"You could take it home and read it for yourself," I suggested but she was already shaking her head, which, with her long auburn hair, was enough to turn every head in the bar, women included.

"Oh, no," she said, with a smile. "The author's rendition has to be the best tool to deliver his own product. Go ahead – sing it out – although not literally. I would need to hear you sing in a disco first!"

"Now remember, this was just before Christmas seven years ago. The City, late at night was full of inebriates. Every train headed home was unpleasant. By this hour, even Fenchurch Street Station had closed down and the journey to the East had to start from Liverpool Street, by far the worse of the two East End termini."

I hesitated, took a deep breath and, without needing to refer too often to the sheet of paper, began to read.

## Chapter 7 – The search is over

"As finally the train began its slow, painful haul up the hill from Prittlewell into the terminus at Southend Victoria, I crept away from the debauched debris of the rear late-night carriages towards the front car, the one nearest the buffers, the one closest to the only taxi that might possibly be waiting on the rank.

"Advancing through the sliding door into the first carriage of the train, I stopped in my tracks. Absolutely stunning, there she was. Seated, upright, dainty, elegant and beautiful. Her hair was long, silky, sparkling and bouncy, her image demure. She sat there, pert from her ankles to the tip of her head. Her lips, slightly parted, were moist with sensuality. Her skin was soft, creamy and smooth. Her whole body was poised, ready to pounce. Her perfectly manicured right hand was resting so lightly on her smooth but taught right thigh. I returned my gaze to her inviting lips, glistening with expectant taste, oozing sexuality with a natural gloss that beckoned, almost demandingly. She was dressed ready for a banquet, a ball, a military presentation. Every last detail was perfect.

"Her very body smiled from within. She radiated warmth, hospitality and love. Oh, how I fell instantly. Never had I encountered such natural magnetism.

"Her coat, a perfect white leather, not at all cheap, beautifully shaped so that it caressed her exquisite body, was parted sufficiently to draw attention to her strong but oh so sensual pin-striped trousered thighs, whilst in no way detracting from her perfectly formed torso, unbelievably pert breasts – so natural but so thought evoking – a vision of total beauty.

"In her other, her left, hand, with a delicately crooked little finger was the ultimate evidence that before me was seated perfection personified.

"Sound asleep, but totally faultless, sat the object of my life's desires – clutching so graciously, in her silk-gloved left hand, a quarter-pound burger from which exactly one small but delicate mouthful was missing. Not a French fry nor brown paper bag in sight.

"My Perfect Lady."

I put my paper down, not sure whether to smile or duck.

## Chapter 8 – What now?

The silence was long and the colour was red. Both of us. I decided that I needed to apologise. It was, after all, far too personal, far too detailed and far too presumptuous. I lent forward and placed my hand on top of Veronica's. Her hand, however, didn't move. She just sat there with her sweet, happy smile on her face then, totally unannounced, punched me in the jaw.

"I thought it was absolutely lovely," she said, to my complete surprise, "but why does everybody have to keep harping on about my tits?"

"I'm sorry," I muttered, not knowing whether to laugh or cry. I chose, foolishly, to smile, long before I read the signs. Wrong – badly wrong! Her fist came at me again but this time, she controlled it and stroked my cheek.

"Seriously, it was lovely, and I'm sorry I punched you but I still think you deserved it."

I felt wet and cold again and then realised that Veronica had knocked my beer into my lap. At least she was consistent about how she treated her men.

Now we both laughed and this time, for the first time, it was relaxed. Our hands met and we both smiled. I stood up and headed for the bar.

"A large dry cloth for my suit, please, and two glasses of champagne." I could see through into the other bar, where Jonathan Duffy was sitting open mouthed, staring venom at me. Bad loser at rugby, he was obviously no better in matters of the heart. I hadn't a clue that I had been so close to Veronica all that time. I was the one who should have felt resentment.

I returned to the table carrying, with a tea-towel over my forearm, two glasses of champagne and had the answer ready immediately for Veronica's "Am I not worth a bottle, then?"

"If one pint of IPA gets me a punch in the jaw, I thought that a bottle of champagne should be consumed somewhere far more private. The sight of a grown man crying is not pretty. Apart from which, the quality of champagne here is restricted by the fact it probably comes from Spain and is therefore designated bubbly." I was not doing well here and needed for us to leave and go somewhere else.

"If we throw this down, I'll order a cab and we can go to Louis Quatorze .........but only if that appeals to you. They do a mean Château Briande."

"I'd rather have a diet Coke," Veronica giggled, putting on a fake Essex girl accent and ridiculing me totally. One very big point to her.

"OK, you win," I said reluctantly, "but would you care to join me for dinner, Ma'am?"

"Ma'ameoiselle," she responded instantly and I could tell that the lady was quick witted, intelligent and intellectual, something that I admired, in addition to her looks.

A cab was already outside, ordered by somebody else, who had disappeared, so we stole it and, leaving the two half consumed glasses of something bubbly and sickeningly sweet, we hopped into the back, before agreeing on a venue.

"What do you like to eat?" I asked tactfully, not expecting the cab driver to answer.

"Curry, mate," came his smart-arsed response, "but not round 'ere. Red Fort in Westcliff is good but the Governor is sellin' up soon, so may not be around tonight, mate."

"Actually," replied Veronica, "that is good and I wouldn't mind – if you eat curry, of course."

So, thanks to a local cabbie, our first meal together was going to be in the Red Fort. At least, on that basis, there was no indecision and trying too hard to be polite on a first 'date.'

## Chapter 9 – A 'First Date' to forget.

Hey, I like this chap. He has a sense of humour, a good taste in wine, women and food and seems to be remarkably resilient. And he's resourceful. Having stolen someone's cab, he's now taking me out for dinner and to somewhere I like. All that after I kicked him to the ground and punched him in the face. Sounds like my kind of man.

Mind you, I'm not so sure about the cab driver. I thought the Old Town had a twenty miles an hour speed restriction, both sides of the railway. This guy's doing nearly fifty and we haven't reached the Ship yet.

"Hey, slow down, John, we would like to get there," just fell out of my lips. He half turned towards me to remonstrate. "No – just keep your eyes on the road and slow down. Otherwise we're out of here."

And, as we reached the corner by the Ship, there was a small car backing out from the full car-park, slowly into the road. But our driver just wasn't prepared and we glanced the back of it.

With our speed, we didn't stand a chance and our stupid driver lost it. The left hand side of our cab just took off and we started a roll to the right, which might have been alright, had not the road turned to the left. Now up on the two wheels of the righthand side of the car, we were confronted with another car coming head on round the bend towards us. So we hit it. This third car stopped dead but we were already on two wheels and the impact just threw us into the air, spiralling to the right. After what seemed like forever, but was probably only for a second or two, we flew up and nearly over the footbridge coming across the railway. But not quite. Some part of our car clipped the footbridge and we cart-wheeled. For a second I saw an advertising hoarding and then we went through it and landed upside down on the railway track, accompanied by the horrible screeching of metal against metal. We skidded along on the roof, facing back towards Leigh Station. The skidding, sliding motion didn't seem to slow us down, until we collided with something heavy and metal. Probably an overhead electric cable stanchion or a signal but it spun us round viciously, so that there we were, twisting upside down like a spinning top. And then the spinning stopped, followed by the silence, the total silence. Nothing but the howling wind and the lashing rain. And the drip, drip, drip of...... petrol. And the distant rumble of train wheels on the track coming towards us. The rumbling, the drumming, the vibration of the track below us.

Then came the screeching. The hissing and the screeching drew closer and closer. I recognised the sound of a train being braked as hard as possible. The headlights were bright and dazzling. We were powerless to do anything. We. I didn't know who we were. I was just about alive but I didn't know about anybody else. That damned train was still coming. I could sense that the driver was trying all he was worth but two hundred and forty tons takes some stopping, particularly in the rain. The hissing and screeching was now almost deafening and then, with a crunch, it stopped, seemingly very close.

I heard the driver's door slide open and he was clambering down the metal steps towards the ground.

"Hang on, in there," I heard him call – a young man, with a sense of urgency. "Oh, my God. Petrol. It's everywhere. Is anybody in there? Speak to me!" and suddenly there was a face about a foot from me. I groaned. "Hold it, love, we'll have you out of there in no time. I'll get the power turned off first, though," and with that he was clambering up the steps again. Smart guy – no mobile phone usage by him. But by this time I could hear people climbing down from the road. I bet they all had mobiles. And they wouldn't think about the petrol fumes.

And then I heard a moan next to me. I didn't know who but I couldn't do anything about it because I couldn't move.

"Not my best day of the week so far," came the voice. "Seem to have lost my head twice tonight."

"Mike! How are you?" I asked stupidly.

"I don't have a clue," he said, "but I'm talking, so I'm not dead. How about you?"

If I could have held his hand, I would have cried. But I couldn't feel my hands – or my legs. All I could feel was scared.

Then I heard shouting. The train driver. He was trying to get people away and shouting at people to put their phones away.

"The power's off now," he assured us. "Anybody else alive in there? I've called the Fire Brigade and an ambulance and the police are on their way – I can hear them coming down the hill now," as the wail of sirens approached.

"There's at least two of us but I don't have a clue about the stupid driver," I said, surprising myself. I was obviously angry at him. The smell of petrol was now becoming intrusive and making it difficult to breathe. I could hear more sirens in the distance.

"Can you move, Mike?" I asked.

There was no response.

"Mike. Answer me! Talk to me! Mike!"

"Sorry," came the reply, "I've had a hell of a week and I just fell asleep."

"Mike! Don't do that to me! We've got to get out of here and quick. We're swamped in petrol. This lot could go up at any moment. Stay awake, for God's sake."

Silence again. "Mike! Come on – stay awake. It's important. Mike?"

Still nothing.

And then I heard the rustle of waterproof clothing.

## Chapter 10 – How to bat an idea around.

"Don't anybody touch their phones. No smoking and let's have all engines turned off." I can hear a strong, assertive voice.

It must be a dream, a very strange dream. I seem to be looking down on a scene of mayhem and debris. I feel upside down. I can hear sounds but they keep fading away and drifting back. Someone keeps calling out my name. "Mike." At least, I think that's my name. I think I'm having an "out of body" experience. But somebody is there. A girl, a woman. I can't see. It's dark. Very dark. There is wind and rain...... and petrol. I can smell petrol.

It's not the only thing I can smell. I can smell fear.

I'm tired, very tired. I think that maybe I need to sleep.

I can hear voices. "Mike! Come on – stay awake. It's important. Mike?" What are they saying? I don't want to stay awake. I'm tired. Just leave me alone. I want to go to sleep, don't you understand?

"Mike! Come on – stay awake. It's important. Mike?" It's those voices in my head again. OK, OK. I'll try to stay awake a bit longer. But I'm cold. Very cold. I really do just want to be left alone up here, looking down, like a bat. I bet bats don't get voices telling them to stay awake. Bats sleep hanging upside down. I want to be a bat. I think I'm becoming a bat. I wonder what bats eat? I'm hungry. That's it – I'm tired and hungry – I'm a tired, hungry bat.

*Just one step back, outside my skin,*
*I look down on my life within*
*I breathe a sigh and all release*
*At bedside now, I rest in peace.*

I like that – that's what I really need, peace.

"Mike! Come on – stay awake. It's important. Mike?"

"Oh, come on, lady. I'm just shutting my eyes. Let me sleep for just another few minutes. Then I'll get up."

"Mike – thank goodness. Now stay awake. They'll get us out of here really soon. There are medics and firemen out there. Hang on in there, please."

See – even she knows I'm a bat – hang on in there! Say, what is this? I'm wet. I'm upside down. I can smell petrol. What is this? "Hey, get me out of here."

"OK, Sir. We'll have you out of there in no time, don't worry." I have never heard any words so pleasing. Activity, at last.

"I'll just undo my seat belt."

"No, stop. Don't do that, Sir. You'll get the mother of a headache." Oh, yes, of course. If I'm hanging upside down...... doh!

I can hear that girl's voice again now. She must be trapped in here, wherever that is, with me. "Mike, they're going to get us out now. Just relax. These guys know what they're doing, they're professionals." And with those words, some stupid bastard undid my seat belt and I fell on my head. All my lights flickered and then went out.

## Chapter 11 – Hardly the great escape

I heard an horrendous crash and a deep moan. I think someone had released Mike from his inverted position somewhat ahead of the plan. As he landed with a thud on the roof, the whole car rocked and then twisted onto its side. I was out, I was free. My side of the car had no windows and not very much of a door. As the car crashed over, I was thrown out of the hole where most of the door had been. I was clutching my bag and a handful of hair, although from where, I don't have a clue. Mike, however was still inside and I saw a couple of burly figures clothed in Day-Glo jackets diving through the gaping hole from which I had been thrown to try to drag him out.

I saw them grasping a pair of legs and hauling the rest of his body out of the window when suddenly there was a horrifying sound that sounded like a slow-motion "woompf" and we were all thrown into the air as the car exploded in a sheet of searing flame. After that, all I could remember was hearing a shriek, a woman's shriek, I think. I also vaguely remember seeing at least three people on fire. And then my world went dark.

## Chapter 12 – Slowly does it

I've never felt like this before. I can't actually feel anything but I can feel so much pain from limbs that I can't move or see. Whatever has happened can't be good because the world is dark – I can't see anything. Can't see? Can't feel? Maybe I'm dead.

"Good Morning, Veronica." I can hear. It's a man, a young man – perhaps mid-twenties and he has an accent, possibly Welsh. "You're going to be alright. It probably won't feel like it for several weeks but you are going to make it. By the way, I'm Doctor Latif and I saw you when you were brought in last night."

Brought in? Brought in from where? To where? Doctor? Am I dead? He thought not, so this must be a hospital. Mind you, I feel dead. With this amount of pain, if I'm still alive, I think I'd rather be dead.

"I need to ask you some questions, though." It must be that Welsh Doctor Latif again. I don't think that guessing accents is one of my strong points. "But I must warn you that you have got bandages on – lots of them. You got burned last night but not seriously. At least your hair will grow again. I'm going to take the bandages off your head in a minute to examine the rest of your head but they will need to go back on quickly, but that is quite normal in these cases."

What does he mean, these cases? And my hair will grow again? Hey – how much damage is there. Why can't I see?

"In a moment, you will be able to speak. Now I would rather that you don't scream or shout because it has been a very long night and I have just a bit of a headache. And, by the way, whose fistful of hair did you pull out last night. It wasn't yours. Bit of a pity, really because we might have been able to transplant it to help your hair grow back more quickly."

His accent is worrying me now – more Wolverhampton than Wales – I wonder where the Latif comes from? Could be Bradford, I suppose.

"Right – are you ready now? This might be a bit bright, so I suggest you keep your eyes closed for a bit. I can always put the pads back on your eyes if it's too painful."

Bradford now – definitely Yorkshire. And I'm not keen on all this talk of pain. Still at least I'll be able to talk soon, when the bandages come off. Bandaging my mouth is like making an Italian or Frenchman sit on his hands. Talk? Scream? Shout? I'll bloody sing if I want to. Who does this guy think he is? I'll sort him out. Just let me get my hands on him. Actually, I'm feeling better already – although I must admit I'm a bit scared about my hair. I don't think I could do a Britney or an Annie Lennox.

"Are you ready now? I shall need you to sit up a bit but I'll give you a hand – here, let me help." Ooh, his hand is warm. But he does feel quite strong. Yes, I like that. Up I come. Actually, that doesn't hurt very much at all.

"OK. Well done. There, that wasn't too painful, was it? I'm now going to start unrolling the bandages but, please, no screaming. And no asking for a mirror. That is definitely out for a while."

Oh. I don't want to know now. Now I really am frightened.

"Right, here we go. Let me know if it hurts too much. I'll be as gentle as I can but sometimes the bandages can stick. Just sing out if you want me to stop."

This guy's bedside manner isn't bad – all apart from the mirror bit – although I suppose he might be right about that too. I just hope not. At least the bandages seem to be coming off alright, although we haven't got down to the skin yet. It could even be Manchester. It's a most weird accent.

"Well that was really good. Nothing caught at all. I'm going to leave the pads on your eyes for a minute or two while I just clean you up a bit first. I shall wipe round your neck, your face, your forehead gently to start with."

Stratford upon Avon. Who is this guy? Actually, I love all this attention. I don't know who you are but you can keep doing this for a lot longer. I wonder how long I can drag this out? Perhaps I don't want to open my eyes and see the mess? Perhaps Dr Latif could be persuaded to hang around a whole lot longer?

"Now let's see about those pads. Your eyes won't like the sudden exposure but you will feel a cool flow of air. One thing, though. You haven't screamed yet. From what I saw last night, I'm surprised. You certainly have great lungs and managed to wake many of us up. Do you feel alright, or would you like me to give you something?"

Right! Now I've got it – he's from Middlesbrough. His accent isn't true Geordie because it goes all over the place. So he's not from Newcastle or Sunderland. It must be Middlesbrough.

Anyway, what does he mean – great lungs? Hey – he's stroking my eyes now. That's a bit much isn't it? "Excuse me, Doctor Latimer or whatever you're called, why are you stroking my eye lids? That's not really a recommended medication, is it? If you don't stop soon, I might just scream – to see if I can."

"Veronica, I was wiping your eyelids delicately with the pads. This is the recommended practice because your skin has been burned and I am just applying some soothing, antiseptic cream, which will make it better. Just keep your eyes shut a little longer, please, and soon this will be finished."

He is, of course, right. The air flowing over my eyelids is beautiful, soft, soothing and cool. Relief.

"Now I have a special treatment. I am going to replace the pads but, just before I do, I am going to apply something different. Now it won't hurt, well probably not very much, but it will have a lasting effect – for the better, I hope."

And as I am sitting there, being stroked and pampered, would you believe it? – the bastard has just kissed both my eyes and then replaced the pads. Hey – you're out of order, Mister. Well, I'm not taking this and rip the pads off my eyes, open them and there, right in front of me, well, more on my lap, is Mike.

"You bloody creep," I shout, "what the hell is all this about?" and, as I look around me, it is true. I am in hospital. I am in a bed. I am swathed in bandages and Mike is sitting on my bed in one of those gown things that would probably expose him from behind, except he's in front.

Suddenly his arms are around me and he is wincing in pain. He looks dreadful. His face is burned, his skin is red and blistered and he has an enormous hole in the hair on his head. Oh, my God, no. Did I do that?

"Yes, you did that," he responded to my unasked question. "You tried to drag me out of the cab but I was trapped in my seat belt. You ripped an enormous chunk of my hair out – heaven knows, I can ill afford it – but you yanked it all out of my head nevertheless. But we were both still stuck inside. And then somebody in a yellow jacket undid my seatbelt and you were gone. The Day-Glo jacket man then reappeared through the side of the car with another Day-Glo man, and they started to drag me out – by my feet. They nearly got me out when the whole lot went up. I have never heard such a loud "woompf" in my life and then all three of us were flying. We just took off and flew onto the tracks. My jacket was on fire, as was my hair but the other two guys were just brilliant. They rolled me over instantly and smothered me in seconds. I couldn't see you but I could hear you screaming. As I said, you've got really great lungs. From every angle."

I would have hit him but I just needed a hug. And tears. I don't do tears but today I do tears. Big. We can't stop hugging and crying.

## Chapter 13 – Faster now

What a lady. She really is that perfect lady. OK. So she's gullible and soft but that's what she should be. I just love playing tricks on people and even I have to admit, that that was a bit much. But she was burned and I am training to become a doctor. I'm just not very good at accents. Apart from that, I now need to go back to my bed because I am exhausted and I've got a big hole in my hair. In my head, it feels like. Goodness, she is strong.

Her burns aren't that bad at all but her concussion was, so being kept in overnight was essential. For me, anyway. It is helping my recovery no end. I am burned quite badly but, with time and a bit of skin grafting off my bum, it appears that I shall look like my bum forever. Yes, I had a doctor with a sense of humour too.

"I'm afraid that the driver didn't make it but he wasn't a driver anyway. He had actually stolen the cab from outside the pub about five minutes before. He had been drinking there for a couple of hours and had got lost on the way back from the gents. So his love for curry was actually the death of him."

The one thing that did come out of the evening, though, was the fact that we met and, pushy though this might be, we are going to meet again, if only so that I really do buy that dinner and bottle of champagne. I don't think it will be tonight – but it won't be long after."

"But now, if you don't mind, I need to finish my rounds, so please excuse me."

And with total confidence, Mike turned and walked away to the bed next door, exposing his bare backside to me totally.

Yes, I think we two might well become one.

# Dylan the Dog

By Simon Woodward

It was early in the morning,
and there was lots of fog.
But Sophie didn't mind that there was fog;
because she knew that very soon she would have a dog.

And a dog called Dylan would be short.
His legs wouldn't be long and his height would be naught.
But Sophie didn't mind that her dog would be naught,
because he would be hers.

In the morning she opened her eyes
and to her surprise there *was* a dog.
A short one whose legs were naught,
and when he jumped he could be caught,
by Sophie.

But Dylan was a different kind of dachshund.
He wasn't like the others, being the only one of his kind.

The short dog whose legs were naught,
was orange.
But Sophie didn't mind; she was happy
that her dog, whose height was naught,
was hers to keep ...... and orange.

And she knew, in her heart of hearts,
that with her dog, she could sleep,
safe and sound throughout the night –

Because she had an orange dog whose height was naught,
And had been bought to look over her –
Her protector.

# Transplant

By Paul Bunn

## Prologue

My name is Bryan Locksmith and I'm going to die soon. Two very simple facts put together by me for the first time and I am elated.

You may think, dear reader, that knowing your name and the fact you have limited time left aren't exactly eureka moments in one's life but in my case they are. Having arrived at this conclusion for me was vital.

What has happened over the past few weeks has made me doubt my sanity, with anything seemingly possible. It means now, after all the mistakes I've made, I have finally accepted who I am and the fate that has befallen me.

I expect you want to know what this is all about and, knowing the clock is ticking, I'd better tell you...

## Chapter 1

Louise looked down at me with a mixture of hope and uncertainty reflected in her strikingly beautiful deep blue eyes. A tear trickled its way down her smooth, ivory-skinned face as she perched on the bed holding my hand. More than anything I wanted to hold her but didn't have the strength...yet.

"Soon..." I thought, before drifting off to sleep again and dreaming of her in my arms.

It was a few hours before I woke once more and darkness had now encroached into the hospital ward. The liver transplant had gone well and I had been moved from the Intensive Care Unit earlier that day. It was quiet except for a few muffled coughs from someone a few beds down.

Louise had long gone, her vigil finished for today, at least. I hoped she would be back the next day, as she had throughout the dark times over the years. I had another chance that maybe I didn't deserve but was determined to take it. The clouds hanging over me like a threatening storm had dispersed. Life would be good again.

Over the next few days I felt my strength returning, helped substantially by the arrival of Louise every day. We talked about anything, from subjects as diverse as when we first met during a boat trip on the Thames, to our relationship, with its ups and downs. It was during one of these conversations that I first started getting the cravings.

"You haven't got a cigarette have you?" The words came out before I could stop them. Louise blinked in surprise.

"What?" She eventually replied. My cheeks reddened and I laughed nervously.

"Only kidding, its these drugs they're giving me. I don't know what I'm saying half the time."

"But you don't smoke; you never have." Her eyes searched mine with a hint of mistrust.

"I know, I know. I can't think why I said it. I was a drinker, not a smoker."

"And you don't do that now do you?" Her question was part statement and part accusation, which hurt me.

"Louise, I promise you it's been 18 months since my last drop, I swear."

For a terrifying moment I didn't think she was going to believe me but then her shoulders sagged and she sighed.

"I do believe you but it's hard after you know… everything that's happened."

"Come here." I said.

Gingerly holding out my arms I hugged her, deeply breathing in her sweet perfume. For a precious moment that was all that mattered – until the hunger for a cigarette returned with a vengeance. I didn't understand why.

## Chapter 2

A few weeks later I was back home. My new liver hadn't rejected me – yet and I was healing up nicely. Sitting on the settee watching TV, I felt tired and happy. Louise had come back for good. We had broken up, whilst I was still drinking; she had been unable to cope with me anymore. That was my wake up call. Spending nights down the pub or having a few cans at home was my life, I was rarely sober in the evenings. Things came to a head when, a week after I'd sworn to give up, she found a bottle of vodka in the wardrobe. I cried and pleaded but to no avail, she was gone and my heart was broken.

I don't remember much for a while after that, apart from crying and wallowing in self-pity. All I thought about was how could I get her back and would she ever forgive me.

I held onto the photograph that had stopped me going over the edge. It was of both of us on honeymoon in Barbados, on the beach hugging each other tightly. It wasn't the best photo ever taken but it encompassed the feelings we had for each other. Louise peered over my shoulder.

"That was a great honeymoon," she said, gently resting her head on my arm. Smiling I tucked the photo back into my wallet.

"The best," I said and kissed her on the lips.

## Chapter 3

"I'm just going for a walk to the shop." Slipping on my shoes, I eased open the front door.

"Do you want me to come with you?" Louise called from the bathroom. She still worried about the effect of my transplant operation, even though it had been four months ago now. I felt fitter than I had for a long time and would be starting work soon.

"No, I think I'll be able to make it on my own. Send a search party if you haven't heard back in half an hour."

Louise mumbled something which I didn't catch as I stepped outside, shutting the door with a firm click. The sun was low on the horizon, so I had to squint and shade my eyes. We needed some more milk and the small corner shop was just down the road. Getting out as much as possible was important to me. Louise worked during the week and spending time on my own wasn't a great deal of fun. Daytime TV had its limits in relieving boredom.

Once I turned the corner, I took the cigarettes from my pocket and lit one, inhaling deeply. After that initial urge for one in hospital had passed, I found it difficult to think of anything else. I still didn't understand why, as it was something that had never even crossed my mind before. Still, it was only one or two a day and from my point of view, it was better than drinking. There was no need to tell Louise about it at the moment; she had enough on her plate with her job and looking after me.

The shop was one of those tiny premises that seemed to sell everything from tinned salmon to batteries. The shelves were crammed full of goods and there was barely enough room down each aisle to breathe, never mind look for something you needed. Not being well lit meant Geoff, the owner, was always being asked where a particular item was. Fortunately I knew where to look.

An excruciating pain shot through my head like a thunderbolt as I reached for the milk and I slipped to the floor. Geoff rushed over, his pasty round face initially a blur but he soon came into focus.

"Are you alright, Bryan?" His watery brown eyes were etched with concern.

"Yeah, I'm fine," came my embarrassed response. It had come and gone in a couple of seconds and I felt numb. Like a computer that had crashed and was now re-booting, my mind was empty, waiting for everything to come back.

"Let me help you up."

"No, I'm OK, really." I said.

Was I? I didn't know the answer.

Leaving the shop, I could feel the eyes of other customers boring into me. I wanted to shout back at them, hadn't they got anything better to do with their lives rather than stare at me? A trickle of sweat rolled down my temple as I hurriedly walked home, a finger of fear worming its way around my stomach. There was an instant in the shop, when Geoff had said my name, which didn't make sense. In that vacuum of a few seconds whilst on the floor, my first thought had been: "Who's Bryan?"

It seemed to take an age to get back home again and the safety of those four walls. All of a sudden I didn't want to be out in the open anymore.

I approached our bright red front door taking some deep breaths, composing myself before entering. Standing in the hallway, I looked in to the full-length mirror. There was a little paleness to my face but otherwise I looked fine and relaxed.

"Did you get it alright?" Louise's call came echoing down the stairs. For a moment I wasn't sure what she meant and then I remembered.

"Shit." I said under my breath. In my haste to leave the shop, I'd forgotten the milk. "They didn't have any but are getting another delivery later," I lied. "I'll pop back then."

Feeling tired, I collapsed onto the sofa resting my head on the back, with my eyes closed. It had to be some sort of side effect from the anti-rejection drugs I was taking. There couldn't be any other explanation. With this thought in my mind I drifted off into a fitful sleep.

When I awoke Louise was asleep, her head resting on my shoulder. Not wanting to disturb her, I didn't move and thought back to what had happened earlier. It wasn't so much the sudden headache that concerned me, but the fact I'd forgotten my name, even if it was only for an instant. Was this caused by the operation? I did know you could suffer from anxiety and depression but this sensation didn't feel like either of those; in fact, I was very happy.

Maybe I was reading too much into it. Pushing myself hard to get back to some sort of normal life, was always likely to produce a reaction, even though I was pleased with my progress overall. Feeling better, I listened to Louise's gentle snoring and smiled.

## Chapter 4

It was great to be back at work. I was itching to start using my brain again but also nervous of everyone's reaction to me. I didn't like to be the centre of attention at the best of times, so wasn't looking forward to that aspect of it. The first couple of days were the hardest; colleagues were continually coming up to me and asking how I was in their sympathetic tones. This soon died down as it became old news and more up to date office gossip took over, which was a relief. Although other people's concern was appreciated, I sometimes wished I'd put my trials and tribulations on tape so, when asked, I could just play them back and get on with my work.

On the way home at the end of that first week, the traffic was bumper to bumper. This was just typical, reasonable the first few days, but like this on a Friday. I drummed my fingers impatiently on the steering wheel, watching the pedestrians easily outpace the motorists. I'd forgotten how frustrating commuting could be.

A few minutes later the reason for the snarl up became apparent. The blue flashing lights of a police car and ambulance had blocked one lane of the dual carriageway dealing with a traffic accident. Getting closer, I saw a motorbike lying on its side, with a car a few feet away. My heart froze. The motorcyclist lay motionless next to his bike his left leg twisted in a way it shouldn't have been. There was a pool of blood spreading out from beneath him. I wrenched my eyes from the scene, not wanting to see anymore. An image flashed through my mind of a paramedic trying to revive him, and I shook my head to clear it, forcing myself to concentrate on the road.

Two miles further along I had to stop. Shaking uncontrollably with sweat pouring off me, I got out of the car, just in time to be sick at the roadside.

"Christ." I held my head in my hands in a state of utter terror.

Seeing the accident had triggered this reaction but there was something else clawing at my mind. It was as if I'd seen a relation or close friend get knocked down, the fear of what might happen to them had coursed through my veins like ice.

Taking a few deep breaths, I sat back down in the car, needing to regain my composure before continuing home. Reaching across to the glove compartment, I took out a packet of tissues. Taking one, I tried to wipe away the bitter taste I still felt on my lips.

The first drops of rain spattered against my windscreen, as I drove back into the traffic. Glancing at the sky and seeing the thick, gunmetal grey clouds, it looked like it was going to be more than just a shower.

Stepping through the front door after that awful journey, I sighed deeply. The rain had made the journey long and tiresome and I was desperate for a drink. For a moment, the thought of an ice-cold beer flashed through my mind and I licked my lips in anticipation. Closing my eyes, I banished the image. One would no doubt lead to two and it wouldn't stop until I was unconscious.

After today's events, that was very tempting. Something alcohol free would have to do.

Louise had left me a note on the kitchen table.

> *"Hope your first week back has gone well. Dinner in fridge."*
> L x

After seeing what was in the fridge, sealed on a plate with a piece of cling film, my heart sank. Pieces of tuna sprinkled over a bed of lettuce, cucumber and tomatoes wasn't my idea of a filling meal. Whatever happened to pie and chips? Reluctantly, I removed it from the shelf and spent the next half an hour picking at it with my fork. I'd had enough salads over the last few months to last me a lifetime and didn't really feel in the mood to eat more of them; besides my stomach still felt delicate from earlier. Pushing the plate away, I gave up on it.

Going back to the fridge I grabbed a can of coke, took a big swallow and enjoyed the feeling of the fizzy liquid going down my throat. Staring at the can, I smiled and shook my head. This was something else I now had a liking for. Again, like the smoking, it had started with a craving that just wouldn't go away, so the next day I'd bought 18 cans of the stuff. Louise just looked at me in disbelief after she saw them in the fridge.

"But you hate coke," she'd said.

I just shrugged and continued watching TV. "I like it now."

I knew it was weird, but at the time it didn't really bother me. I guessed it was caused, like everything else, by the trauma that had been part of my life up to that point.

## Chapter 5

Checking my watch, I saw it was just past 6pm. Louise wasn't going to be home for another hour, so I decided to go for a walk, just to clear my head. The night was pleasantly warm, so I just slipped my thin jacket on, before stepping out. When I came back, Louise was frantic with worry.

She flung her arms around me squeezing me tight before pulling away. "Where the hell have you been?" Her eyes were bright red with recent tears.

"What do you mean; I've only been out for a breath of fresh air."

It was then that I noticed the mud on my trousers, not just at the bottom, by the shoes, but all the way up to my knees. My hands were also filthy, even under the fingernails. I stared at them in disbelief. These weren't my hands, how could they be? It was as if someone had removed mine and replaced them with someone else's. Time seemed to stand still, as I tried to comprehend what had happened since I'd left the house earlier.

> *Walked down the garden path… turned left, reached the corner and then… and then… nothing.*

I turned despairingly to Louise, feeling my world slipping into a nightmare, from which there was no escape. "Louise I…what's happening to me?"

"Where have you been?" This time there was an edge to her voice, no tenderness and just a hint of anger.

"I honestly don't remember."

She came up to me again, her eyes searching mine for answers, but I had none. Then she sniffed my breath. "Have you been drinking?"

My immediate reaction was to say "no," but I checked it. I wasn't sure, because I didn't remember. There was no feeling of drunkenness on my part, not even of being a little tipsy, so I was reasonably certain I hadn't.

"No," I finally said.

She wasn't convinced.

"You have to believe me." It came out in a whisper.

"How can you not remember, Bryan, you've been gone for ages." She was agitated, pacing up and down the room, only occasionally glancing in my direction. "Have you seen the time?"

Looking up at the wall clock, I was stunned to see it read 11:15pm. I'd been out 5 hours.

"If you've been drinking again, that's it this time, you know that."

The words stung me, like a slap in the face. "But Louise I..."

She stopped in her tracks. "I don't want to listen to your excuses, go and have a bath and get that stinking mud off you." With that, she turned her back and stormed out of the room. I knew there would be no further talking that night.

The bath eased the tension I felt in the muscles on my back and shoulders. I could hear Louise clattering around downstairs, her annoyance apparent.

The problem was, I couldn't remember anything at all. There was a blank space in my memory, from the time I left the house to when I arrived home – as if I'd been asleep the whole time. What the hell was happening? The thought of losing Louise again wasn't worth contemplating. I tried to think, screwing my eyes shut in concentration. I felt I was speeding through a deep, dark tunnel, headlong towards some terrifying realisation, and was unable to stop myself.

Something happened tonight, something terrible. I sat up in the bath and gasped, fear gripping my heart in a vice like grip. I didn't know where that idea (voice?) came from but it left me cold, despite the warmth of the water. I had caught glimpses of myself running across an empty field and almost cried out, it had felt so real. Scrambling out of the bath, I grabbed my towel, not wanting to see any more strange images.

Slipping a shirt on, I noticed the scar from the operation. It wasn't something I thought about much now but was always thankful that it (along with a brilliant surgeon) had saved my life.

As I traced my finger along the inverted "T" shape that it made, a thought struck me. Maybe the transplant had affected me more than I'd let on?

Tonight's "blackout" had frightened me more than anything else before so it was vital for me to try and find out why it was happening. Dressing quickly, I made a mental note to make an appointment with Dr. Truman, my doctor, the next day. He had been the one who'd spotted my liver failure symptoms in the first place and I trusted him.

The surgery was five miles away, just off the High Street in the town centre. The car park, as usual, was virtually full and it took me a good five minutes to find a parking space, by which time I'd nearly given up and turned around to go home. I was embarrassed because I didn't know what I was going to say to him. Checking my watch, I hurried to the surgery.

## Chapter 6

Dr. Truman sat back in his chair and stretched, before folding his long slim fingers together and resting his hands on his lap. His hazel coloured eyes studied me through gold-rimmed glasses and I looked away, unable to keep eye contact.

*This wasn't a good idea.*

I began fidgeting in my chair, like a naughty schoolboy and picked at my fingernails.

*Definitely not a good idea.*

"What seems to be the problem, Bryan?" He had been my doctor for twenty years, taking an especially keen interest in my well being since the transplant.

My mouth locked up, not wanting to say what my brain had formulated earlier that day.

"Bryan?"

"Nothing and everything," I said finally. "I don't feel physically ill, in fact I've never felt better but…things have happened."

Once I started, I couldn't stop, telling him everything, including the previous day's blackout.

Dr. Truman sat listening, asking questions occasionally, and making notes. I couldn't discern any reaction on his face, which remained passive throughout our discussion.

Once I'd finished, I felt drained, all my energy gone. "I want you to take this to the pharmacy and keep to the recommended dosage." I took the prescription from him. "What's this?"

"Anti–depressants."

"What?"

"Transplants are very traumatic and stressful experiences and it's obvious you are not coping with it very well. These should help."

Staring at him I was stunned. "Is that it?"

Seeing my confusion, he leaned forward, a brief smile crossing his lips. "Come back in two weeks, if these don't help, then we can look at doing some tests."

Speechless, I stormed out of the surgery, throwing the prescription in the bin on the way.

I was fuming. He had dismissed me and made it sound as if I wasn't coping, which, in my opinion, was absolute bullshit. There was no way what had happened over the last few months was down to being depressed. I had expected my doctor, whom I trusted implicitly, to show a bit more concern than he actually did. Sitting in the car, I fished through my pockets for the cigarettes I'd bought earlier; lighting one up I took a deep drag and blew the smoke out through my nose and tried to calm down. My first instinct was to go back in there and try to see him again. I actually put my hand and arm on the car door ready to get out, but stopped myself. The only thing that would achieve would be to reinforce Dr. Truman's theory – that I was depressed and stressed out. No, there had to be another way of finding out what was going on. The trouble was, I had no idea what that was.

## Chapter 7

Louise was waiting for me at the front door, the note I'd written earlier grasped in her hand. I didn't want to go through my reasons for seeing the good doctor then.

"Can we talk about it later?" I said walking passed her, deliberately avoiding eye contact. Going straight upstairs, I collapsed on the bed, not even bothering to remove my coat first.

When I awoke, the room was pitch black, and, for a moment, I was disorientated, not sure where I was. The dream I had just had was still vivid, though, and it was that which had disturbed me the most.

> *It was the motorbike accident I had seen some time before but now I was the motorcyclist, lying broken and dying on the hard, cold tarmac. The pain had been unbearable; I wanted to shout help but could only feel the coppery taste of blood filling my mouth. My emotions were of rage and frustration, which masked the fear of my mortality. The periphery of my vision narrowed in a red haze leaving just a tunnel of light. Then, just before my sight disappeared completely, a voice spoke to me in reassuring tones, a familiar voice, but the words were lost as I fell into unconsciousness.*

Lying there in the darkness, a cold sweat enveloped me and I pulled the coat up, around my neck. I'd never been on a motorbike before, so why should the dream disturb me? The only reason I could think of was that it had seemed so real.

The bedroom door opened, squeaking loudly on its hinges, (something that I still needed to sort out), and Louise's voice drifted quietly to me.

"Are you awake?" She sounded agitated. I wasn't really in the mood to talk, so kept still, keeping my breathing even. She tutted and turned the light on, banishing the night in an instant. I squinted my eyes as I turned to see her standing in the doorway. I could tell she had been crying, her eyes bright red with recent tears.

"What's happening to you, Bryan, you seem so…distant at the moment?"

Seeing the anger and hurt she was feeling struck me like an arrow through the heart.

"I'm sorry, its just there's so much going on in my head, I'm not sure who I am anymore."

She showed me the note I had left her earlier. "What's this all about?" Getting slowly to my feet I reached out, grasping her hand in mine. "I've been trying to get some answers and I thought Dr. Truman may be able to help."

"What did he say?" I saw fear flicker briefly on her face, instantly changing to concern. I shook my head. "Anti-depressants…he gave me a prescription for bloody anti-depressants."

Louise held my other hand and fixed her gaze on me. "Are you depressed?"

My gut instinct was to say "no" but I stopped to think first. Despite my obvious concerns, I'd never felt what you might consider unhappy or depressed. The fact Louise had stuck by me was enough to keep me going through thick and thin, no matter what.

Before I could answer, the telephone rang and Louise picked it up. "It's Dr. Truman," she said handing it to me.

My stomach flipped over. There must be something wrong with me, why else would he call?

"Hello."

"Bryan, Dr. Truman here." He sounded excited. "I've got to see you."

"You couldn't get rid of me quickly enough earlier."

Sensing my hostility, he gave a nervous laugh. "Yes, sorry about that, I was rather blunt but I wasn't sure then."

"Sure about what? Am I ill?"

"No, no, no, nothing like that. Come and see me tomorrow morning at the surgery, say 9:30."

The phone went dead, before I could ask any more questions. I stared quizzically at the handset, as if that would give me some answers.

"What did he want?"

I turned towards Louise, my expression unchanged. "He wants me to see him at 9:30 tomorrow."

## Chapter 8

The receptionist, her glasses bathed in the reflective light of the computer, did her best to ignore me, as she concentrated on whatever task she was involved with. In the end, I had to clear my throat, before she reluctantly dragged her eyes from the screen.

"Please take a seat Mr. Locksmith. Dr. Truman will see you shortly." She gave a thin smile and then went back to her computer screen.

Waiting was never a strong point of mine. I sat down. Perched nervously on the edge of the waiting room chair, I watched the clock crawling around to my scheduled appointment with the doctor. I hadn't slept well that night, my mind constantly churning over the endless possibilities as to what he was going to say. He'd said I wasn't ill but what else could it be?

Louise had wanted to come with me that day but I'd said no. It was something I needed to get my own head around first but had promised to tell her everything on my return. Reluctantly, she had agreed but wasn't happy about it. I sensed the doubt in her as she saw me off that morning but my determination (stubbornness?) held back any guilty feelings I had. How I regretted that now.

"Dr. Truman will see you now." The receptionist peered over at me, with another false smile, and indicated the double doors that led to his room.

Without acknowledging her, I made my way through, heart beating ever so slightly faster.

He was sitting at his desk, hands folded neatly on his lap, watching me carefully when I opened the door. "Hello, Bryan, do come in." He indicated the chair at his desk was for me.

Saying nothing, I sat down, a brief flutter of anger knotting my stomach, before settling again. I was eager for an explanation from him regarding his offhandedness with me the previous day but also intrigued, if not a little apprehensive, with what else he was so keen to tell me now.

"Firstly, Bryan, my apologies for the way I treated you yesterday. It was very...unprofessional of me." He stood up unable to look at me, his face turning a faint red colour. He cleared his throat. "Unfortunately, once I'd heard your story, I knew I had to check against similar, researched cases before I could be certain..." His voice trailed off.

"Even now, I can't be one hundred percent sure." He picked something up from his desk and pushed it under my nose.

"What's this?"

"Enlightenment?"

"What do you mean?"

"Read it and I'll do my best to explain afterwards."

"But I don't understand, how will this help me."

"Bryan, trust me. It will help."

His eagerness for me to read it was apparent. "Go on." He turned over the first page and pointed. "It won't take long."

This wasn't what I had been expecting – to sit and read a few pages of A4 but I could see it was important to him. So, I began to read.

Ten minutes later, I closed the file with a slap, my patience at its limits of endurance. "What the hell is this crap, this cellular memory?"

Dr. Truman stood up, went to the surgery window and gazed at the passers by before gathering his thoughts. "There are many slightly differing definitions of the term but the one that sticks out is what is written on the front cover of that report."

I again picked it up; a lot of what I'd read earlier hadn't really sunk in. Under the title "Cellular Memory – Fact or Fiction?" was this: —

> *Definition: The transfer of characteristics and behaviour from the organ donor to the recipient via the cells of the transplanted organ.*

"There have been many documented cases and I believe you could have become another one of them."

I stared at him incredulously. "So are you saying all my recent problems have been caused by my new liver?" For the second time in two days, I wanted to walk out of the surgery, having felt like I'd been brushed off. "Do you think I'm stupid?"

"No, no, not at all; look, I can tell you why I think it is the case with you." He picked up his notepad and flicked through until he found what he wanted, finger tapping the page in satisfaction. "From what you told me yesterday, it started with smoking?" He looked at me for confirmation and I nodded. He continued scanning the page. "Ah yes, a sudden liking for coke, the blackouts, and most strikingly of all, the reaction you had to the motorbike accident."

He noticed me shifting uncomfortably in my seat at this last point. "Something else has happened hasn't it?" His eyes shone with anticipation. As far as I was concerned, it still made very little sense to me and I wasn't in the mood to indulge him.

"Tell me," he said, unable to hide his eagerness.

"I'm not going to tell you anything, unless you explain what this cock and bull story you're spinning me is all about."

Seeing my intransigence, he placed his notepad on the table and told me. As he explained how he had been the first on the scene of a motorbike accident, which fitted perfectly with my dream of the night before, my fear grew.

"I know I'm not supposed to tell you this but I'm determined to prove my theory is correct – even if it is unethical." He still hesitated; perhaps some part of him was fighting against revealing the truth he was about to tell. "You see this person was your donor."

At that moment, I knew. It was like a wall being smashed down in my mind. I knew everything about the donor and my heart felt like it was seized in a vice. It was as if I was living his life, as well as my own. Fleeing the surgery, I had to get home, pack my bags and run. What about Louise? My eyes filled with tears, as I made my way across town. She would be safer and better off without me that was for sure.

## Chapter 9

The donor's memories continued to flood through to me...

## Chapter 10

People were always following him, always wanting a piece of him. They couldn't leave him alone. "Get away." he used to say, but they ignored him. His brother always got very angry with him. "It'll be your fault, if they get you," he would say. "You're not as clever as me." How he hated his smart arse brother. He could still hear his booming voice; see the coldness in his dark brown eyes;

smell the stale tobacco on his breath and sense the hate that coursed through him. "Oh! The glory of killing one of those bastards before they catch you." He would then laugh wildly.

He wouldn't kill, like his brother wanted, and was ashamed by that, but why? All that he knew was that he liked people but that other voice (his brother?) told him incessantly that he was useless and if he couldn't escape then he would never get any peace. "Kill them," his brother kept saying. It was driving him mad. He'd had enough; it was time for the pain to end, time to banish it all on a one-way street to oblivion.

The motorbike would be his angel of death...but it wasn't enough. He didn't care what his brother thought about him anymore, he'd show him. The donor card was in his pocket on that last fateful ride. How his brother hated him for it. But... just before impact, he knew he'd lost the battle.

## Chapter 11

The police car was parked outside my house and the two officers were standing at the front door talking to Louise. I just felt a numbing cold, deep inside me, as the final piece fell into place. The night I went "missing" for several hours, I'd killed a man.

"He finally did it, through me." I murmured.

The policemen had spotted me and were making their way warily down the footpath towards me. How could I explain this? I thought.

"*You can't*," came the gleeful reply. I put my foot down and sped off. The driver of the articulated lorry didn't see me – mainly because I pulled out without looking.

## Epilogue

So, there you have it. Am I a monster, or did recent events have an impact? Well, I guess you've already made your own mind up about that. Whether you believe in cellular memory, or whether I was going mad, I personally don't know. I will tell you one thing though, the donor, one Stuart Judd, was schizophrenic. How do I know? Well let's just say Dr. Truman was compiling some very interesting case studies in his report.

Anyway I think my time's almost up. People are gathering around my bedside now but I can't make them out properly. It doesn't matter I can think about Louise. I hope she's all right. And then I see her and she's smiling. I try to smile back, hoping she sees it...my breathing stops.

*Just one step back outside my skin*
*I look down on my life within*
*I breathe a sigh and all release*
*At bedside now I rest in peace.*

## The Home

By Colin Butler

The lounge, silent as a sepulchre
Save for the Television that reigns,
With wallpaper sounds for unhearing ears,
And flashing pictures for unresponsive brains.

Suddenly the silence is punctured
By shouts of an elderly toddler sound.
Whilst most are lost in their private world,
Where many strange thoughts abound.

Visitors arrive with flowers and fruitless fruit,
Shouting to be understood above the moan,
They talk of grandchildren and future plans,
While other residents sit silent and alone.

Residents huddled in easy chairs,
Snoozing and dreaming of youthful days,
Of work, of love and friends now gone,
All memories muddled by a misty haze.

Mealtime comes and they shuffle in
With zimmers, or sticks for the not-so spry.
Pitting false teeth against crusts and pies,
And dreaming of delicacies of days gone by.

Carers wash and feed the residents
With Caribbean or Oriental smiles.
Accompanied by a shrug of resignation - homesick,
For their homes distanced by so many miles.

Tick, tock, goes the grandfather clock
Chiming each hour as day follows day,
Ticking remorselessly on, till each resident
Bids their last goodbye and finally fades away.

# Interview with Sir John Cleggs-Bennett

By Simon Woodward

Sir John Cleggs-Bennett (now deceased) was not your ordinary type of man. It is only because of his fairly recent death it is now possible to publish the transcripts of an interview with him. Just to put the importance of this event into context, this is the only interview he allowed to take place and be transcribed.

His life and his involvement in everyday society across the world had to be kept secret; he was a person who always worked behind the scenes to guide and direct the society in which we live, from the last vestiges of the 1800s to the latter half of the 20th Century. However, a lot of his efforts were in vain.

It was only when the time of his imminent demise became known to him that he decided to contact the editor of the world renowned publication "The Recent Emissary", who then engaged me, Richard Simonson, to set in writing the story of his life, in his own words.

Sir John had a strong belief that, if his work ever became public whilst he was alive, then whatever he had put into motion would have been rendered impotent and of no use to anyone.

The man had worked fervently in the background of major governments, unions, the odd fringe party, and market stall to direct and drive the way forward.

The editor of "The Recent Emissary" has determined it is now time to publish and reveal to the world how much we owe to Sir John Cleggs-Bennett.

As a journalist, I cannot describe absolutely his affect on society today, but what I can do is present the questions I asked him and his responses. The determination of his influence is up to you.

When I interviewed Sir John Cleggs-Bennett at his bedside, I asked him his age and he told me the incredible figure of 121. This is fact, as far as I could ascertain, as he produced his birth certificate, which certainly backed up his claim.

Could he have been a skilled forger? Possibly. Might he have been a skilled forger to influence society's development? Probably.

During the course of the interview, he described times, places and situations that could only be described if he had been there.

As a person he was kind, considerate, patient and, on occasions, very obtuse. He saw ill in very few people and appeared to take criticism gracefully, most of the time. However he didn't suffer fools gladly and being politically correct was not something he thought about.

On occasions, Sir John went into great detail. All I can say is; stay with him, you never know there may be points he made that are relevant to our lives today.

**Simonson:** Sir John you have graciously allowed me to interview you about your life. Why have you decided to allow an interview about your life now, when you have steadfastly refused any interview in the past?

**Sir John:** Young person, throughout my life I have seen a lot and have understood a vast amount more. It is only through this experience that I have come to know the date of my death. However, this knowledge is not old. To be quite honest, I found out only yesterday, when I visited the corner shop.

**Simonson:** The corner shop?

**Sir John:** Yes, exactly.

**Simonson:** This is interesting. Why is it, do you think, the trip to the corner shop revealed the time of your imminent demise?

**Sir John:** It's quite simple. The corner shop is a place I have always visited throughout my life and, in particular, the one very near to my home of the last five years.
**Simonson:** Yes, but how did this recent visit differ from all the others?
**Sir John:** To be quite honest, I'm not exactly sure; suffice it to say that the door didn't open in the way it had done in the preceding five years.
**Simonson:** Right. So the door did not open in its usual manner?
**Sir John**: Correct.
**Simonson:** So how did this differing door behaviour lead to the knowledge that your time on this planet was going to be curtailed somehow?
**Sir John:** Let me ask this; have you ever opened a door with unusual consequences?
**Simonson:** Ermm, I can't say I have... actually... thinking about it... I did pull on a door once and it didn't open as expected, but all that happened was that I ended up walking in to the edge of the door, bruising my shoulder and chest, all the while holding a somewhat detached door handle.
**Sir John:** So you agree that, in some instances, doors do purvey some strange behaviours?
**Simonson:** Well, having thought about it in that way, I can't say otherwise. All I obtained, through that door interaction, was a bruised shoulder and chest. Why, Sir John, do you think that your experience with weird door openings provided you with this glimpse?
**Sir John:** It didn't. But I think it was a portent.
**Simonson:** It didn't?
**Sir John:** No. It was only when I got into the shop, after dealing with the sticky door, that I found I was in a cloud of strange mist and, of course, I thought this was not that unusual, as most corner shop proprietors burn all sorts of things; it's their culture you know.

**Simonson:** So you carried on into the shop and into the not so unusual mist?
**Sir John:** Absolutely; I've seen much stranger things abroad.
**Simonson**: So when did you receive the premonition about your demise?
**Sir John:** That's simple; it was when the mist coagulated into a large sphere, which then proceeded to absorb me. Not that it was a premonition, though.
**Simonson:** The mist turned into a sphere and then absorbed you?
**Sir John:** Yes.
**Simonson:** Weren't you worried about this?
**Sir John:** No, I've been involved in much stranger things abroad.
**Simonson:** But this absorption revealed to you the circumstance of your imminent death?
**Sir John:** No.
**Simonson:** No?
**Sir John:** No. It was only when the proprietor popped the sphere that I then found out the date of my leaving.
**Simonson:** When you say leaving you mean death?
**Sir John:** I suppose you could call it that.
**Simonson:** So, the proprietor popped the sphere and...?
**Sir John:** He told me, "You will die the day after tomorrow".
**Simonson:** And that was it? That's why you called the editor of The Recent Emissary?
**Sir John:** Yes.

As you can probably tell by now Sir John's life is extraordinary, to say the least, and, in the next part of the interview, I asked him about his beginnings.

**Simonson:** Sir John, when were you born?
**Sir John:** You impertinent scallywag; where's your etiquette?
**Simonson:** Sorry, Sir John, what I actually mean is; when was it that your mother gave birth to you?

**Sir John:** Well... that was... hold on a minute, you've just asked me the same question again. This is outrageous.

**Simonson:** Sir John, I didn't mean it that way. What I meant to say was; on which day did your father give you your first birthday present?

**Sir John:** Ah. If I remember correctly that was the fifth of March 1875.

**Simonson:** Do you remember what your father gave you?

**Sir John:** Yes, I can't forget. He gave me a folded piece of paper.

**Simonson:** Folded paper?

**Sir John:** Absolutely.

**Simonson:** And this was interesting?

**Sir John:** Very.

**Simonson:** What made this particular piece of paper interesting?

**Sir John:** After he gave it to me, he told me to throw it.

**Simonson:** And that was the interesting part, being able to throw a piece of paper?

**Sir John:** Yes.

**Simonson:** Can you describe this event any further?

**Sir John:** Of course I can. What a question to ask. I'm on my death-bed, you fool, not suffering from some type of brain dysfunction. Were you the best they could send?

**Simonson:** Sorry, Sir John. Please allow me to re-phrase the question.

**Sir John:** Carry on then.

**Simonson:** Once you had thrown the folded piece of paper, what aspects of that action stuck in your mind?

**Sir John:** When I threw it, the piece of paper circulated around the room for some moments.

**Simonson:** It was flying?

**Sir John:** Of course it was flying. What else do you think it was doing? I was most intrigued. I just loved throwing it around the nursery.

**Simonson:** So, at the age of one, you were throwing pieces of paper around your nursery?

**Sir John:** Yes, of course. I had to please my papa. Wouldn't you have done?

**Simonson:** Let me get this straight. You were playing with flying pieces of paper, perhaps what we would call today, paper planes, in 1875, on your first birthday?

**Sir John:** Yes. That's what I've said isn't it?

**Simonson:** But, but, flight wasn't invented until the Wright brothers flew in December 1903.

**Sir John:** Ah, the Wright brothers, I remember them well; they used to come around, with their father, to see my mother; she did enjoy his company and the brothers often used to play with me, though they were a little older than I. I don't exactly remember when they started to visit but I do remember their father enjoyed my mother's pies. Yes, quite often he turned up and my mother was happy to give him one, and one for each of his sons, if I recall.

I remember throwing my Father's flying paper and they used to run after it, picking it up and bringing it back to me, in my cot, to throw again.

Strange thing though, after they left the house I could never find the pieces of paper and had to cry, until my Father made me another one.

That was very strange, now I come to think of it.

Soon after that we left Indiana and travelled to Kansas. My Father had heard from his brother, Albert, Albert Bennett, that there were opportunities to be taken advantage of in Kansas.

Sir John mentioned his father a great deal in our discourse about his first few years, so I decided to delve a little deeper into his father's history and ask him a little more about his relationship with his father.

**Simonson:** You mention your father a lot, was he important to you as a young child?
**Sir John:** Yes, I have and, of course, he was. I mean, without his history, I wouldn't be here, would I?
**Simonson:** Possibly true. In what way did his presence in your life influence you?
**Sir John:** Ah, now that is an interesting question. I can definitely say that, without him, I would not have been able to achieve everything I have done, up and unto this point, this point of our interview, I mean.
**Simonson:** Very good. But how did he contribute? In what way did he avail himself so that you were able to follow through in your life, until this point?
**Sir John:** I think it started when he laid down his seed and my mother took it on, if I recall correctly, if you know what I mean. I believe that was the start.
**Simonson:** Right, right. Apart from him laying down his seed?
**Sir John:** Well...
**Simonson:** Hold on a minute, you remember your conception?
**Sir John:** Of course I do. I have a very good memory you know.

It was at this point that it became obvious to me that I was certainly interviewing an extraordinary person, who had had an extraordinary life.

**Simonson:** Sir John, your recollection of your past is amazing to say the least. Are there any particular instances you can recall about your father's life you are willing to divulge?
**Sir John:** I can tell you about his time in Dodge City.
**Simonson:** By Dodge City, I take it you mean the Wild West?
**Sir John:** If you want to call it that, you can. It was certainly wild.
**Simonson:** Wild in what way?

**Sir John:** Wild in the way of wild animals, wild country and wild weather.

**Simonson:** OK, back to Dodge City. What did your father do, after moving the family to Dodge City?

**Sir John:** If I remember correctly, he became a cobbler.

**Simonson:** A cobbler? A person who made shoes?

**Sir John:** Yes, exactly, he also repaired shoes you know.

**Simonson:** Right, he repaired shoes as well. So, whilst in Kansas, he had trained as a cobbler?

**Sir John:** No, he was what we would call these days, an entrepreneur, and this is one of the reasons I respect my father. He had no idea about how to make or repair shoes but he saw the need and made a decision to fulfil the need. There were no brakes on the horses in those days.

**Simonson:** What do you mean, there were no brakes?

**Sir John:** At the time, before horses were fully domesticated for the whites, the only way to stop a horse was to lean over to one side and put your heal down hard in the earth.

**Simonson:** So the cowboys wore out their shoes trying to stop their steeds?

**Sir John:** Exactly. You don't think the Indians told them how to do that, do you?

**Simonson:** No, but weren't the horses trained?

**Sir John:** A very few were, because they had been brought over from the Motherland, but the majority were native, caught on the plains, if you will.

**Simonson:** So your father took up cobbling because there was a need?

**Sir John:** Absolutely, that is what he did. There is an area of Kansas named after his struggle to become a skilled cobbler.

**Simonson:** Which area?

**Sir John:** Boot Hill.

**Simonson:** You mean the cemetery?

**Sir John:** No, it's where my father threw all of his reject shoes, boots and soles, while he was trying to learn the cobbler's trade. It did take him a while, quite a long time in fact.
**Simonson:** But Boot Hill is where the notorious criminals of the time got buried.
**Sir John:** Yes, that's also true, but not the notorious criminals you're thinking of. That was Boot Hill in Tombstone. As far as I am aware there are at least seventeen Boot Hills in America.
**Simonson:** OK, so not Boot Hill in Tombstone, but Boot Hill in Dodge City. How did that name come about?
**Sir John:** Well, after my Father got the hang of cobblery [sic], he no longer required the land he'd used to scrap all of his rejects, so he sold it.
**Simonson:** He sold it? Who to? Who would want it?
**Sir John:** Yes, exactly. He sold it to the undertakers, who were expanding their business at the time, for one reason or another. I vaguely remember it having to do with bullets or something. Suffice it to say, he didn't need the land anymore, so he got rid of it, and for a good price, if I remember.
**Simonson:** What you're saying is; your father got rid of a piece of land, which contained all of his scrap, to undertakers of the time and it was those undertakers, who named their cemetery Boot Hill?
**Sir John:** This is exactly what I'm telling you.
**Simonson:** And it is called Boot Hill because it is made of boots?
**Sir John:** I can't say that, it was the undertakers who named it and the only relationship between them and my Father was the sale of the land.

When he found out they'd called it Boot Hill, he couldn't decide whether they were trying to be ironic or they'd just given it the first name that had popped into their heads.

In hindsight, I think they'd just named it after the first thing that had popped into their heads.
**Simonson:** So, after your Father sold the land, what then?

**Sir John:** He gave up being a cobbler and moved on. And, as far as I can recall, he felt that addressing problems of the feet was not his vocation in life.

**Simonson:** So he was striving for a vocation then?

**Sir John:** Exactly.

**Simonson:** Was it ever clear to you, at that time, where your Father would seek his vocation?

**Sir John:** No, not really. All I knew was that Mother and I would be heading north easterly. Father had said, "Kansas is not for us" and he wanted to leave. In recollection I think father was fed up with all the death and he didn't want Mother and I to have to experience that negative side of society any longer. I believe he was after a revelation of some sort, something that meant more than providing shoes for the death sayers.

**Simonson:** Before I ask any further questions, can you clarify what you mean by "death sayers"?

**Sir John:** Death Sayers, Simonson, were those people who would creep up to a person when they weren't expecting it and say "death", quite loudly in their ear. Mainly it was the sheriff types, if I recall correctly, and, if it wasn't the sheriffs, it was anyone else they felt disagreed with them.

**Simonson:** So your father moved on, because of the slaughter that ravaged the area you were living in, at the time?

**Sir John:** That's the reason we moved on, as far as I understand it, but, you must remember, I was very young at the time and may not have grasped the true reasons why my father decided to start travelling again.

**Simonson:** I think your recollections of the reasons are more than valid. Where did your father take you after you left Dodge City?

**Sir John:** After procuring a donkey, he took us north east-ish through Nebraska and then on to Wyoming.

**Simonson:** That's quite a journey. How long did that take?

**Sir John:** I believe it took about a year.

**Simonson:** During this journey, which you say took a year, there must have been instances that stick in your mind. Is there anything you can tell me about this trip?
**Sir John:** The trip, as I remember, was uneventful. We did come across some Indians on our journey, the Arapaho and the Pawnees, but they didn't give us a second look. However Father did make camp near one of their settlements for a while.
**Simonson:** You weren't attacked?
**Sir John:** No, of course not. Why would we be?
**Simonson:** Because the Indians were after the blood of white men.
**Sir John:** The Indians didn't give a hoot about white men, as long as their rites were respected.
**Simonson:** OK. So for a while your father, yourself and your mother were in Indian territory. Did anything happen?
**Sir John:** During that time my father had to learn how to survive. Although we had money there was no where to spend it to get the things we needed to survive. So he had to make do with the resources that were to hand.
**Simonson:** What were they?
**Sir John:** They were the shrubs, trees and the wild life.
**Simonson:** How did he make use of these natural resources?
**Sir John:** Father said the first things needed for survival, after shelter and warmth, were water and food. Father thought that if he could find some food then this would mean there would be water nearby.
**Simonson:** By food, what exactly do you mean?
**Sir John:** Whilst we were on the journey, Father wanted to make sure we all had decent helpings of meat.
**Simonson:** How did your father go about locating meat for you and your mother?
**Sir John:** Father knew of this beetle called the Carrion Beetle; he knew it would hunt down carrion to feed on and lay its eggs in.

The only problem he had was how he was going to find one of these beetles to follow.
**Simonson:** Your father was going to follow a beetle?
**Sir John:** Yes, he had a natural instinct for tracking invertebrates.
**Simonson:** OK. So how did he find one of these beetles?
**Sir John:** Father was fortunate that he had a small canary left over from the shoe shop. He had brought it along so that on the cold prairie nights, whilst we were sitting around the camp fire, we could have a good sing song before bedding down for the night. Those nights of singing with the canary ended when Father killed it, so he could use its dead body to attract the attentions of wayward Carrion Beetles.

Father had devised a survival strategy whereby he would leave the dead canary somewhere which was obvious to carrion beetles and wait for one to turn up. As soon as the beetle arrived, he would quickly hide the dead carcass away, leaving the beetle confused for a short time, before it would go off and hunt down carrion elsewhere and, as soon as it did, Father packed everything up and we began to follow. This is how we made most of our way across Nebraska.
**Simonson:** Living on carrion?
**Sir John:** Not all the time, because, where there was carrion, there were the animals that became the carrion. On occasions, we did have to eat carrion, but, cooked with the right seasoning, it was quite edible. Even today, I wish I could pop to a restaurant and ask for a carrion bhaji. Mother always turned that meat into something you would want later on. I don't know whether it was the seasoning she used but you always felt full after the meal and then, within a few hours, you felt like you would want to eat again. Very peculiar, the way those meals felt hearty only to become a lost memory a few hours later; very peculiar indeed.
**Simonson:** So, your father took you and your mother across the prairies, following the Carrion Beetle. Did he ever mention where he was trying to get to?

**Sir John:** My Mother believed in everything my Father did and would have gone with him anywhere, but, when he fell ill and we were still stuck in the wilderness, she did feel it was time to find out where we were going.
**Simonson:** How did your mother cope with this problem?
**Sir John:** During our journey, she began to learn how to use the native plants for their curative powers. When father became ill with a fever brought on by a twisted ankle, Mother decided to see what she could do with Saxifrage. She had noticed various clutches of this plant on the way to where we were camped, before Father had fallen ill. I think we were lucky, because it was Saxifrage of the Saxifraga Occidentalis variety. Mother decided to collect the petals of this plant and nearly fell ill with exhaustion. The petals were not very big and she had to collect plenty of them to make the medicine in the required quantity to cure Father. She had to travel many miles to do this.

Once she had collected enough petals, she ground them up with the roots of the plant; then she added donkey urine to make it into a paste. When this was finished, she desiccated the mixture by drying it out over the camp fire. This was the first stage, I recall her singing to me in a lullaby fashion; I think she wanted me to sleep, so that she could concentrate on Father. The final preparation required adding the spittle of a yellow canary. Unfortunately, Father had used the last one up for attracting the attentions of the carrion beetles; so she had to find an equivalent source of spittle, as canaries were scarce in this part of the new world.

By this time, Father had become extremely ill and, in his last lucid moment, he said to my Mother, "*Go, Mirtle, go. Find the spittle of life and save me from a painful death.*"

Mother realized she had to find an equivalent bird species, if Father was going to survive the twisted ankle and the fever it had brought on. She said to me, "*John, stay with your Father, I have to seek out some spittle and I may be gone a while.*"

There was not much I could do but abide by my mother's wishes; I was just coming up to my third birthday. Mother left to seek out the spittle of a similar bird and I was left with Father who, when he was not unconscious, talked about strange things such as "*attaining liberation from the material world and union of the self with the Supreme Being*" and "*the gift of poetic thought, imagination, and creation, together with eloquence of expression*" and "*the hardiness of yellow earth be known to all*". I didn't really understand, at the time, what he was trying to say.

It was three periods of darkness before my mother returned with a receptacle full of mountain plover spit. She poured the contents on the mixture she had made three days previously and this last ingredient completed the salve. She then proceeded to apply the salve behind my Father's ears.

She said to me, "*Dear John, I have done what I can for your Father. All we can do now is await the outcome.*" After that, she consoled herself by dancing around our camp fire singing again.

After four days of singing, Father awoke.

**Simonson:** That is incredible. It sounds like all of you only just survived.

**Sir John:** I think it was at that time, I first became aware of my mortality.

**Simonson:** What happened next?

**Sir John:** My Father told us that during his illness he had had a vision and the vision had told him to go to Yellowstone, the area of Wyoming, which had recently been made a national park, though we did not know it at the time. He said further that there was a special person in Yellowstone, someone we would need to find, a person who knew the meaning of this world and could teach him the meaning, through melodic lingual chants and un-rhythmical metaphors. Father said we would need to find the yogic bard of Yellowstone. So, when he had recovered, that is where we went.

**Simonson:** How did you find Yellowstone?

**Sir John:** As far as I recollect, Father used his compass.
**Simonson:** No, what I mean is, when you got there, what was it like?
**Sir John:** Ah, Yellowstone, Yellowstone, Yellowstone; that strange and wonderful place; with its upward spouting waterfalls, petrified trees and plants. Just one step back, outside my skin, I look down on my life within, I breathe a sigh and all release, at bedside now, I'll rest in peace.

At this point in the interview, Sir John, after his strange words, seemed to pass into a state of unconsciousness and I had no other recourse but to stop my questioning.

It was obvious to me that Sir John's life was gradually ebbing away and he needed to rest a while, if we were ever going to continue.

It was now clear that one of the reasons Sir John had been so influential in his own history was the fact that, during his upbringing, he had been part of a family, which had been wholly extraordinary in their own right.

And although I waited for Sir John to recover, it wasn't to be; he past peacefully away, taking the rest of his incredible life's story with him.

I very much doubt I'll ever get another opportunity to interview anyone who comes close to the greatness this man undoubtedly had.

Rest in peace Sir John.

# Shut the Door as You're Leaving

By David Shaer

I remember, I do, I'm sure I remember
Those warm summer days and the cool of September
I still feel the warmth, the sun's glowing rays
My innocent youth and halcyon days

The sun made us happy, just smiling again
We knew it would finish, to school in the rain
The holiday's over, to my shell I'd retreat.
Forgotten the summer, the colours, the heat

We'd stayed on a farm with chickens and cows
With lambs and their mothers, like piglets and sows
We'd played village cricket, with rules from the dales
Our cousins were heroes, especially the males.

They talked very strange with accents unclear
Us townies were strangers for two months each year.
I'm out of my depth, my trousers I'd hitch
And still get as wet when I fell in the ditch

My uncle was nasty and gave us bad looks
They're never called ditches, they're always called brooks
He hated the townies, we'd not got a clue
Of protocols rural and things not to do

He got me in trouble for being so dumb
I cried in my hankie and ran home to Mum
He told me so often of skills I did lack
He didn't do humble – I will get him back

My Aunt was much nicer and had a just cause
She never had secrets or hid behind doors
Her accent was local but not from round there
She came from Devizes and had pretty hair

But now I've forgotten the stuff that's all near
I really can't handle the reason I'm here
They say that I've lost it but won't tell me what
I stare at the ceiling and cry quite a lot

I used to be happy and find life such fun
But now they all treat me as if I'm still one
They wash me and feed me and keep me in bed
If this is my future, I'd rather be dead.

My mind is all scrambled, there's things I must say
But falling asleep takes my mind off the day
I'm lying here waiting but don't know what for
Whatever's on offer I can't handle more.

I remember the fifties, the sixties and more
But lost what came after and can't keep the score
Whatever was happ'ning is far out of sight
Shut the door as you're leaving and turn out the
light.

True Prologue
I wrote the above with my mind in a mess
And couldn't believe that the words mattered less

To my cousin who's loving and kind by my side,
But as I was writing the silly sod died.
He never really could conquer his thirst
But one thing's for sure he wasn't meant to go first

Dear Michael.

# A New Perspective

By Jessie Hobson

## Chapter 1

Mrs. Geraldine Harrow,
10 Clatterbridge Lane,
Little Merket,
Suffolk.

The heading at the top of the letter conjured up for me a picture of a smiling farmer's wife. She would have worn a flowered skirt and serviceable bonnet of a by-gone era and driven her horse and cart noisily across a hump-backed stone bridge to a small market town in the green and lush county beloved of John Constable. Fantasy came a long way from fact.

Number 10 was a non-descript semi-detached 1930s house in a drab, narrow, suburban street, festooned with vehicles on either side, like a lumpy necklace, except where frontages were deep enough to have been sacrificed as car standing space.

The woman, who opened the door to me, if not actually emaciated, was thin and bony, with a long, austere face and an unwelcoming, almost hostile, stance.

"Well?"

"Mrs. Harrow? You asked me to come and see you. About Sean - Sean Cartwright. I'm Alison Duplessis."

She moved back, one eyebrow raised in appraisal, then motioned with one hand.

"Come in."

The hallway I entered was white-walled, the only colour being pale beige carpeting, with a small diamond pattern in a darker shade. This continued up the stairway on the left. There was a picture or mirror on the wall. I had no time to make sure which, as she indicated a room on the right, so I went in ahead of her. Once inside, Mrs. Harrow directed me to an upright armchair, with polished wooden arms, covered in brown dralon and graced with a plump cushion in quilted cream satin. It seemed the lady liked muted colours. The chair was surprisingly comfortable.

"Sean is my godson," she said without preamble. "You couldn't have known that, of course, because he wasn't called Cartwright as a baby."

She must have seen that this had taken me by surprise, because a wry smile flitted across her face.

"What's more," she continued, "You are my goddaughter."

"How can that be?" I demanded indignantly. “Maman and Papa would surely have told me about you."

"That is because Andre and Julie Duplessis are your adoptive parents, not actually related to you in any way."

Stunned, I sat silent, disbelieving at first, then certain things, that had puzzled me over the years, clicked into place. Very early memories of a little boy being in my life - but my brother Rene was younger than I, so it could not have been he. The little boy. Oh, no, not Sean.

"Are you telling me that Sean is my brother? And that we cannot marry?"

"Let me explain. Maureen Amis was my cousin. She wrote a document, I think it was in the nature of a confession, one which was weighing on her soul. The doctors believed at the time that she was a manic-depressive, and she gave the paper to me when I visited her in hospital, shortly before she died. It has become relevant only now, which is why I am passing it to you. Take it and show it to Sean, and, yes, the world once knew you as brother and sister."

Geraldine Harrow, a cousin of mine? I watched her go to a slim bureau and fetch a large envelope, bulging with paper. My face must have shown my horror, because she smiled again, and said "It is not all bad, you will see."

## Chapter 2

It is a blur in my mind how I left that house, clutching the fateful bundle of papers written by a woman, whom I, most certainly, could not remember as my mother.

My first impulse, as I drove to Harwich, was to ring Maman - Julie, wife of Papa, Andre Duplessis. My own identity - Alison Duplessis. Not this - this adopted child. I felt confused. Why had they never told me?

But it didn't seem quite right to tackle this any other way than face to face. Whatever else, I needed to read the document before speaking about it to them, and, more especially, before showing it to Sean.

Arriving at the docks, I went through customs like an automaton and drove aboard the ferry, trudged to the upper deck and looked for a quiet corner, where I could maybe start to unravel the mystery document.

Frustrated at every turn by knots of passengers gathered on all available seating, I abandoned my attempt to be alone and went in search of refreshment. One or two predatory males eyed me up and down speculatively, but they were rewarded with a withering look from me, and I approached the counter unmolested.

"Madam?" queried the assistant, also somewhat wary of my uncompromising manner, which she clearly saw as haughty and unfriendly. I was in no mood to put her at her ease, and gave my order briefly and succinctly, in French. She served me, without comment, and I moved to the checkout to pay. As I moved away, a voice behind me said:

"Bonjour, M'mselle Duplessis."

There was laughter in the tone, and I wheeled to face my friend, Marie Louise, my mouth agape with astonishment.

"Marly. What on earth are you doing here?"

I had lapsed into English, her nickname from days at Norwich University automatically transporting me back.

"I could say 'snap' to that. It wouldn't get us far, though, would it, Lissie?"

She too had reverted to the short version of my name we had used in the past.

"I'm on my way home," I said. "It is all complicated, I can't really explain at the moment, but I've had some staggering news I can't come to terms with yet, so perhaps you had better tell me your side of things."

"That sounds mysterious. I shall look forward to hearing more when you're ready. As for me, I'm off on holiday to Paris for a week. To some extent, it is a working holiday, as I want to do some research into the Maigret stories, to see whether the locations really existed, and if real people formed the basis of the stories."

Marly's enthusiasm helped to take my mind off my own problems and I was glad we were both aiming for the French capital.

"Do you have a car?" I asked.

"No, I plan to travel by train."

"Not any more. You shall be my passenger and we can chew over old times."

My recent news made me refrain from giving an immediate offer of hospitality at home - did I have the right?

We spent the rest of the journey aboard wandering round the deck in the evening light, the sea calm and sparkling with reflections from the setting sun. She confided to me that she had a flat at Sheringham, on the Norfolk coast, and that she worked as a librarian at one of the Norfolk towns. My recollection of the exact location is hazy, as my mind was not fully attentive. In my turn, I told her of my business trip on behalf of Papa, to collect some antique porcelain from an auction house in Suffolk, for which he had entered a phone bid. I omitted to mention my visit to Little Merket. That could wait.

## Chapter 3

The journey to Paris was uneventful, apart from a couple of hooray henries exasperating everyone with their antics, in an ancient open-topped sports car, and we arrived in time for breakfast at my parents' home, on the outskirts of Paris. My parents, I told myself firmly; adoptive or not, my beloved Maman and Papa.

Marly was made welcome, as I knew in my heart she would be. She and Papa enthused over the porcelain pieces I had brought back for him, and he promised to take her to visit the antique flea-market at St. Ouen and to advise her on purchases for her flat. I found myself looking at Maman with new eyes, and she must have realised my unease, because she drew me aside, away from the others. "Something is troubling you, Alison."

As usual, we spoke French en famille.

"Oh, Maman, where shall I begin? I had a letter from a Mrs. Harrow to go and see her."

It was clear Maman knew what I was about to divulge, as her face tightened with distress and she clasped her hands together, twisting her fingers distractedly, her head bowed and unwilling to look me in the eye.

"So it's true. I'm adopted. Why didn't you tell me?"

"These things happen, dear. Time passes and it doesn't seem to matter. You were, and are, our beloved daughter, and the longer we put it off, the harder it became."

She raised her head suddenly, startled by a thought.

"Why did she choose to tell you now? For what reason?"

"It must be to do with Sean. I'm in love with him, and, according to her, he's my brother."

"How does she know this?"

"My birth mother left a document with Mrs. Harrow with all the facts. I have it here, but I have not yet had time to read it, because I bumped into Marly. I'm supposed to let Sean know where we stand."

"You must read this document, whilst Papa takes Marie Louise exploring Paris tomorrow. Have you told her anything yet?"

"No, but I told her I had had some astonishing news, so she is bound to ask before long."

My wise Maman took Marly off clothes shopping for most of that day, leaving me to tell Papa my news. He received it gruffly and with a Gallic shrug of the shoulders, as if it were really of little consequence, which seemed unfeeling to me. But then, he did not like Sean very much.

## Chapter 4

In Marie Louise's presence, we all spoke English over our evening meal. In spite of her name, she was from Norfolk stock and had been a natural candidate for graduating at University of East Anglia, whereas the co-incidence - as it seemed - of both Sean and myself studying there was astounding. I had been told that money had been left in trust for me to do my degree there and, in the arrogance of youth, had taken it for granted, nor yet had thought to ask the source of the money. It now seemed likely that Sean had had a similar arrangement, but why bring us together?

Perhaps the answer lay in the documentation. Maman was right, I should read it. I was able to have the solitude I needed in my bedroom, as Marly was using the guest bed in a separate room. With fumbling fingers, I drew out the dreaded sheets from Geraldine's cousin Maureen and began to read.

Wasn't it Shakespeare who said, "What a tangled web we weave, when we practice to deceive"? Nobody in the picture emerged as a wide-eyed innocent from Maureen's tale. At least Sheila was single when she fell in love with her neighbour Maureen's husband, Bernard. But, when she had a baby girl by him, she wanted her adopted. That baby was me.

So Maureen was not my birth mother after all; but she agreed to accept me, for Bernard's sake, and because she wanted a girl. She chose to call me Erica, which puzzled Bernard. He did not know that soon after they married, Maureen had got involved herself with a married estate agent called Eric, and had fallen pregnant with his child. He, in his turn, had laughed her to scorn when she suggested leaving Bernard, and pointed out that, with a beautiful wife and three kids at home, what need did he have of a new family? So Maureen let Bernard believe the child was his, and never let on about her infidelity. In the fullness of time, a boy was born and named Barry, after Bernard's dad. Sean, of course. Three years older than I, so we each had unrelated parents. That far through Maureen's story, I was over the moon that Sean was apparently free to marry me.

I read on, it becoming clear that Maureen's acceptance of me had been conditional. She expected Bernard to end his affair. It seems he paid lip-service to this, but actually secretly continued to meet Sheila.

Both were killed some months later in an accident, when it appeared the brakes of their car failed beside a lake and the vehicle rolled into the water, where both drowned. Maureen continued to care for both children but ended up in hospital. She was told she had a terminal brain tumour. This was when she contacted her cousin, Geraldine, with the document I was now reading, and arranged our adoption, Barry/Sean to a Yorkshire couple and me, Erica/Alison to......

At this point, I burst into tears, as I recalled the happy years I had spent with Maman and Papa and, at the same time, mourned a little for Sheila and Bernard, my birth parents, consoled that they were together at the end.

There was still one small envelope left, sealed. 'For Alison's eyes only. Open only after reading the rest.'

What special thing could Maureen have to say that was so secret?

## Chapter 5

Before I had a chance to open this last missive, there was a tentative knock on my bedroom door, then Marly popped her head round, her eyes wide with anxiety.

"Lissie? I heard you crying. Are you all right?"

"Yes, yes," I answered hastily. "The news I got is better than I thought, and I was just relieved."

I was not ready yet to explain it all, and in any case I still hadn't found all the answers, until I had looked into the sealed package.

"I'm sorry I disturbed you," I added. "Please go back to bed - I'm fine."

Marly gave me a hug and went out again, with a reassured smile on her face.

It was as well that she went before I opened the ominous 'For Alison's eyes only' envelope. By the end, my heart had turned to ice.

'Dear Alison,' it read, 'for such I must now call you. When I named you Erica, it was out of spite, because I felt that both Eric and Sheila had betrayed me, never mind Bernard, and I needed to unload my hurt in some way. I was never unkind to you, you understand, and, in many ways, I am glad that you no longer bear that name.

What I have to tell you now, I beg you not to tell to Sean. He is, after all, really my son, Barry, as he was then.

I have already said that Sheila and Bernard were drowned. I must admit that in truth, I was responsible for their death. One afternoon I went with you and Sean, (Barry), for a picnic to a quiet greensward clearing in the woods near our home. There was a small lane nearby, just large enough for cars, giving access to a lake, with a couple of osiers on the rough banks. I put your pram in the shade by a hawthorn shrub and spread a blanket and cushions on the grass for Sean and myself and, when we had eaten, I settled Sean for a nap and rocked you to sleep in the pram. All was quiet, when a car drove up. Our group was not easily visible.

I was shocked to see that it was Bernard's car and that he had Sheila with him. I watched as they started to cuddle and kiss, and I went berserk.

I racked my brains for something to hurt them, and scrabbled in my bag for some hair-spray I carried. I ran silently across the clearing and pulled open the car door and sprayed their startled eyes. While they were briefly blinded, I released the brakes, slammed the car door, and, in my fury, found the strength to push the car towards the lake. It soon gathered momentum, and plunged into the water, where it quickly sank below the surface. I stood there for several minutes, then quite calmly packed up our picnic gear, woke Sean and wheeled you home. I was never connected with what happened. At the time, I acted the distraught widow to perfection, with no thought of remorse. As I am now dying, it is on my conscience - they were your blood relatives. So, you will see, I found it necessary to take just one step back outside my skin. I looked down on my life within. I breathe a sigh and all release at my bedside now. I rest in peace.

Forgive me.

Maureen.'

## Chapter 6

This tormented woman, capable of cold-blooded murder, was Sean's mother. She had cast her burden on my shoulders. I thought bitterly that, maybe, she could rest in peace, but I would have to keep her secret from the man I wanted to marry. I spent the night in turmoil, sleepless and miserable. How could I face everyone in the morning, without it being obvious that my whole world had fallen apart? By dawn, exhausted, I slipped into a fitful doze, my dreams unrelated to the problem, but nightmarish and ominous in character, leaving me wracked with feelings of guilt, for which I could find no reason when I woke.

How to react to the family was solved for me by the arrival of my brother Rene, who had heard that I'd come home. His cheerful chatter and gossipy news kept people's attention, so I was able to sit in the background, without anyone noticing me.

In my head, I began to plan how to approach Sean. If I gave him Maureen's document, except for the separate envelope, it might be simplest. I knew that he had never really been fond of his Yorkshire parents - perhaps he had known he was adopted, although he had never said so to me. Would he be pleased to know about Maureen? The straightforward answer was to phone and arrange to meet him. He no longer lived at the Cartwright home.

Since leaving university, with an honours degree in economics, he had built an empire of his own, a minor one it is true, but sufficient to set up home both here in France and in East Anglia. He worked as a trouble shooter for several businesses needing to liaise across the Channel, and travelled frequently on both sides. We often crossed paths, when I was acting on Papa's behalf as a courier, and our relationship blossomed from the camaraderie of university life into a close and personal awareness and, yes, love. On my mobile, I called Sean's number.

The sound of his deep voice answering made me gulp momentarily with longing, but I recovered quickly and found that he was available in a couple of days time, after a conference in Marseilles, to which he would be going that afternoon. We left it that he would come to meet me at home and, as he could not be specific about what time he would arrive, he would let me know on the day. I mentioned that Marly was in Paris with us and told him about her proposed trip to St Ouen.

"Oh, her. I remember. Nice girl." he said. But he seemed more interested to know what momentous news I had in store for him, so I said he would have to wait till he came.

Listening to him had cheered me and I felt emboldened to confide in Marly what had occurred.

"Sean is coming on Thursday and I shall show him this bulky paper package, which is what all the mystery is about."

"Am I now allowed to hear what it is?" asked Marly.

"Yes - here - take it and read it. It will be easier than trying to tell you in my own words."

"You realise I am not staying here the rest of the week, don't you? I've already booked a hotel room, and your father is leaving me there, after our trip to St Ouen."

"In that case," I laughed, "you must get reading fast right now."

Marly curled up in a chair with the document, minus the small envelope, which I had already hidden away, locked in a safe drawer. I left her to it, as I sorted my room, hummed happily at the prospect of seeing Sean soon. From the corner of my eye, I could see the locked drawer and a niggling doubt crept into my mind how I would cope with this devastating knowledge. One should expect to share secrets of any calibre with someone whose life is to go in tandem, not hide them guiltily away. I stopped humming and stood pensively at the window, seeing nothing, feeling unfamiliar emotions whirling in my thoughts. I felt angry with Maureen and not a little afraid of how much her personality and that of her lover, Eric, would influence Sean's temperament. Returning to where Marly sat, I found her just ending the document.

"Mm," she said. "What a mess. You are welcome to handle that. Interesting about Sean, though. Not your brother, only a near miss." She grinned and handed the package back to me. "Have fun." Her light-hearted answer seemed to me almost as strange as Papa's indifference.

Papa came in just then to collect Marly and her baggage and we said farewell, with all the usual promises to be in touch. Once Marly had gone, I took some time before Sean was due to come, firmly cementing my relationship with Papa, Maman and brother Rene; for me, my true family. We shopped, we gossiped, we played cards and made plans for future purchases for Papa's antiques business. Rene dragged me off to look at cars, most of which were way outside his price range, and Maman cooked my favourite meals, as if I might disappear before her eyes, unless I was well fed. It was a happy time, with the joy of anticipation added, waiting for Sean.

## Chapter 7

Sean's call was short and simply said when he would arrive, so I spent time making the best of my appearance and setting out the package he was due to read.

When he came, his kiss seemed perfunctory, which I put down to Papa's presence in the room. Maman tactfully called Papa to help her elsewhere and, as Rene was already out, we were alone at last.

"What did you want to see me about?"

No 'How are you darling?' No 'Give me a proper kiss'. He was not usually so formal and abrupt.

I responded in kind, in honesty with some relief, by curtly handing Maureen's document to him and saying simply, "I've been asked to show you this."

Sean took the package, gave me a quick look, and then settled to read. I wandered round the room, fiddling with flowers in a vase, tidying pictures, which were quite straight anyway, lining up books on a shelf, anything other than look in Sean's direction.

"When I was quite small," he said suddenly, "I was told I was adopted. Weren't you? What's the importance of all this guff? Does it really matter whether we are brother and sister? As it happens, it seems we are not, anyway."

"Matter? I love you, Sean. Of course it matters."

I was sorting my hair by the mirror as I spoke, and glanced towards his reflection. He had flung the package down and stood up, not looking at me, and I was appalled to catch a calculating look of sheer malice on his face. I turned swiftly, but when he looked me in the face, his expression was bland. Surely, I had been mistaken.

"I thought you Frenchwomen were more amoral than that. We've come pretty close to committing incest, if we had been brother and sister."

"Sean," I said, shocked. "I said love, not lust."

"Oh, forget it." he answered testily, "It doesn't alter anything."

"No? Then why are you so disagreeable today? Even before you read 'this guff'' as you call it?"

Sean took a deep breath.

"I can see we are having a bit of a spat, so perhaps I'd better go. You have given me the information as requested. Let's leave it at that, for the present. I'm back off to Southwold."

Then he just left. My whole day crumbled to dust.

## Chapter 8

Two things stayed in my mind. Sean had said 'it didn't alter anything', which surely meant we were still looking to marry one another. The other remark had been flung over his shoulder as he left. His cottage in East Anglia was near Southwold, in Suffolk and he had said he was going back there. Was this a back-handed invitation to follow him there, for a loving reconciliation? For the present, I was too hurt to make such a move. Leave it a while, I thought. Maybe he would ring and make amends.

The phone call, which did come several days after I had wallowed in misery, was not from Sean but from Marly. She wanted to know if I was likely to be in England the following week, as it was her turn to give me some news.

Papa had asked if I could attend an auction at Acle in Norfolk, to which I had agreed. Perhaps, at the back of my mind, had been the idea to visit Sean's cottage. I said to Marly that I would be staying in Wroxham, a bigger town than Acle. She was delighted and said I could have a tourist's treat by travelling to Aylsham on the tiny steam train from there to meet her at the station. My car could stay in the hotel car park until my return. It all fell into place to our mutual satisfaction. I did not tell her of my plan to call on Sean.

I arrived in Norfolk two days before the auction, and set off across the countryside from Wroxham, an hour's drive or so, and left my car some distance from the cottage, as I hoped to surprise my beloved. The day was hot and sunny, my mood expectant, and I tiptoed lightly around the back of the house into the back garden, to be brought up short by the sight of two naked bodies embracing ardently under a gazebo on the lawn. They were too engrossed to notice me but, with a feeling of inevitability, I realised it was Sean and Marly. I retreated as quietly as I had come, all my dreams shattered, and stumbled back to my car, where I sobbed uncontrollably.

Tears exhausted at last, I drove to Wroxham. Back at the hotel room, I flung myself on the bed, my mind in total confusion. I recalled the look of malice I had intercepted several days before on Sean's face. Did he really hate me? How long had he been seeing Marly? — surely longer than his casual reference to her as a 'nice girl' when I told him she had been staying with me in Paris. Even Marly had seemed rather flippant about the document when she returned it to me.

I decided to carry on with the arrangement I had made with Marly, as there seemed no better time to find out the truth. I had never actually told her that Sean and I were 'an item,' as people say. Clearly, we were not. My mind began to get into gear. I was very fond of Marly, and Sean, it seemed, had a good deal of his actual father's character, a philanderer.

Marly's parents were very wealthy, she was their only child. Was he after her money? That calculating look on his face - did I stand in his way? Was he his mother's son, too - would he kill me? If Sean could kill me, he might just as easily destroy Marly's family and Marly herself to get his hands on their money. These horrifying thoughts flitted fitfully through my mind. The shock of knowing that I had been living with only the illusion that Sean loved me, left me feeling very empty and drained. I began to feel angry and cheated, a woman scorned, if you like but, frightened at the strange turn of events, the need to protect myself. How dreadfully naive I had been.

At this point, I was thankful that I always write about my activities in a diary. I would make up a package, as Maureen did, of all that had happened since I went to Little Merket, and leave it with a solicitor in Wroxham, with instructions to send it to Geraldine Harrow if I should die within five years. If I am still alive then, I can retrieve it, no harm done.

## Chapter 9

Geraldine Harrow made her way slowly to the front door. She was still deeply affected by the sudden death of Alison, and her grief showed in her face as she opened to the postman's knock.

"Sorry, missus. This one's too big to shove through the letter box and needs to be signed for as well."

"For me? Are you sure?"

The postman held the package up for her to see the inscription. With a small sigh, Geraldine wrote her name on the proffered board and tucked the official-looking envelope under her arm, as she thanked the postman and closed the door again.

It was a bulky package, seemingly from a solicitor. She eyed it with disfavour and set it down on the small coffee table by her armchair. It could wait until she had made herself a cup of tea. Even this she did without enthusiasm, and it was fully half an hour before she made a move to look at the new correspondence. As she unfolded the pages, she found first a letter from Hatchett, Brown and Gorrison, solicitors, stating that the enclosed had been entrusted to them, with specific instructions to forward it to her under certain circumstances, which they deemed now to have occurred. She opened the letter from Alison, and began to read.

As the account from Alison proceeded, she became more and more engrossed, until she came to Maureen's confession, about which she had never known. She hissed, and moaned aloud as she read this, then stood up and went to her bureau. A framed photograph of two girls stood on the top. One, although much younger, was clearly Geraldine herself. The other......

"Oh, Sheila, my dear, dear sister. So it was no accident. Maureen killed you and Bernard. Why, oh why, did you give her your baby?"

She picked up the photograph and cradled it in her arms, returning to her chair. She recalled that, at the time, her husband Harold had been diagnosed with cancer, which would have made it difficult to undertake to care for a tiny child herself. With guilt, she remembered being angry with Sheila for parting with her child at all, for Geraldine had been childless. Harold's death soon after had diverted her attention and, by then, Bernard and Maureen had formally accepted the baby as theirs. So she had had no choice but to see the children adopted, as Maureen stipulated on her deathbed.

For some time, Geraldine sat with her chin resting on her hand. After a while, she realised there was more to be read and she renewed her perusal. At the end, her face was grave.

Her mind returned to Alison's funeral, where she had met with Sean and Marie-Louise, now engaged to be married. In conversation, Marie-Louise had told her how they had been walking with Alison in single file through Aylsham, near the library, along the very narrow paving of a tiny winding road, really not designed for present-day traffic, when Sean had tripped and stumbled into Alison, sending her flying into the road in front of the car, which killed her. There had been an inquest, exonerating Sean from blame.

The letter from Alison gave one pause to consider whether Sean, like his mother, had stooped to murder, to achieve his aims. If Marie-Louise ever suspected him, she would be in serious danger of suffering a similar fate. Geraldine had lost her sister and her niece. It must stop there.

She gathered the package together, tidied her hair and put on a neat corded coat in her favourite beige colour, then left the house with Alison's account, her destination the local police station……

# A Moment in the Life Of

By Simon Woodward

The ground cracks,
The earth breaks,
Crumbling around.

The new shoot,
That is first seen,
Breaks forth with no sound.

The bud opens,
The petals there,
Displaying glory, above the mound.

Bees arrive,
And take nectar.
Around the flower they abound.

The insects go,
It's autumn,
The petals now, upon the ground.

And finally,
The death,
Of the plant, without sound.

# I Will Remember Them

By Colin Butler

I awoke from my troubled sleep with a shout and a cry for help. The sweat was pouring off me, as I tried to settle down. I had had several nightmares over the previous couple of weeks. In the latest, I had been in the trenches somewhere in Flanders. It was raining heavily and the mud was caked around my feet. Just then, a rat began to climb my leg, but the sound of a shell landing nearby frightened him off and he ran scampering down the trench. As I stood watching it, another shell landed just a few feet away, knocking me off my feet and as I fell, I saw that it hit my colleague and he fell screaming in agony.

My wife, Charlotte, then woke up and enquired, "What's the matter, Pete? Are you having another nightmare? It's those diaries and letters isn't it?"

I nodded silently and then said " I just can't get them out of my head."

Why was I having these nightmares? Well......

My wife and I had moved into our new house, well actually, it was an old Victorian house, which needed a lot of decoration and modernisation, just a few weeks previously. I had decided to put a number of things we had brought with us from our previous house up in the loft. These were items that we never used, but which would 'definitely be needed one day'. I climbed up to the loft, peered into the stygian gloom and decided to go back for a torch.

I proceeded rather apprehensively – what would I find there - spiders, mice or rats? What I did find were numerous items of junk - an old tin bath, an old pram, minus one wheel, a broken rocking horse, a clothes dummy and lots of other useless items.

Tucked away, in a far corner, was a large metal box and, upon examination, I discovered that it contained various papers. I was intrigued and decided to carry it downstairs and examine the contents, at my leisure. My first concern was to get rid of the junk in the loft, to make room for my junk - sorry, reserve items. Consequently, it was about two weeks before I got around to examining the mysterious box. All the items were covered in a thick layer of dust and I discovered that a number of spiders had taken up residence and spun several intricate webs amongst the contents.

After getting rid of this detritus, I found a bound red diary with a beautiful floral cover. I carefully opened it and read the title "The Diary of Ann Williams" – I turned over the pages to discover that it was for the year 1913. Who was Ann Williams? She must have been a previous occupier or daughter of an earlier owner. I was intrigued and began to read the diary, logically starting with the January pages. As I read, it opened up a world far different from mine - a world without television, computers, mobile phones or even telephones – a much simpler and slower world.

It soon became apparent that she had resided at this house with her parents, living a quiet and uneventful life, at that time. From the diary, I learned that Ann spent the evenings reading, crocheting and helping with the domestic chores. She was then aged 18 and, although she did not have a regular boy-friend, there was a boy, named George, who lived down the road at number 84, that she rather liked. According to Ann, he was rather handsome, but was some two years older. Ann was too shy to talk to him, but merely smiled at him and said hello in the street.

Later in the year, it became obvious that Ann was a very determined young lady, who had joined the suffragette movement. Throughout the remainder of that year's diary, she recorded her attendance at meetings and described how she took part in demonstrations. I was very intrigued and soon found the diary for 1914, this time bound in a green cover. In May, she had been arrested and taken to Holloway prison. The pages gave a very graphic description of her ordeal – how she refused to eat for several days and was eventually force-fed by the warders. I was really moved and felt angry that, nowadays, so many women did not even bother to vote, - they were too busy, going to discos, parties etc, - after all that the suffragettes had endured to get it. Reading the diary, I followed her hopes and dreams, as the world trembled on the brink of war and disaster. She was very politically aware and reported her thoughts on the assassination of Archduke Ferdinand and the mounting crisis, followed by the outbreak of war in August 1914.

Ann reported a meeting of the suffragettes, who had curtailed their operations with the onset of war. The meeting emphasised their determination to get the vote, but not to jeopardise the war effort in the process. In her diary, she clearly followed the progress of the war in Belgium and France.

I was very interested in her comments about the Suffragette movement. I had heard of Mrs. Pankhurst and the movement, but did not know too much about them.

I then picked up another diary, this one in a blue floral cover for 1915. I read her description of how her father had applied to join the army, but had been refused, due to his poor eyesight, and how disappointed and ashamed he had been to suffer this indignity.

I read on and found that she had met a boy named Cyril Peacock and it soon became apparent that she was very keen on him and she wrote about various meetings with him, although she did not go into much detail. I planned to read more of the diaries at a later date. Then I discovered a sheaf of letters, tied with a piece of pink ribbon, and rather guiltily began to read part of one of them -

*Dear Ann*
*It was lovely to meet you again last evening, I did enjoy the meal at Lyons Corner House, I was a bit nervous, but you put me at my ease. I also enjoyed the Cinema afterwards – "The Pawn Shop" was a good film and that Charlie Chaplin was so funny, and at the same time so sad!*
*I was very interested to hear about your job as a secretary in that big insurance office in London, it sounded so much more interesting than my job as a plumber's mate.*
*I hope we can meet again soon.*

*Yours with love Cyril*

I then read part of another letter.

*Dear Ann*
*I really enjoyed our walk in Hyde Park on Sunday. You looked really beautiful in your new dress. I was so proud to be walking arm in arm with you. One of my friends saw us and yesterday commented that I was such a very lucky man to be walking out with such a beauty!*
*I did enjoy listening to the band – they played lots of popular songs like "It's a long way to Tipperary," and "Pack up your troubles in your old kit bag," songs sung by our boys in the trenches!*
*I'm really fond of you Ann. I can't wait to see you again. Perhaps we could go out next Sunday – to the park again, if it's fine.*
*I'm, however, very worried about the war. I feel guilty that I have not volunteered, as a lot of my friends have already enlisted. Listening to the military band really brought it home to me.*
*Yours with much love*
*Cyril*

Then part of another letter.

*My dear Annie*
*I was so pleased to meet your Mum and Dad. They were both very nice to me. I hope I didn't show myself up. Your mother made a lovely tea and that fruit cake was really delicious. As you know, sadly, my parents died when I was quite young and my Aunt Lil brought me up. You will have to come and meet her soon. I will ask her if you can come to tea.*
*All my love Cyril*

I found many more similar letters. As the weeks went by, the terms of the letters became more passionate and more intimate. I began to feel rather ashamed to be reading these personal letters, like some sort of voyeur. But the next letter had some worrying undertones.

*Dearest Ann,*
*When we met last Saturday, I really enjoyed the meal at the restaurant. It was so romantic with our table lit by candlelight. I was so thrilled when you said that you loved me.*
*My happiness is, however, clouded by the situation in Europe. The war seems to be going badly. All those 'experts,' who predicted it would be over very quickly, have been proved wrong. Many of my friends have joined up and I feel very guilty that I am still at home.*
*Still I mustn't bother you with my worries, my darling. Let us look forward to our walk on Sunday.*
*All my love Cyril*

The next letter read

*My dearest Ann,*

*We had a lovely walk in the park last Sunday. The weather was lovely and it was so nice for us to be together on our own. I really love you Ann and can't wait till we are together again. Don't forget, my aunt Lil has invited you for tea next Sunday.*

*All my love Cyril*

Then in July 1916 there was a really heart-rending letter.

*My dearest Annie*
*I hoper you liked the tea with Aunt Lil, she thought you were really beautiful and liked you so much.*
*You know what we were discussing on our way home. Well, I have some very important news – I have signed up for the Army. All my friends have already joined and I am joining the Royal Middlesex Regiment. I went along to the recruitment centre and they gave me a quick medical and passed me fit. I shall miss you so much, but as Lord Kitchener says "Your country needs you". I shall be in England for a few weeks yet, while we do our training. So I will see you on my leave.*
*All my love, Cyril*

The next letter was dated August 15th

*My dearest Ann,*
*Well we are halfway through our training and I will have some leave next weekend. Can I meet you then and perhaps we can go to the cinema? The training is going well, but it is hard going. We do so much square-bashing, as they call it. This consists of running round and round the Parade ground. If you fall behind, the sergeant-major shouts at you. He is a real so-and-so, I won't tell you what the lads call him- it would really make your hair curl. I fail to see how the square-bashing will help us to beat the Germans. Still I am getting fit. I expect we*

*shall soon be off to Belgium to fight the Huns. All the boys are excited and looking forward to it. But I shall miss you so much, my darling.*

*All my love*
*Cyril*

I flicked on a couple of letters to find one dated September.

*Dear Ann*
*Well we are being posted to France next week. Don't worry, my love, they say it will be over before Christmas and I will be back with you. Perhaps we can get married when it's over – this is a sincere proposal, I will buy the ring when I come home on leave and do the whole kneeling bit- all proper like.*
*Missing you so much, Cyril*

The next letter was also dated in September

*Dear Ann*
*Well we have arrived in France, but I am not allowed to tell you exactly where we are. We spend our time digging trenches ready for a big attack soon. I am sure that we will beat those Germans and that the War will soon be over.*
*I have made some very good friends here. There is a wonderful spirit of friendship amongst the men. My special friend is Billy McDonald. He was born in Scotland, near Glasgow, but has lived in London for several years. He worked as a bricklayer and we get on very well. He has a wonderful sense of humour, even when things get difficult. The only trouble is, I cannot understand all he says with his broad Scottish accent.*
*Our commanding officer is very young and has only been out of university a few months, but I am sure he has been trained well – he went to Eton and Cambridge University, so is very well*

*educated. He mixes well with the men, joining us in having a drink and the sing-songs, unlike some officers over here.*
*Well I must get back to the digging, even though my back is aching.*
*Longing to see you my love*
*Cy*

Then I found some letters in a different hand — a feminine one and it seemed that Ann had decided to write out a copy of her letters to Cyril, in case they didn't reach him or were censored, before he read them.

*Dear Cyril*
*I am missing you so, so much. My life seems so dull without you. I feel so useless, so I am applying to drive a bus in London. I bet you would never have thought that would you? It will be so different to my work in the office, but one of my friends from the suffragette movement is already a driver and recommended me.*
*Please be careful, my darling. I read of the casualties every day in the paper and dad says that we are losing too many troops in the trenches. Please, please look after yourself. Every night, I get down on my knees and pray for your safety.*
*Your dearest Annie*

Then there was another letter from Cyril and blue pencil had obliterated several parts, but I could still read most of it.

*My Dearest Annie*
*How are you getting on driving a bus? I think your bus could be a lethal weapon in your hands and we could do with you out here. Sorry, only joking, my love. Try not to run too many people down! I am sure you will be a very good driver and I am*

*glad you have found a job that will satisfy your desire to help with the war effort.*
*It is terrible out here. We are in a trench waiting……. and the trench is full of mud, rats and lice. We feel so unclean – we live in mud and filth and I cannot get rid of the lice in my hair and on my clothes. The rain never seems to stop and the mud gets deeper and deeper.*
*There is a continual bombardment for hours on end. My head aches with the noise and there is no relief. I feel as if I am going mad at times. But we have to keep our spirits up and support the officers. I really dread going over the top. This means we all go over the top of the trench and run towards the German lines. As we run, men on either side are hit. They shriek with pain and fall to the ground, but we are told to ignore them and run on. Sometimes we can collect them on the way back, but often they have to be left in pools of mud and blood. The result of this carnage is often only an advance of a few hundred yards or even none at all. It all seems so…… I am afraid the officers are……*
*Still I suppose it will all be worthwhile, in the end. We must fight for our country, our King and for good, against the evil, dreadful Huns.*
*After each attack, the officers read the roll call and there are so many tragic silences, when friends' names remain unanswered. Yesterday when my pal Billy's name was called, there was this awful silence that went on and on. He has been officially classed as 'missing presumed dead' – I shall miss him so much, he was the life and soul of our group – always a joke, whatever happened.*
*I am missing you so much Ann and long to be back with you.*
*With all my love Cyril*

I was fascinated with the details of the war. I had always been interested in the First World War and recently there had been a number of films and documentaries on television, recounting the horrors and futility of that "War to end all wars."

As I continued to peruse them, in November the letters from Cyril suddenly stopped. What had happened?

There was a copy of a letter Ann had sent:-

*My dearest Cyril,*
*I haven't heard from you for some time and I am so worried. I pray that you are safe. I tell myself that you haven't had time to write or that the post has been delayed. In your last letter you described the terrible conditions. They must be awful – all that filth and so much useless killing. I know we must fight for the country, but is it worth such suffering?*
*I cried when I read about Billy – perhaps he might just be missing or just injured. Each day I read the papers, scan the lists and pray that your name will not be amongst the missing or injured. I am praying for you morning and night, my darling. Don't forget, you promised to propose when you returned.*
*Try to write as soon as possible.*
*God be with you, my dearest*

The next day I delved further into the box and found a scrapbook – On the front page was emblazoned the words 'THE STRUGGLE FOR VOTES'

It contained a number of newspaper cuttings about the suffragette movement, including articles about Emily Pankhurst and a picture of Emily Davison throwing herself under the hooves of the King's horse, Anmer, at the 1913 Derby. In the caption below, it reported that she had died later in hospital, a martyr to the cause.

In a couple of cuttings the name of Ann Williams was mentioned. There was a report that she had been arrested for chaining herself to the railings in Downing Street and had been sent to Holloway prison, where she refused food for a week and was eventually force-fed. With the onset of the 'War to end all wars', the suffragettes had decided to curtail their activities for national unity, and there were no more cuttings after 1914.

The scrapbook also contained reports obviously written by Ann herself, detailing some of her experiences in the Suffragette movement. I thumbed through the pages quickly, with the thought that I would study them more closely at a later date.

I stopped at a page entitled 'MY ARREST AND IMPRISONMENT.'

She detailed how she had taken part in a march down Downing Street, carrying a banner with the words 'VOTES FOR WOMEN NOW'.

> *"When the police tried to stop the march, I, together with two other young ladies, had chained ourselves to the railings in Downing Street. After an hour, I was cut free and immediately arrested by the police and taken straight to Holloway prison, where I was charged and the following day appeared in court and found guilty. I was shocked to be sentenced to six weeks in prison and taken to the cells. I had been brought up in a quiet family environment and was now suddenly mixed with common prostitutes and thieves. Many of the wardresses were very kind and I believed that some of them were sympathetic to the cause."*

The women decided to refuse to eat, to bring attention to their cause. In her report she graphically described the force feeding procedures.

> *"I starved for several days before the authorities decided to act. Then a doctor accompanied by two wardresses entered the room. They asked me to eat voluntarily but when I refused, they produced the equipment. I was given the option of a wooden or steel gag. The doctor offered the wooden gag as it would hurt less, but I had my fingers in my mouth and when I did not*

*reply or open my mouth, the doctor had recourse to the steel one. He then proceeded to force my mouth open and inserted the gag. He then pushed a long tube of about four feet in length down my throat and proceeded to pour food down. I retched and was immediately sick and as I struggled the doctor leant on my knees and the wardresses pressed my head back. I was immediately sick all over the doctor and the wardresses. I find it very hard to express the horror of the experience. This procedure was repeated each day for a week, as they noticed that I had lost weight. I repeatedly appealed to the doctors not to put the tube down so far and not to pour so much food down as these actions were self-defeating, causing me to be continually sick. After the week, the force feeding ceased and our conditions improved, with the result that I reluctantly agreed to eat. The women had vowed no surrender and we all felt we had won a moral victory."*

Then I found a photograph of a tall young man in uniform, obviously Cyril. He looked very young, but was obviously proud of his new uniform. He had dark hair and a small moustache – almost an apology for a moustache, in fact, and a nice boyish grin. On his arm was an attractive young lady in a flowered dress and with mid-brown hair. She was quite a bit shorter than Cyril, but they both looked so happy and obviously in love. They had been photographed in a park by the bandstand, and in the background, significantly, a military band was playing.

Next to the photo, I found a neat blue box, which I carefully opened to reveal a medal with its ribbon - It was 'The Military Medal' and on the back was inscribed 'TO CYRIL ALBERT PEACOCK- AWARDED FOR GALLANTRY IN THE FACE OF THE ENEMY – THE SOMME – 25TH SEPTEMBER 1916.'

Under the box was a copy of the Daily Telegraph for Thursday 5th October 1916. The paper had turned brown with age and was very creased. It had been folded so that page 3 was on top. The headline read 'HUGE BRITISH LOSSES AT THE

SOMME', and underneath was a seemingly unending list of those severely wounded, missing or dead. The list was in alphabetic order and there was the name - Cyril Albert Peacock- Royal Middlesex Regiment –severely wounded.

Attached to the paper was a letter from the field hospital.

*28th September 1916*

*Dear Ann,*
*Cyril Peacock has asked me to write this letter to you, as he is unable to write himself, at the moment. I am sorry to have to tell you that he was badly injured at the Battle of the Somme, when he was hit by a bullet after he went over the top.*
*He is making some progress and is as well as can be expected.*
*He specifically asked me to express his undying love for you.*
*He keeps saying your name and hopes he will soon be home to see you. Yesterday, he showed me a photo of you both in a park and you do look a lovely couple.*
*I must close now, as the ward is very busy – so many casualties and us nurses are rushed off our feet.*
*Emily Jones (Nurse)*

I then found a letter in an official envelope, marked O.H.M.S., addressed to Miss Ann Williams. It read

*Dear Miss Williams*
*It is my sad and painful duty to notify you officially that Cyril Albert Peacock was severely wounded at the Battle of the Somme. I am sorry to have to report that after a period in the field hospital, Cyril passed away on the 12th October 1916 as a result of the wounds received in the Battle.*
*May I offer my sincere condolences and inform you that Cyril fought with great gallantry in the battle. He was a model soldier*

*and I was very proud to number him in my platoon. During his time in the hospital, he asked me specifically to write to you as he had no close relatives apart from a young sister and he expressly asked me to convey his undying love for you.*
*Yours sincerely*
*James Fitzwilliam (Lieutenant)*

The letter was obviously tear-stained as the ink had run in a number of places. As I read this, I felt very sad and very humble. I had to swallow deeply to get rid of the lump in my throat.

I replaced the contents back in the box, carefully and with a certain reverence. Over the next few days, I could not get Ann Williams or Cyril Peacock out of my mind. I was determined to find out what had happened to Ann after her tragic loss. Genealogy has always fascinated me and I have always intended to trace my family tree, but never got around to it. Now was the chance to trace a person - one I had never even met!

Where would I start? I searched on-line under the Royal Middlesex Regiment and discovered that they had been merged with other regiments in reorganisations, but after much searching, found a suitable web-site. I duly wrote to the relevant address about Cyril Peacock asking for his last address and the details of his next of kin. After about a week, I received a reply and it transpired that his parents had pre-deceased him and his only remaining close relative at the time of his death was his younger sister Rose – hence the Army's letter to Ann. Rose had lived at 25, York Road, Peckham, and so I decided to visit that address.

It turned out to be a rather run-down terrace house in an ordinary suburban street. When I knocked, the door was opened very suspiciously by a tall black man with a bald-head and wearing a dark red track suit. He was very polite and in answer to my enquiry, said that his name was Leroy Gardiner. He explained, however, that he had only lived there for about a year and regretted that he knew nothing about the previous owners. He did say, however, that the lady at number 29 had lived in the road for a long time.

I duly knocked at number 29 and an elderly lady slowly came to the door. She was very friendly and asked me in. Her house was spotlessly clean but in serious need of decorating. She invited me into the lounge and said, in a rather weak and shrill voice,

"Won't you sit down?"

I looked around and saw that books, newspapers and a large, tabby cat, occupied the sofa and armchairs. The cat eyed me suspiciously and protested with a loud miaow, when the lady forcibly moved her to the floor to make way for me.

The lady introduced herself as Miss Spalding and she was very thin and frail, but had a kindly face surmounted by wispy, silver hair.

She smiled gently as she said, "I remember Rose Johnson – that was her married name, but her maiden name was Peacock. She had lived at number 25, until she had to go into an old people's home about 5 years ago."

She then went on, "Unfortunately she died a couple of years ago, but, when she lived here, she talked about her brother many times. It was such a tragic story, he had really loved Ann Williams, and he died so young."

"What happened to Ann after his sad death," I asked.

She replied "After Cyril's death, Ann decided to give up driving the bus in London and volunteered to drive ambulances in France. I think she wanted to visit the hospital where Cyril had been treated and also to help Cyril's fellow soldiers.

Tragically she was herself killed when her ambulance ran over a mine, quite near to the area where Cyril was injured. The ambulance was completely destroyed and Ann was taken to the same hospital that had received Cyril. In a grim re-run of his ordeal, she was treated but died three days later of her wounds."

I thanked Miss Spalding while we drank a cup of tea and we both hoped and prayed that they would be somehow together in the hereafter. I left feeling very sad and thought to myself that the couple who were inseparable until his call-up and were then tragically parted, were in a strange way united in death.

I was determined to try to find out more about Ann. I had already ascertained from Miss Spalding that Ann had had a younger cousin, Lettie Lloyd. Miss Spalding had said that her last address was 97 Acacia Avenue, Forest Gate. Consequently I visited that address, but the door was opened by a young couple, who explained that they had only been in the flat for about a year. They said, however, that there had been a Miss Lloyd there previously and that she had gone into an old people's home in Bermondsey. I subsequently visited the home and was introduced to Miss Lloyd, who was dozing by the fire in the lounge. She was huddled up in a blanket, but seemed to be 'with it', as they say, unlike a number of the other residents. Sadly, she was rather deaf, which made the interview rather difficult.

"Good afternoon, Miss Lloyd," I said.

"Sorry, I can't hear you," she mumbled

"I am trying to find out about your cousin, Ann Williams," I said very slowly and deliberately

"She was a suffragette, you know," she shouted, obviously believing that I was also deaf. .

"She wanted to get back into the movement after the war – but sadly it was not to be. She didn't live to see women get the vote," she spoke so loudly that some other visitors turned around in alarm.

"Oh, and she's dead, you know- died in the First World War"

"She was now in full flow and continued. "I was only about fifteen when she died, I was so upset, as we used to get on well together- we played a lot and she was like a big sister to me."

"That was until she met Cyril, of course. After that I didn't see much of her, as she was infatuated with him."

"Did you meet Cyril?" I asked.

"Yes, he was a lovely boy, very quiet, but kind. I would have fancied him myself, if I had been older. It was such a tragedy, when he died in the war and then she went out to France and also got herself killed. Her parents were grief-stricken."

I thanked Lettie for the information and we went on talking for about an hour. Lettie said how much she had enjoyed my visit.

"I don't get to talk to many people nowadays, apart from the staff here. All my relatives and close friends have gone now."

I promised to visit her again very soon and left.

As I look back, I feel that I really knew both Cyril and Ann as if they were friends. I had dreadful nightmares for a few weeks. The nightmares concerned the trenches and force feeding in prison.
I could not get them out of my mind. It seemed so strange, as I had never met them – but they had got under my skin.

When the middle of November came round, my thoughts concentrated on Ann and Cyril. As I watched the Festival of Remembrance at the Albert Hall and the crimson poppy petals silently rained down on the servicemen and nurses below, I imagined that two of those petals represented the ill-starred lovers. I picked out two poppy petals and followed them, with my eyes as they fell silently and slowly down to land eventually on the cap of a young army private.

Then the President of the British Legion read the traditional words of Lawrence Binyon.

> *"Age shall not weary them, nor the years condemn*
> *At the going down of the sun and in the morning*
> *We will remember them."*

I am not ashamed to say that my eyes filled with tears as I listened and remembered Ann and Cyril.

So many died or were injured in the dreadful carnage of the First World War, and Ann and Cyril were just two of millions, but they brought home to me the tragedy and senselessness of war. Tragically, we still haven't learned our lesson, as men are dying in Iraq and Afghanistan at this very moment.

Afterwards I decided to write an article for the local paper about the story of Ann and Cyril. They had been heroes, at a time of so many heroes, but had been unrecognised in their time. The writing of the article seemed to bring closure for me – a feeling that I had helped to bring their tragic love and lives to people's attention. The article was quite well received and I had several letters of appreciation.

The nightmares had ceased for me, but nevertheless, I vowed always to remember them.

# The Thrill of the Moment

By Paul Bunn

Almost touching ninety
Under the baking sun
The roadside just a blur to me —
The thrill of the moment

Sweat trickling down my neck
Wind buffeting my body
This is the only place to be —
The thrill of the moment

Giving it just a little more
Feeling the power surge
My lips crack into an ecstatic grin —
The thrill of the moment

Passing all the traffic
Crawling along like a snail
I didn't see the car door open —
To be crushed in a moment

On a gurney, at death's door
Bleeding on the hospital bed
With my kith and closest around me —
My life extinguished in a moment.

# Displaced

By Simon Woodward

## Chapter 1

I was an ordinary soul in our village, just a young twenty-something farm worker, trying to make my way in life. The village I called my own was Trelevern, it was small and just a rural farming community in the South West of England. But we did have our grocery store, and we did have our petrol station, in essence though, that was it. The Cornish town of Trelevern wasn't on the coast and it wasn't next to any of the moors and I suppose this was why we were uninterrupted by holiday makers and truly uninterrupted by the rest of the world: it was a good place to live.

After my father died, I was willed the cottage I now live in, attached to farmer Pengowan's land, a few miles away from the village centre. It was quiet and serene, if you could call nature quiet; but that's the way it felt. There's something peaceful about nature's natural cacophony.

Fortunately for me, Mr. Pengowan believed in perpetuating the rite of the workers and, although I didn't work for him often, my father had, and that was enough; I was allowed to call Pengowan's cottage my home.

When the sun came up, I got up also; whether it be 4am in the morning during the summer or 7am during the winter; I followed the sun — this was the way; very rural, but nothing could beat it.

On occasions, Pengowan asked me to perform the odd task; herding the sheep or using the great combine to harvest his crops.

It didn't matter to me what he asked, I was pleased to be a part of Earth's natural cycle; sowing, seeding, and reaping: I enjoyed this life.

After finishing my chores, I would collapse in my bed, which overlooked the fields, exhausted and happy; fulfilled; and this was how I had continued for the thirty-six months, three seasonal cycles, since my father's death, until today.

This morning I had awoken, feeling groggy, as if sleep had eluded me for most of the previous night and, as I sat on the edge of my bed, trying to shake an unusual consuming tiredness from my mind, I recalled strange dreams of dazzling brightness; images of corn fields somehow below me, ones that were moving away becoming smaller until they seemed nothing more than scale models.

For a short while, I struggled to grasp the dream-memories, trying to get hold of them, trying to visualise them in the clarity they'd had but, as I did, they slipped away, becoming more elusive as my tiredness receded.

Eventually, they were nothing more than wisps of a memory I was no longer interested in and I got up as my thoughts turned to my usual routine.

Every few days, I visited the village store; purchasing the bread, milk and eggs Pengowan's farm didn't produce — I was Ok for meat, particularly lamb, and sausages were available, intermittently.

But this day, Mrs. Cottral, the owner of the store, ignored me. Ignored me is too strong — she didn't recognise me as a regular; she didn't recognise me at all. She also seemed a little afraid by my presence in her shop.

"But Mrs. Cottral..." I implored, "I'm Joseph. You know, Joseph Meveres, from up the lane." And, as I indicated my road, pointing in its direction, she stepped back from her side of the counter before answering.

"So you say, but you're not the Joseph Meveres I know." Though she was robust in her reply, I could tell by her stance fear had taken hold. "You are not entitled to any discounts." she continued, "Now pay me what you owe and get out. Go away and don't come back. I know what you are... changeling."

Though confused and having no clue as to what she was talking about, I didn't want to upset her any further so I purchased the food I could afford at the going price and left; I certainly didn't want to upset the owner of the village shop any more than I had done.

But the situation was strange and I could not figure out why she'd decided not to know me anymore, apart from that peculiar word she'd used — changeling. I shook my head, nothing clear becoming apparent: I knew she was getting on a bit and dearly hoped that this wasn't the onset of one of those degenerative mental illnesses; she was too nice to have that happen to her.

I left the village centre and made my way back to my cottage, trying to reconcile what had just happened with the woman I knew her to be from past experience.

Just as I was approaching my front door, I was distracted from my thoughts as Farmer Pengowan stepped out in front of me, blocking my way.

"Joseph." he said, "I need to know what you have been doing."

"Nothing," I answered immediately in my defence, then considering what had been said, I asked, "What do you mean?"

"What have you done to my crop?" he said. I had no idea of what he was talking about. I was just making my way back from the village to my cottage.

"At least seventy percent of the corn has been irrecoverably damaged." He told me, "You look after it; what have you done?"

"Nothing, Sir, honestly." I said, "I haven't even started to harvest it."

"Are you responsible for the field?" Pengowan asked me.

"Of course I am." I said.

"Then how do you explain the state it is in now?"

"I don't know." I said, "What's wrong with it?"

"Have a look for yourself." He told me. He let me go past him, so I could dump my shopping in the house.

Once I'd put the carrier bags on my kitchen table, I stepped back outside my cottage and he spoke to me again.

"Well?" he said.

"Sorry Sir, I still don't understand what you're talking about." I said, shaking my head.

"Come with me," he instructed.

I followed him around the back of the cottage and along the path towards the fields.

He waved his arm across the vista and I looked; I couldn't see anything of a worry: but then he pointed it out.

"See," he said.

What I saw was a field of corn, that had somehow been flattened, in places. My first thought was that there had been a localised storm, some wind or something, perhaps even some heavy rain; but seeing how the corn had been flattened, I began to wonder.

There were twirls and circles, lines and more circles, spirals; all interconnected — a very strange pattern. And I began to feel Mr. Pengowan was blaming me for the damage.

"I didn't do this," I told him. But he just looked at me. "I didn't ruin the crop, honestly, Sir," I affirmed.

Pengowan, and his family, had known my family for a long, long time, and I think he believed me because of this, though his demeanour glinted with an edge of doubt, but, if he didn't, then the reasons were beyond me.

Saying no more, he turned for his Land Rover, got in it and left me, driving up the unmade road, which led from the cottage to the farmhouse, some half mile up the hill.

I looked at the crop again and the damage, now that it had been pointed out to me from this vantage point, was obvious.

Between the remaining upright sandy-yellow corn stalks that were rocking gently in the slight breeze, around the edges of the field, I could see that the centre of the field had been pressed down, to the earth, in some way.

There'd be no harvesting of this field in a few weeks, I knew; if anything it would need ploughing straight back into the ground: what a waste of a season.

I left my vantage point, next to the low leafy green hedgerow at the rear of my cottage, and made my way back, entering the kitchen and putting the kettle on. Whilst the water was trying to get up to the boil on my gas cylinder driven stove, I climbed the short stairway to my bedroom, beneath the cottage's thatched roof, to look out of the window over the field.

I was stunned when I saw the full extent of the geometric designs that had been imprinted on Farmer Pengowan's field, and, although I'd heard of such things, I'd never seen it but, for sure, this was one of those crop circles you read about in the newspapers, from time to time.

I began to wonder about who could have done this; who in our village would have such a malicious but artistic bent.

None of the families I knew would; perhaps it was the out-of-towners, attempting a laugh at our expense. At least none of the fields further away from the cottage had been damaged, as far as I could tell from my window.

The kettle began to whistle, summoning me, and I left the view to go back down the stairs to the kitchenette to make my tea.

As I sat there on my chair at the plain wood table in the middle of the kitchen's dusty grey slate floor, I wracked my brains, trying to think of anyone who may have something against Mr. Pengowan or me, but no-one would come to mind. I decided the destruction of the crop was down to a misguided practical joke by some townies.

As I had an early start the next day, I quickly washed up the crockery and cutlery and turned in for the night.

Morning broke and I woke up. I didn't need an alarm clock, as my bedroom window was without curtains and the early morning light always roused me from my sleep and, if not the light, then nature always had a way.

Gingerly, I got out of bed, my body felt as if I had been stacking straw bails for four hours straight, but I hadn't. That onerous task was to come in the next few weeks. And again, I felt as if my sleep had been poisoned by strange dreams of dazzling lights and the view of fields below me but even these memories had been tainted further, by images of sleek glistening black-walled triangular rooms, illuminated by purplish UV light, and gangly humanesque surgeons.

All my muscles ached and my head throbbed terribly; each way I turned to look, it felt as if my sinuses were filled with fluid and in my ears I could hear the sounds of light kindling, crackling, as if in a fire. I hoped I wasn't coming down with a summer flu, but, if I was, it would explain the fevered dreams.

Standing up on my feeble legs, I got dressed and made my way downstairs for breakfast, though I didn't feel like eating. Ultimately, I opted for a cup of tea and nothing else.

After putting the kettle on, I opened the fridge and poured some milk into my cup, the milk trickled out of the bottle sludge-like; it was off. Just to make sure, I sniffed at it and recoiled, smelling the wet sour smell that indicated it was no good anymore.

I'd bought it only yesterday, so I checked the fridge hadn't turned itself off during the night, by looking for the frost that always built up in the freezer compartment – it was still there, the milk had not been exposed to a warm summer night and there was no icy caking along the bottom of the freezer box.

I made myself another cup and took my tea neat, swilling down a couple of Paracetamol along with it.

Knowing the chores I had to complete for this morning, I checked the clock to see how long I could rest before getting on with them. I hoped there would be enough time to allow the pills to work, but there wasn't.

I rubbed my eyes to make sure they were free from sleep and it wasn't affecting my vision, but it didn't help.

The clock said 8am, somehow I'd slept through the sunrise at 5:30am and, although the quality of light coming through my kitchen window told me it must be later, I still reached for my wrist watch I always left in the fruit bowl on the sideboard, before I went to bed. Looking at it, it told me the same thing, it was 8am.

Now I knew I wasn't well at all and, for the first time since I'd started working for Mr. Pengowan, I picked up the phone to call him, to let him know it was not possible for me to work today.

Dialling his number, I waited for the connection to click through and for him to answer but, after the numbers had stopped clicking, all I got was a single pitched tone telling me I'd either rung the wrong number or he'd been disconnected. I tried again, dialling the numbers for his farmhouse, more slowly this time, but the result was the same.

As the painkillers began to ease my bodily aches, I decided to go to the village to get some more milk and replace the pint that had gone off.

I picked up my moss green jacket from the back of my battered sofa and, putting it on, I left the cottage; then stopped abruptly after shutting the front door behind me.

I stared at the path which led to my front door; the path I regularly cleared of weeds at least once a week, normally twice;

but the path I now saw had at least three weeks' growth on it, I assumed, if not more.

If I was going to do anything today, I would clear the path, but first I would get some more milk.

I began to walk the two miles into the village, down the single track road, which led up to my cottage; it was lined by hedgerow on either side, interspersed by the occasional tree and had, in places, the odd tuft of grass poking through the road's surface along its centre-line.

As I made my way, I started to notice inconsistencies in my next day's life, all of which were pointing to a wholly different season from the one I went to bed in.

I noticed red holly berries that were beginning to show themselves in the hedgerow, the leaves on some of the trees that lined the lane had started to turn autumn's orange golden-brown. The acorns from the oaks, which grew at random intervals on either side of the road, were scattered across its uncared for tarmac.

If I was perceiving all these signals correctly, then, without a doubt, it was autumn, but I knew for a certainty I had gone to bed in late August, the summer.

Knowing I was unwell, I decided to put these thoughts to the back of my mind; I would get my milk and then I would tackle my path.

At the end of the lane was the village petrol station, and arriving here always told me that I was only a few more minutes away from the grocery store. I nearly walked past the garage without a second's thought but, as I got to the furthest end of its forecourt, something triggered in my head and I stopped.

I turned to look at it. There was a rusty iron chain across its entrance and exit; there were no lights illuminating the inside of the little shop that was a part of it, and there was a sign, which stated it was closed.

In my entire life, this petrol station had never been closed during the day, especially at this time of the morning, but today it obviously was. I wondered where the owners were.

I was certain that Mrs. Cottral would know what was going on. So I stepped up my pace and made my way to the shop, as quickly as I could manage with my aching limbs.

Even if she still didn't know me, she would definitely know what was going on; she was the village's information centre, though this was not an official title or anything, it was just the way the village worked.

Mobile phones were next to useless, as the operators had not considered getting a decent signal in Trelevern a priority and, those of us who did need mobile communications, stuck with the trusty walkie-talkie, and this was the way we liked it.

Walking past the small concrete based, tubular open sign on the little bit of pavement that existed in the village, I pushed open the olive-green framed door to the store and entered, the brass bell above it announcing another customer's interest.

The interior had changed somewhat, since my visit the day before and it took a few moments more than usual before I found the open faced fridge containing the plastic milk cartons; I picked one up, a two pinter this time.

As I didn't need anything else, I walked around the new shelving, which filled the centre of the shop, to find the checkout and, finding it, I waited to be served.

There was no bell to push on the counter that I could ring any longer; it seemed that this style of service was no more; so I coughed.

Eventually, a woman in her early forties, I must guess, wearing a dowdy brown knitted cardigan, walked up to the counter from the back room, which was still separated from the shop by multi-coloured vertical strips of 1970's plastic.

I didn't recognise her at all.

Seeing the milk carton I had in my hand, she asked me: "Will that be all?" I told her yes and she rang up the cost on the till.

"That'll be £1.15" she said.

Before handing my money over to her, I was determined to find out where Mrs. Cottral was, so I asked.

"Where's Mrs. Cottral today?" I got a blunt reply.

"She died two weeks ago," was the answer and, although I thought that would be it, she continued, "I haven't seen you in here before, did you know her?"

"Of course I knew her. She served me..." I nearly said, yesterday, but quickly changed my tack, "only the other week and I live just up the lane, here." I indicated the direction I had come from, "Was it dementia?" I asked.

"No, no." The woman in the shop started, "My aunt was sound as a bell; it was a heart attack. Though, if you believe what some are saying in the village, she'd been scared to death." I just blinked at this answer and then Mrs. Cottral's niece continued, "Have you heard that Farmer Pengowan has disappeared?"

All I could do was shake my head; my mind was in turmoil, surely only yesterday I'd had a minor confrontation with Mrs. Cottral; and Pengowan? That was another question.

Suffice it to say, I handed over the money and left the store.

I now felt very confused — all my timelines were off somehow. I wandered back home, trying to figure out what was happening.

As I walked up the lane, I saw a grey squirrel grasping at one of the acorns on the road, putting it in its mouth. When it spotted me, it leapt into action, keeping the acorn in its mouth, as it dived through the hedgerow, to wherever it needed to go.

Sitting at the table in my cottage, I glanced at the clock; it told me that it was only midday.

And as I waited for the kettle to boil. I looked around my kitchen, not knowing what else to do, noticing the heavy cobwebs that had appeared in its corners.

I rubbed my head round and round with my hand, trying to get a handle on the situation I found myself in — but it didn't help. The only conclusion I could draw was that I'd lost some time out of my life, somehow. And, before I could think further about it, the kettle boiled, whistling, so I picked it up and made my tea.

Pouring the warm refreshing liquid down my throat, my thoughts turned to the chores Farmer Pengowan expected me to complete; barring the field that had been flattened, there were three others to harvest, but I couldn't do this today – I needed some rest; tomorrow would be the day, I decided; but the thought that I was not like this – or I shouldn't be – instilled a sense of guilt I wasn't used to feeling.

As I supped my tea, I knew today was not the day I should climb into the great yellow and blue combine to start my task.

Tomorrow; I would do it tomorrow. And that was fact. And that was my decision.

As I sat at my table, looking out of the back window of the kitchen over the hedgerow and into the un-harvested fields that lay beyond, I rested within myself, just being, with no thoughts as to doing.

Gradually, the sun continued its path from the day-time sky and started its descent towards the horizon; all the while, I watched the colours the sunset generated, as its light made changes to the contrast and brightness that had accentuated the life force the crops seemed to emanate and, not moving from my seat in the kitchen, I sat there watching, somehow being a part of the cycle. And, as I did this, I attempted to put all the things I now knew into some kind of logical form, some neat little scenario, that would explain everything I'd experienced so far.

Darkness enveloped the outside, with the hedgerows disappearing into blackness beyond the beige corn fields.

I got up from my table; it was time to go back to bed and rest: getting ready for the coming morn and the tasks I would have to complete as a part time employee of farmer Pengowan, though I wasn't sure I needed to anymore, if he had truly disappeared; but I had been charged with these duties and, just because he wasn't here at the moment, it didn't really mean I was discharged from them.

## Chapter 2

I awoke in my bed suddenly, thrown from another traumatic nightmare, fleeting glimpses of a chilled dark room, which now included too real visions of a three-pronged instrument sizzling, as it pushed through my abdomen; I leant over the side of the bed and dry heaved, no contents to expel.

As I sat back up, I began to feel a little better, the retching seeming to purge my illness slightly and, as I recovered, whatever had woken me was gone and it was morning again.

My body still ached: but, as I looked through my bedroom window, the pains I was suffering disappeared into the back of my mind.

I now looked out over fields, hidden beneath a severe blanket of white; the hedgerows and fences that separated them were now walls of white… something.

As I breathed out, I noticed a cloudy vapour and then the penny dropped; I was looking at snow; but snow in August?

Easing myself out of my bed, into the bedroom, the cold hit me with a force I was not used to at this time of year. I got dressed as fast as I could and made my way down the wooden stairs to my kitchenette; I had to get the heating on. This was my first concern, before I could try and tackle mentally, the un-seasonal weather.

Within a few moments, I had the fire burning in the hearth and, although I'd achieved this fairly quickly, I knew it would be a good forty minutes before it began dishing out the required heat to the rest of the cottage.

Wrapping my dark blue cotton dressing gown around me, over my clothes, I sat in front of the fire, waiting for it to do its work, wondering why I should have had to take such actions. Perhaps this was just one of the problems supposed climate change wrought.

As the heat permeated the cottage, I took off my dressing gown and threw it over the back of my sofa; very soon I could have a shower, the water in the back boiler being hot enough to do so.

In the meantime, I made myself a hot drink, tea seeming the simplest option. I didn't bother with milk this time, as I desperately needed to warm up and, as I poured the boiling water onto the tea bag, I began to feel like this drink was all I was living on; but, as they say, starve a fever, feed a cold.

As I supped my drink, the wood in the fireplace began to burn low and it was apparent that I ought to top it up, if it was going to continue to heat my home.

Putting on some Wellington boots and a jacket, I left the comfortable heat of the kitchen, cum living area, and crunched through the snow in my small back garden, to the shed, that housed more fuel for the fire.

After clearing the snow from the shed's entrance, I pulled its rickety door open and began removing the logs I would use, placing them on the roped flat piece of hardboard I had for these occasions.

Almost full, I picked up three more logs, continuing my automaton style of stacking I'd developed over the years from tasks such as this, my mind focusing on heaving the load back up the garden to the kitchen.

Turning, I pulled the hardboard sled away from the shed's door, so that I could close it easily, then, turning back, I placed my hand on the edge of the door, about three quarter's of the way up, ready to close it and, as I did so, I glanced at the depleted pile.

The sight I saw made me collapse on to the make shift sled, heavily. Two boots, ones you could call farmer's boots, were poking out from the bottom of the stack.

I blinked my eyes and shook my head, in an attempt, I suppose, to clear what I was seeing from my vision.

Within seconds, my consciousness began to register the odour of death, but not the usual smell of an abattoir that housed dead pigs or sheep; there was a very subtle difference; a difference I instantly recognised, because I could see the boots.

I had to find out who it was, though my mind was already telling me. As fast as I could, I worked through the remainder of the pile, chucking each log to the other side of the shed.

One by one, the removed logs began to uncover shins, knees and waist, all still clothed but, after that, the torso was bare; but not just bare, it was mutilated: the internal organs, those that still existed, were there to see, exposed as nature hadn't intended them to be; their covering missing.

I'd done a fair bit of butchery, as part of my chores for Farmer Pengowan, and saw immediately that the liver and heart were gone, though the strangest thing of all was the lack of any blood. It was almost as if this body had been prepared in some way, perhaps even, for exhibition.

I didn't pause for long contemplating this, I had to know who it was, for definite. I cleared the last of the logs away — then froze.

The dull open eyes, which stared at me, belonged to my father's friend and employer; it was Farmer Pengowan: my empty stomach retched.

It was only the uncontrollable shivering that brought me round; I'd passed out and fallen into the snow that had enveloped my garden.

With as much control as I could muster, I pulled the loaded sled back towards the cottage, not looking back, not wanting to acknowledge that which existed in my shed.

Eventually, I pulled the back door closed; the logs were now stacked up, appropriately, next to the fire and, although the cottage was warm and cosy, I still shivered, deeply, as if my very soul had been chilled to temperatures that only existed in the minds of scientists.

In an attempt to rid myself of these shakes, I picked up my kettle and held it, clattering, against the silver nozzle of the tap in my kitchen; as it rattled, so it filled, very slowly; my shivering making the water's flow a hit or miss affair, but I did it and, once completed, I placed the kettle on the stove, after which I fell back into my sofa to wait, still riven by the shakes.

The kettle began its whistle and, unsteadily, I got up, reaching for the cupboard, taking a single tea bag from the steel container marked 'Tea'.

After pouring the hot water onto the tea bag, I open my fridge to get the milk, reaching for it.

I didn't pick it up. This time I knew it was off, the fur on its surface, a very light avocado in colour, spoke volumes. I poured the hot water into my mug and sat down again, ready for yet another cup of neat tea.

I now knew that it wasn't August anymore, no more than yesterday had been late August; somehow, my life had been skipping weeks at a time and, during these periods, I had slept, but I felt this couldn't be right; the times I'd awoken full of aches and pains surely meant that, during my unconscious moments, I'd been doing something. As these thoughts went through my mind, I finished my tea and, putting the mug down, I made my way to the shower, thinking that perhaps this action would afford me some clarity on the situation I now found my self in.

Stripping off in the bathroom, I turned towards the shower, reaching in and turning the taps to the positions I knew, from experience, would deliver a comfortable stream. I then turned to face the full-length mirror.

At first, what I saw I believed to be an artefact of the steam that coated it but, as I rubbed it down with a towel, the illness I had been suffering showed itself in its entirety.

I was looking at an exhausted man, whose pallor was that of a person tinged a light grey-green, one who had three open and weeping suppurate welts, two just below each rib cage and one where the belly button should have been, each as raw as they looked.

Logic told me that these wounds on my torso should be extremely painful, should be hurting, but there was no sensation at all; no irritation and no feeling. It was almost as if the damage to my body had been anesthetised in some manner.

I looked at my eyes, as I now felt that all parts of me ought to go through an examination of sorts, and saw desperation, encapsulated by heavy brows and dark rings.

I closed them to this vision and rubbed the mirror once more, hoping, beyond hope, that all I was seeing was part of some fevered hallucination. But, as I slowly opened my eyes and saw my hand, I stopped.

What was before me, holding the towel against the mirror, wasn't my hand and, although I had accepted, sort of, the colour of my skin, the webs between my fingers were plain to see; I dropped the towel and checked my other hand; it was the same.

Whatever I was suffering was more than just a summer flu, but what it was I couldn't fathom. One thing was for sure though, I was changing, metamorphosing in some way; I was becoming not me anymore, physically at least.

I turned the shower off, knowing in my heart it wouldn't help.

## Chapter 3

Everything I'd seen and acknowledged so far was a trauma but one part of me, deep down, was exerting normality; a way to survive this experience, I guess. And, in this vein, I decided to go back to the village to pick up milk, once more. This was the way I would survive what I was going through. Perhaps Longlife was what I should choose this time, my mind told me; but not on foot, don't be silly, the snow had put paid to that.

Of course it had. It would be easier to use my mountain bike, as I had done in previous years, when the snow had fallen; the bike would cut through the snow quite simply.

I would go to the village and stock up on the milk and any other food *he* required.

My bike was kept in the outhouse, a flimsily built attachment to the cottage; well it looked flimsy to me but it had been there as long as I could remember.

Normally, I would enter the outhouse from the rear of the cottage but, not wanting to clap eyes on the shed ever again, I went out of the front door, traipsed across the snow covered overgrown path and opened the front of the wooden building, entering.

I saw my bike leaning against the old wooden walls, its tyres deflated through lack of use and care, but this was the norm; I only ever used it when walking was going to be too slow and, strangely, when it snowed, cycling on a mountain bike was a lot easier than walking.

Knowing where the pump was, I pulled the canvas covering from the top of the oil and muck stained bench to retrieve it, dumping the canvas on the floor.

Reaching for the pump, I nearly picked it up, but impossibly gleaming silver tools stopped me and I looked at them and, for some reason, a smile that felt knowing, graced my face.

These tools, ones I'd never seen before, were lying on the bench, calling to be held. They were vaguely similar to a butcher's kit but more perfect in some way; and, as I looked at them, I noticed a few were discoloured.

I leant closer to get a better look, sniffing the air; then moved away quickly. Two of them, the ones with unrealistically thin silvery blades, had been tainted by hardened reddy-brown glutinous lumps, which had formed almost perfect spherical droplets on their surfaces.

None of the other tools was discoloured in this way and none of the other silvery tools looked like anything from any person's toolbox that *he* knew.

Just the view of these tools made me wonder whether Farmer Pengowan's body had been carved up here, in the outhouse, and that thought was promptly followed by the question of who had done it.

*You*. I heard a distant voice call out in my mind, but dismissed it as a bizarre ethereal insight, that had been induced by the fever I was suffering.

Feeling my bile rise, I retreated back to my kitchen; the urge to gather any food today being completely usurped.

I made myself another neat tea and, as I drank it, I looked out of the kitchen window at my small garden and the white fields beyond, without passion and without being. I was completely drained of everything that made me, me.

The light began to dwindle and, automatically, I made my way to bed, rubbing my hands together knowingly, a small part of me wishing that, when I awoke, everything that had gone on would disappear, as if part of some cruel and vicious nightmare.

Without any energy, I collapsed into bed fully clothed and, for a second time, a smile crossed my face; I hadn't the wherewithal to change for bed and I hadn't the wherewithal to be bothered about it.

## Chapter 4

My eyes flickered open, in response to the sun hitting them; I think it was the sun, but I couldn't move. The ache that *he'd* felt in the passing days had gone, only to be replaced by nothingness in *his* limbs.

As my consciousness rose, I felt a tightness on my chest; it was like the shirt *he* wore had become tighter in some way, smaller by a fraction, but I couldn't lift *his* arms to assuage the feeling.

I tried to exclaim, 'What the hell?' but my voice was just a mere whisper of its former self, my throat being terribly dry.

I wondered where I was but, looking to my left, I saw the windows without curtains and knew I was in *his* father's house, lying in *his* bed and all was calm.

Not resisting the paralysis, I lay there looking out of the window at this planet's natural day, then, suddenly, my serenity was shattered. The noise sounded like the door to *his* cottage was being smashed in, rending cracks filling the air.

The sirens piercing this new day assailed my ears. I wanted to get up to see what was happening but, every time I tried, nothing moved; my transformation was not yet complete.

Then *his* bedroom door swung back against the room's wall, banging loudly, and people in blue clothing jumped on us, turning us over, handcuffing *his* hands behind my back.

I tried to ask what was going on but I only exhaled, no sounds coming forth from my mouth.

As they lifted me onto a stretcher and carted *us* down *his* wooden stairs, prone, I heard *him* screaming inaudibly in my head, 'What have I done, WHAT HAVE I DONE?' with no recognition that I was now in control; soon *his* voice would be no more.

And then *we* were in their vehicle, and travelling; going to who knows where.

As I tried to struggle, only by turning *his* head violently, no other part of *his* body able to move, the image of a blurred man crossed my vision, as he leant over me, placing a transparent mask on my mouth, holding it firm.

The man turned to someone behind him, talking, and although the words he said I knew I ought to know, their meaning was lost on me; an alien language to my ears.

I heard a hissing sound and a distantly familiar, almost sweet smell filled my nose, and with each breath I took, so light changed into darkness.

## Waiting

By Paul Bunn

They crowd around
Deep in conversation
Can they not see me?
Lying on this bed

I notice a glance
In my direction
I see no pity
Only greed

If only they knew
The pain I felt
My body ached
Tired of life

The moment approaches
Waiting nearly over
Their voices diminish
One more breath

All eyes upon me
A smile crosses my lips
They want the money
The cat's home will get.

# The Villa

By Jessie Hobson

## Chapter 1

SEPTEMBER 1930

The September Saturday had been mild and sunny and Lucy was engrossed with the little jointed dolls she had been given for her eleventh birthday. They had been specifically chosen to fit in the miniature villa, which her father had built in the tree house at the end of the lawn. Constructed some years before, when her older brother James had been a boisterous lad, the lofty room had been a refuge for him and gave peace for a short while to his exasperated parents, but he had now left home and was apprenticed to the local locksmith, and only came home for occasional weekends. Lucy and her younger brother, Thomas, now had possession.

At the moment, Thomas was on the ground sorting some lead soldiers, not the least interested in Lucy's suggestion that they play doctors and nurses, using the little beds in the doll's house to act as a hospital. Neither child was old enough to remember the Great War, when Father had been a soldier and Mother had struggled alone with baby James. They knew that Father had gone to an army hospital when he was wounded; their mother proudly recounted to them that his bravery had won him a medal. He himself said nothing, preferring to put the horrors of war behind him and provide for his family.

He was a formal man, and could not abide names to be shortened, so his wife was always addressed as Elizabeth, and James and Thomas were never allowed to be called Jim or Tom.

He particularly detested anyone calling him Bert, and would gruffly correct whoever did so, saying his name was Bertram, thank you. To his work colleagues, he was Mr Berringer, having returned to being chief accountant with Ledbridges, a quality haberdashery firm, with branches throughout the Home Counties. It was through one of the shops that he had encountered Elizabeth, who had accompanied her mother in making purchases there, and he had contrived to court her and marry her, just two years before war broke out. It was not a popular decision with his own parents, who regarded Elizabeth as a 'poor thing,' because she was quiet, gentle and unassuming.

However, Bertram had seen what they had not, that she was also loyal, hardworking and resilient, faculties which enabled her to endure the years of separation, bringing up her baby, and to make her man welcome on his return, without overplaying her independence. She only ever opposed his wishes, if she felt strongly enough about an issue to voice her opinion firmly.

In the tree house, Lucy was re-enacting what she imagined must have been Father's stay in the army hospital. She adapted her voice to imitate the high-pitched tone of the nurse doll in her left hand or the growly grumble of the doctor doll in her right hand. A third doll, representing her father, lay abed swathed in bandages made from an ancient cotton handkerchief torn into strips. She set the dolls down carefully and unwrapped the wounds and squeakily pronounced them healed. She then stood 'Father' up and made the jointed legs walk him out of the hospital. Game over, she climbed down the ladder and contemplated Thomas and his soldiers, for a moment, then walked indoors.

Elizabeth was busy at the scrubbed deal kitchen table, rolling pastry for some meat pies. She looked up with a smile as her little daughter entered.

"Hello, dear," she said. "I'm glad you have come in. I have got a job you can help me get done."

Lucy scuffed her shoes sulkily – she had thought to go and find a favourite book to read, and was not feeling at all like running errands. She cheered up, however, when her mother asked her to take some freshly baked scones next door, to the Harrison family. They had only one child, a girl of fourteen, but Lucy worshipped this smart, worldly-wise nearly adult young person and would say to Elizabeth "Dora does this" or "Dora says that" with great admiration in her voice.

The scones were wrapped in a clean damask napkin and put into a wicker shopping basket. Lucy left the house by the side door. She walked along by the red brick wall of the solid Victorian house that was her home, and went into the road, turning towards the neighbouring house.

The Harrisons had moved in only eighteen months before, and their house had been built just a few years earlier, in an innovative Art Deco style, with curved window frames and severely plain lines. The path from the gate lay between neat, orderly flowerbeds and a tiny patch of grassed lawn. The glass in the front door had an ornate geometric pattern. Lucy knocked on the door and waited.

## Chapter 2

Leo and Patricia Harrison were a well-to-do couple, indeed, Patricia came from a long established county set; 'old money' people said, whereas Leo had proved his worth as an industrialist, although the more class-conscious among Patricia's acquaintance muttered disparagingly under their breath about 'nouveau riche'. Moreover, they wondered how he had avoided military service in the trenches. It did not prevent them taking advantage of his generosity, when opportunity presented itself. He was too wise to be taken in by them, but tolerated the position out of confidence in his own abilities and the knowledge of exactly why he had been in a reserved occupation. Besides, he adored his svelte, sophisticated little wife. Although Dora had come on the scene early in their marriage, this did not interrupt their social life in the Charleston era of cocktails and tea-dances, which had enchanted Patricia or Patsy, as she was more often called. They simply employed a nanny for the baby. This matronly soul had long outlived her duties in the nursery, but had consented to move on with the family, in the position of housekeeper. So it was that Nanny was given the courtesy title of Mrs Green, although she had never married. It was she who opened the door to Lucy.

"Hello, young lady. What a beautiful basket you have there."

Lucy smiled with mischief. "You sound like the Big Bad Wolf in the story of Red Riding Hood, Mrs Green. But I am not going to my grannie's – these are for Mr and Mrs Harrison, from my mother."

"My, they will be pleased. Come along in and I will let them know you are here. I expect Dora would like to see you, if you have time?"

Lucy nodded eagerly and stood obediently in the hallway, while Mrs Green disappeared into the heart of the house. She looked with keen interest, and some degree of envy, at the light clean lines of the stairway, so different from the heavy knobbled brown wooden balustrade in her own home. She was not yet old enough to understand that the opulence before her was that of wealthier folk than her own, simply that it appealed to her senses.

It was while she was gazing up the stairs that Dora came quietly from the doorway of the lounge.

"Nanny says you've brought us some scones, Lucy. May I see?"

Lucy held out the basket. "They are all wrapped up."

Together, Dora's dark sleek bobbed hair and Lucy's fair plaits bent over the basket, and they carefully turned back one corner, delighting in the fresh smell of baking.

"Caught you in the act," said a deep baritone voice behind them. They looked up to see Leo with a mock frown on his face.

"We weren't eating them, Daddy," said Dora, "just looking."

Her father, who was beginning to run to middle-aged spread, put an arm round each child's shoulders and answered "They are exactly what I fancy right now. Let's find some plates and have a feast." He propelled the girls towards the kitchen. "Don't tell Mummy, though," he continued. "She thinks I am putting on too much weight. Oh, dear, I am too late, here she is."

Indeed, Patsy was already in the kitchen, wearing a crisp apron over her low-waisted floral dress, as she sorted some goods, which had been delivered from the grocer's store a few moments before. The boy, with his bicycle, had come to what swanky people, (in his view), called the tradesmen's entrance and had been met by Mrs Green and her mistress, while Leo and the girls had been chatting.

The little group worked together to butter the scones and carry the trayful into the dining room. Lucy looked, with awe, at the small square plates and angular cups, which the adults were using for tea drinking to accompany the impromptu feast. Mrs Green produced two glasses of homemade lemonade for the girls. Dora opened her mouth to protest that she was not a child, but saw the look of delight on Lucy's face, and held her peace.

Perhaps it was unwise of Leo to talk openly to his wife while Lucy was in the room, but he announced that, because there were to be alterations at the office the next week, he would need to bring home some papers to put in the safe with Patsy's pearls and other jewellery. He said he intended to get a locksmith to check out the safe and introduce some security measures, as the papers were confidential and could be of interest to rival companies if stolen. Probably, Lucy would not have taken heed, if Leo had not mentioned the word 'locksmith,' which immediately led her to think of her brother. She wondered if he would be doing some of this work.

## Chapter 3

James had been blessed with sensible parents in Bertram and Elizabeth. Early on, they had realised that his school reports showed better results for sport and woodwork than for more academic subjects. They knew he would be unlikely to settle for a white collar desk job, and Bertram was fortunate to have made the acquaintance of Henry Walker, through the local Rotary Club, to which both belonged. As a locksmith, he was able to take the boy into apprenticeship, an active enough career to suit both his liveliness and his manual skills. James had left school at fourteen and was now nearing the journeyman stage in his training.

Henry had been busy after the weekend and, on the Tuesday, entered the austere tidy workshop with more time to carry on his instruction. He selected the various parts to form a cylinder lock. He laid the pieces carefully on the work bench, and called James to come and observe the process of assembling the parts.

"Watch with care. I will expect you to locate a similar cylinder in your own set of drawers afterwards and to set it up in the right order," Henry instructed.

In spite of his tendency to be a scatterbrain, James was a quick and apt pupil at this type of task and, after a few false moves, was able to fit the pieces together to Henry's satisfaction.

"Right. Now we will fit the whole lock into the practice door and then we can do the fun bit," said Henry with a grin.

"What's that, then?" asked James.

"To teach you how to pick the lock. Not much good being a locksmith if you cannot undo a lock when necessary."

"That could lead some people into the temptation to take up safe cracking, couldn't it?" queried the surprised apprentice.

"Obviously, you need to give this kind of training to only trustworthy workers. I think I have known you long enough to judge you to be honest."

A gratified James took out an assortment of picklocks from his own selection of tools and watched and learned, before attempting to emulate his master.

"Did you know," said Henry conversationally as they worked, "that we have a contract with the Harrisons who live next door to your parents?"

"Really? What do they need from us?"

"An upgrade in security, not just the safe, but the exterior doors as well. Personally, I find, from experience, that burglars tend to ignore locks on doors – I mean, nobody in their right mind is going to leave a key conveniently in the lock on the inside. Thieves are more likely to break in through a window."

"That would be too noisy, surely?"

"No, James, not if they cut the glass with a diamond and catch it with a suction pad. Or I have known one enterprising villain plaster the window with sticky flypapers and give it a tap with a hammer."

James laughed. "My mother uses those in the kitchen. She can't abide flies."

After the day's work was completed, James made off to go home to his digs. He had taken out lodgings with a stout lady called Mrs Jarvis, who had been the cook with landed gentry, until she retired. James was the long, lean type of young man who can eat like a horse, but not put on an ounce of weight, so his landlady tried with all her might to feed him up, but only succeeded in increasing her own girth.

His evening meal was stew with dumplings and she had already planned, in her mind, to make some deep crust pies the following day, which suited James fine, as he enjoyed his food. He helped Mrs Jarvis clear and wash the dishes, when they had eaten.

She always addressed him as 'Mr James,' as if he were the son of the family she had served, which amused him.

"May I ask a small favour of you, Mr James? The evening is a bit chill and I thought to light the fire and sit by it with my wireless. I think there is a play on, and I can knit as I listen. Would you be kind enough to fill the coal scuttle for me, please?"

"Yes. I'll do that before I get changed. I am going to the men's club to play billiards. I won't be late," James added as he saw her look.

While he prepared to go out, Mrs Jarvis made some twists of newspaper and cut open a bundle of kindling ready to light the little open fire in her sitting room, and by the time James went out, there was a cheerful blaze in the hearth.

"Have a pleasant evening, Mr James. I will leave some sandwiches for your supper."

"Thank you. I shall probably be glad of them."

The men's club was a few streets away from where James lived and, when he entered the billiard hall, he saw, to his disappointment, that the young men playing were a group he preferred to avoid. His parents would have called them 'common,' as they were ill-educated and ill-mannered for the most part. They kept company with an older man in his thirties, Fred Butterworth, who sneeringly encouraged them to act as a gang with a reputation for causing trouble. He had been to prison and usually tried to mastermind their activities, without involving himself.

"James, lad," he greeted the young apprentice. "You are just the man I wanted to see."

James did not answer, judging it best to wait to see what Fred had to say.

"George here tells me he has news from his younger brother, Billy, who runs errands for the grocer on his bike. I expect you know him – he delivers to your parents and other neighbours." He laid emphasis on the last two words, and chuckled. "It seems your little sister has been telling him that next door is having some work done by your boss, Mr Walker. What would you know about that, I wonder?"

"That's confidential," said James bluntly.

"Maybe," said Fred. "But we could do with your help in lifting some of their property. They are rich and we fancy a share."

"What makes you think I want any part in that?" said James, taken aback by the menace in Fred's voice.

"Well, if you don't," went on Fred silkily, "we could always tell someone you were behind it, with your helpful little sister. Planning to rob your neighbours. That wouldn't do your career much good; would it? And we wouldn't want a little girl to get hurt, but she might, don't you think?"

The threat of violence to Lucy scared James, and he sought in his mind how best to handle the situation.

"Give me time to find out when the work is being completed and what is being installed. Then I can let you know."

"That's a good boy. Glad you can see reason," said Fred. "Let the lad have a go at the table," he called to one of his gang.

They made room for James under the huge hooded lights over the massive billiard table, and he played there for a while without further reference being made to Fred's plan, long enough for him to leave for home, without seeming in too much hurry.

## Chapter 4

Mrs Jarvis was still enjoying her fire and knitting when James came in, so he sat down and ate his sandwiches.

"All you need now is a nice little cat on your lap to look the complete picture." said James.

"Oh, no. Nasty things; scratch the furniture and leave hairs all over the place. They are a nuisance, except for keeping mice away."

James was stopped in his tracks by her vehemence. A few days earlier, he had seen a friend, who worked at the pet shop in the town centre, and had half promised to find a home for one of a litter of kittens, thinking to give one to Mrs Jarvis. He thought ruefully that he would need to ask his parents to have the furry bundle, perhaps as a late birthday present for Lucy. 'Tomorrow being Wednesday,' he thought, 'is half-day closing at the shops. I will need to collect the cat on Thursday, if Mr Walker will let me keep it on the premises for a couple of hours'.

Thinking about his boss, and how he had shown trust in him, he felt torn as to what to do about stopping Fred and his gang. He decided to sleep on it, but of course, sleep would not come and he tossed and turned well into the night. Next morning he arose looking haggard, and Mrs Jarvis wondered if he was sickening for an autumn cold. He reassured her, but arrived at work listless and jittery.

Henry was already busy with a grinder working on fine-tuning keys he had cut earlier. He looked up and his smile faded as he saw James drooping over his bench.

"You don't look yourself today, lad. What's wrong?

James paused, then made the decision to share his problem with his master.

"Actually, I'm worried, Sir." He chewed his lip as he considered how to put his concern into words.

"In the evening, I play billiards at the men's club, and some of the fellows there are a bit on the rough side. One of them has a younger brother who is the errand boy for Duffields, the grocer's. He delivers to my parent's place, and next door too, that's the Harrisons'. My little sister must have heard about what we are working on for them, and told the boy. She is rather proud of what I'm learning and I'm sure she had no idea she was being indiscreet. Anyway, these chaps want me to help them break in and said they would make out I was behind the idea if I gave them away. But I am not willing to be a part of that. I want to be a good locksmith. And they made threats, in a backhanded way, to hurt Lucy as well."

Henry laid down his work and led James to the small office behind the workshop. He brewed tea and they sat and drank it quietly. Having thus given himself time to think about what James had told him, Henry said, "We may need to let them think you are going along with their scheme. They probably expect you to open the safe. But if I go to the local constabulary and put them in the picture, the bobby on the beat can keep half an eye open and perhaps we can come up with some means to keep you from needing to worry about your sister."

"They want to know details – when the job is done and what we have altered. Should I tell them? Suppose they decide to go ahead anyway, without me?"

"If you tell them you know how to work the combination, they will certainly want you there."

As a safeguard, Henry knew that he would be making it impossible for James, or any other thief, to succeed, by introducing a gadget called a gate into the lock, which needed a highly skilled locksmith to bypass the combination. He felt it would be wiser not to tell James, not from lack of trust, but in case his manner gave the game away to the gang.

James was relieved to have spoken to Henry, and as they had worked out exactly what to tell Fred, he felt bold enough to ask if he could collect the kitten on the Thursday, if his mother agreed to take it.

To his surprise, Henry was enthusiastic, and even said they could go together in the lunch-hour. His reasoning was that his wife had lost her old cat a couple of months before, and he would like to see the litter and choose a tom-cat for her.

In the meantime, Henry reminded James that they would be off to the Harrisons' on the Wednesday morning, to assess what needed doing, which would give them time both to plan how much information should be passed on to Fred and for James to briefly visit his parents to ask about the kitten.

That evening Henry made his way to the police station and warned them of the likelihood of trouble, and James went home with diagrams to study in preparation for the next day's work.

## Chapter 5

That Tuesday, Lucy was feeling very excited, as she had just come home from her very first day at the secondary school. She had set out proudly in the morning with Dora, who was attending the same school. The older girl had seen her safely through the playground, but after that, Lucy had dealt with her day on her own; Dora had a piano lesson after school, and would not be going home until later. Lucy had not noticed a raffish young man watching her walk home, her head full of news to tell her mother. He ambled along behind her with his hands in his pockets, to see which route she took, then wandered past the two houses as if on the way to another destination. Nevertheless, he took a couple of sharp glances at the Art Deco house as he went by. Lucy disappeared into the sideway of her house and made her way through the kitchen door. No-one was about, not even Thomas, so eventually she went into the garden, where she found Elizabeth and Thomas sweeping paths and dead-heading flowers.

"Go and change out of your school clothes, Lucy," her mother directed. "Then you can help us cut some cabbage and pull some carrots from the vegetable plot, while you tell us how you got on."

Thomas stared wide-eyed, and a bit scared, at his sister in her smart school uniform, knowing that tomorrow would be his turn to go to infant school, a new venture for him too. He was not sure he wanted to go, but Lucy did not seem upset, so he supposed it must be alright. Mother would take him and bring him home.

The children had time to play in the tree-house, after their garden tasks, while their mother prepared the evening meal. Lucy pretended the little villa was a school-house and moved the beds out, to make room for chairs for the dolls.

"Shall I ask Father to make us some desks and a blackboard, Thomas?"

"That's a good idea. Can this doll be the teacher?"

"If you like. We should put one of the other dolls in the kitchen to make school meals."

"Do we eat dinner at school, then? I hope the food is nice."

"Well," said Lucy doubtfully, "it wasn't as nice as when Mother cooks it when I had it today."

They chatted on until Elizabeth called them in to wash their hands and sit at table. By this time, Bertram had arrived home from work, and the family ate quietly, the children minding their manners, as they had been taught. Afterwards, they persuaded their parents to play games of Old Maid and Snap before it was time for bed. For once, Thomas did not grumble when his sister was allowed to stay up later than he.

Out in the street, the measured tread of the policeman could be heard walking past the houses. Henry's message had been heeded, and the constable was already on the alert.

Fred, meanwhile, had met with his gang of four, two of whom were fledgling villains, impressed by the older man. Only in George had Fred recognised a kindred spirit – vicious, greedy, unprincipled and willing to take risks. It was to him he entrusted the outline of his intentions, which were to prove Henry wrong in one aspect. Fred had no intention of including James in the break-in. He planned to intimidate him into divulging the combination of the safe, then to knock him out or eliminate him from the proceedings in some other way, then to go in without him. George was to accompany Fred in the burglary, the others were to be posted on look-out and, if his idea was successful, then one would be holding Lucy hostage to force James to comply. It never entered his head that kidnapping was a serious offence or that to harm the victim would warrant hanging, as would a fatal blow to James' head. He believed himself totally capable of escaping with his crimes, without penalty.

## Chapter 6

Thursday dawned cold, with a damp autumnal mist. The children and their mother left early for school, Dora joining them as they left. Leo was not yet up, so Patsy and Mrs Green were waiting for Henry and James to arrive to start their work. Bertram left his house a little later, carrying a valise to the station, as he was due to stay overnight at the northern branch of his firm. Elizabeth had her shopping basket with her, as she intended to collect some basic weekend shopping and to order the Sunday joint from the butcher. The Berringers' house lay quiet and shrouded, making it easy for George and his look-out, Ted, to slip furtively round the side of the Victorian building, to see whether there could be an easy way into the neighbouring house from the back. They were disappointed, as the French doors looked solid and impregnable, so they crept out, crouching hastily out of sight as the locksmith and his apprentice walked jauntily past and turned into the Harrisons' gate. As tradesmen, they went round to the side entrance, which gave George and Ted time to escape unseen.

"We'll have to get in by climbing on to the flat roof of the porch and through a bedroom window," said George to his accomplice. "Maybe a wooden mallet and a cold chisel to break the window catch."

"Who sleeps over the porch?" asked Ted as they walked away.

"Dunno," answered George. "Might need to rough up whoever it is to keep 'em quiet."

Ted was not too happy about this. He had not heard the discussion between Fred and George the night before, and did not realise the gang could possibly injure someone. He was too cowardly to question the wisdom of such a plan.

Henry and James had not noticed anything amiss, as they arrived to begin their assessment. Mrs Green let them in and announced them to Leo, who, by this time, had breakfasted and was champing at the bit to go off to his office. The locksmith gave his suggestions, which met with approval, and Leo hastily kissed Patsy goodbye and left her to finalise how the work should be carried out. Having discussed the various aspects of the job, which took until mid-morning, Henry and James left the Harrisons' house and the two men parted, Henry to return to the workshop, while James called at his parents' house about the kitten, having arranged to return to the locksmith's, as soon as possible.

Elizabeth was home by now, polishing and dusting and making beds, humming happily to herself, with no-one under her feet as she worked. She was pleased to stop as James came. He was not a frequent visitor, so she was delighted to hear that he was working next door. She was more doubtful about the kitten, but relented and agreed that Lucy would love one. She thought to herself, after consideration, that maybe a cat might solve the reason for certain scratchy noises in the pantry – she had wondered if there was a mouse, or worse, mice.

"Your father will not be home until tomorrow," said Elizabeth, "so I will have to make the decision to have the kitten, without asking him. If he is put out, I will say we can do with a mouser."

"You can always get round Father when you make your mind up," grinned James. "I must go," he added abruptly. "Mr Walker is expecting me back. I will bring the kitten tonight."

There was only half an hour or so left to work that morning by the time James got back to the workshop, then the two men set off for the pet shop, where they purchased a ginger tom for Henry and a black and white queen for Lucy. The pet shop was able to provide two cat baskets, at a price, of course, and, amid plaintive yowls, Henry and James carried their kittens back to the workshop and shut them in the office, with food and water, until home time.

Elizabeth had told Lucy that there would be a surprise for her at teatime, if she behaved herself, so she was on best behaviour when James arrived with a basket. The sedate little girl suddenly became animated and overjoyed, when she found the kitten inside, and promptly named her Tiddles. Thomas was just a bit jealous, until he heard it was a birthday present. Someone might give him one, or perhaps a puppy, when he had his sixth birthday, he thought.

James stayed with the family for the evening meal, then he left for the men's club to tell Fred and the gang what they wanted to hear about the security measures at the Harrisons' house, and to let them know the work would be done the next day. He was careful to sound reluctant to let them know this information, and to plead for Fred to leave Lucy out of it.

"Try to find out whether the people will be going out over the weekend, especially during the evening. It would also be useful to know who sleeps in which bedrooms." demanded Fred. As he did not want James to realise the intention to break in on the upper floor, he added, "We could, maybe, find some more jewellery up there too."

George, who was athletic, had noticed in the morning that there were adequate footholds around the door to enable him to climb up the porch and, when James had gone, he discussed with Fred his ideas about how to get in and they both agreed he should come downstairs and open the front door, to let Fred in. Ideally, they wanted the family to be out but they would probably have to deal with at least the housekeeper and the girl of the family, harshly, if necessary.

"Just in case you get any ideas into your head about the daughter, she's a kid, not grown up yet, so don't mess her about, if she's there. I know you like the ladies, but keep your mind on the job." Fred had made the mistake of being distracted by the fair sex when breaking and entering when younger, resulting in being caught and jailed. So his warning to George was heart-felt.

## Chapter 7

The following day, Henry and James packed toolboxes with saws, nails, screws, clamps, the latest Schlage cylinder locks for the doors, smaller fasteners for windows and a new combination lock for the Chubb safe, plus all the other paraphernalia they needed. At the Art Deco house, Henry set James to go and fix the door locks so that without James noticing, he could fix the false gate to the combination lock. Mrs Green brought them a cup of tea each for their lunch – they had supplied their own food – and they worked steadily on through the day, securing the ground floor. Leo had not thought it necessary to fit locks to the windows upstairs. He was not aware how agile some thieves could be. By chance, James overheard Patsy telling Mrs Green that she and her husband were going to a dinner dance on the Saturday, and would probably take Dora if she wanted to go. He was relieved to know they would be out, but he did not find out if Mrs Green was going to have time off. It was more news than he had expected to be able to tell Fred.

Whilst her brother worked next door, Lucy had gone to school without enthusiasm, as she wanted so much to play with Tiddles. Mother had shut the kitten in the kitchen before taking Thomas to school, and she was careful when she came home to keep doors shut, so the animal did not stray, except when taken into the garden to get it used to its new home. Thomas had to be reminded about doors too, when she brought him home; Lucy needed no such warning, as she played with Tiddles almost ceaselessly.

Bertram arrived home early in the evening, kissed Elizabeth and announced, with satisfaction, that the auditors had been well pleased with the accounts he had presented, and that the firm's proprietor had awarded him a bonus.

"We can take the children for a seaside holiday this year," he was saying when he noticed Tiddles, who was stalking a ping-pong ball that Lucy had rolled across the floor.

"What is that cat doing here?" he demanded.

"James brought it for Lucy for her birthday," piped up Thomas. "Can I have a puppy for my birthday, Father?"

Elizabeth tried to keep a straight face as she watched expressions fleeting across her husband's face, but when he looked at her with a baffled, defeated resignation, she burst out laughing.

"It will keep down any mice, dear. And if the children have a dog to walk later, that will be good exercise, don't you think?"

"Just as long as they do the walking, not you. And certainly not me," Bertram said – his old war wound still gave him occasional difficulty with sustained movement. Thomas hopped up and down with glee and longed to be six.

At the lodgings, Mrs Jarvis was a bit huffy with James, because he had not come home for supper the night before, to eat her beautiful pies. He apologised for not telling her that he would be visiting his parents, but did not mention that he had taken a kitten there. Mrs Jarvis was mollified – it was right and proper for the lad to pay his respects to his family. Her larder faced north, as a good larder should, so the pies had kept fresh and she warmed them through in the small oven, being careful not to knock her leg on the drop-down door, which was easy to do in such a small kitchen. Once again, James set forth for the men's club, to bring Fred up to date. Neither he nor Fred knew that a couple of police cadets had been introduced to the men's club, and that these young men had made it their business to eavesdrop on the gang. When Fred was hearing that Saturday would be a good chance, the police made their plans accordingly.

## Chapter 8

The weekend began with light showers, so Lucy and Thomas stayed indoors and played with Tiddles with shrieks of laughter. Bertram tried hard to read his newspaper but gave up in the end. Lucy had asked him about making desks for the school in the villa, so he went out to the garden shed and sorted out bits of plywood and sat at his treadle fretwork machine to cut them to shape. Elizabeth shut herself away in her workroom and mended socks. Next door, only Mrs Green had risen early. She cleaned, dusted, lit a fire in the closed stove and prepared breakfast. Later, Dora appeared, yawning, bored and grumpy, because she had wanted cornflakes not porridge. Mrs Green took trays that included toast and boiled eggs up to Leo and Patsy. She popped into her bedroom over the porch to tidy it, then made Dora's bed in the back bedroom. She bustled back downstairs and made fresh toast for Dora under the grill. That done, she set about clearing the kitchen, ready for preparing the main meal of the day.

For James, Saturday was still a working day, and he and Henry caught up with some of the other jobs in hand. His mind was not fully on the tasks, and Henry had to get quite sharp with him at times. He knew James was worried about the coming night, but there was work to be done, and apprentices should pay attention. The day dragged for James, and he was relieved to come to the end of it. He had arranged to meet Fred and the gang later, after the club had closed. Fred thought it better for James not to be seen with them during the evening, and only he and George had gone to the club, in the usual way. The rest of the gang, like James, would join later. This was what Fred had said to James, but the two look-out members had been told to watch for an opportunity to snatch Lucy and hold her hostage. Failing that, they would take George's younger brother, Billy along with them to make noises, as if he was the little girl trying to escape.

James was too wrought to notice that he met only Fred and George, and he followed them towards the Harrisons' house, with sheep-like obedience. Henry had told him the number of the combination lock on the safe, and he repeated it, over and over, in his mind.

As they got near to their destination, James heard what sounded like a little girl crying, and Fred turned with a leer to him and said, "That's your sister. Ted and his mate have got her. If I say so, they will burn her pretty little face with cigarettes. So, now, Jamesy boy, I want the number of the safe's combination."

James was astounded at the turn of events. The crying grew louder, and he looked at the evil face before him and recited the number.

"Say that again?" said Fred. James repeated it. Behind him, George swung a cricket bat at James' head and the lad crumpled at their feet.

"Drag him into the bushes out of sight," grunted Fred. James' limp body was soon bundled away, and George started to climb. Breaking open the frame made a fair bit of noise, and he held his breath, as he eased the window open. He slid silently into the room, and saw Mrs Green asleep in her bed. He crept past her and down the stairs to let Fred in.

Unknown to James, the gang had not succeeded in capturing Lucy. She was crying, but indoors. Inadvertently, when Bertram came in from the shed, he left the door open long enough for Tiddles to escape into the garden, and Lucy was distraught because the kitten was missing. She was eventually persuaded to go to bed, with the promise that they would look for Tiddles again, first thing in the morning.

Tiddles began the biggest adventure of her little life. She explored the Berringers' garden, then scrambled over the fence into the Harrisons' garden. She trotted up the sideway, sniffed at the strange body under the hedge, and watched, as Fred waited for George to open the door. As he did so, she darted inside.

Lucy felt she could not wait until morning to look for Tiddles. She slipped downstairs and out of the house, wrapped in a shawl, and began to call quietly for her kitten.

Suddenly a hand was clamped over her mouth and a voice hissed "I am not going to hurt you. I am a policeman, and there is a burglary going on next door. If I let you go, will you promise to be quiet?" Lucy nodded her head vigorously. "Then go and climb into your tree house, out of the way, until we have caught the robbers." Lucy fled across the lawn and up the tree, her eyes wide with fright.

In the Harrisons' house, 'Mrs Green' rose from the bed over the porch, fully uniformed, except for a helmet. Earlier in the day, Leo and Patsy had been visited by a police sergeant, who had arranged for Mrs Green to leave the house as well. Men had then been posted at strategic points, indoors and around the garden.

The constable tiptoed down the stairs, as Fred, cursing, was trying to open the safe. Henry's number given to James was totally useless for an amateur thief, but Fred was so engrossed he did not hear as a second constable moved quietly from the kitchen. The two policemen glided to catch the burglars. Just then, George moved back and there was an affronted screech, as he trod on Tiddles' paw. He swung round, to find himself gripped by the strong arms of the law. Fred struggled to his feet and rushed towards the front door, to be met by yet another uniformed man, who overpowered him.

Lucy had heard Tiddles yell, and almost fell out of the tree in her haste to get down. The kitten ran out of the house at full tilt, back the way she had come, over the fence and straight into Lucy's arms. They stood in the dark, comforting each other, as the noise next door subsided and the gang were led away.

As dawn broke, the rattle of milk bottles and the clip clop of horses' hooves along the road heralded the milk cart. The milkman looked with amazement at a body lying under the hedge, and rang the bell frantically. Thankfully, James, who was in a coma for a while, recovered fully and was able to complete his apprenticeship; Dora and Lucy visited him in hospital and, a few years later, James and Dora started 'walking out'.

## Chapter 9

SEPTEMBER 1940

Elizabeth wrapped her coat round her shoulders, as she crossed the lawn with her teenage son, Thomas, to the Anderson shelter. The air-raid siren had sounded, and Bertram was already on his way to the ARP hut, his tin hat firmly in place. At the start of World War II a connecting gate had been installed between the Victorian and the Art Deco homes, and shortly after the two Berringers had settled, Dora, now carrying her baby daughter, joined them in the shelter.

"Where are your parents, dear?" asked Elizabeth.

"They are doing voluntary work at the British Restaurant," said Dora. "The food there is a help to people's rations, especially if they have been bombed out."

Those two words resonated in her memory for many years to come, as there was a deafening explosion which rocked the shelter and left the two women staring with horror at one another. They scrambled to the door and peered out. The bomb had flattened the Art Deco house and seriously damaged the more substantial Victorian one.

"We are lucky to be alive," said Elizabeth shakily.

"We need to let someone know there was no-one indoors," answered Dora, who had always been practical like her father. "Thomas, go and find help."

Their thoughts turned to James and Lucy who were away in the armed forces. For reasons of national security, their civilian relatives did not know where they were. Lucy was in the Women's Auxiliary Air Force, plotting aircraft movements. James, who had married Dora two years before, had joined the

Royal Engineers. Leo was particularly proud of his son-in-law, as he had spent his own years, during the First World War, developing the early tanks brought into service as that war progressed. James was already in Europe and was killed in action later, the only member of the two families to be lost.

As the 'all clear' sounded, Elizabeth surveyed the scene before making a move to reorganise her life and that of the two families. She looked down the garden to the old tree, which had escaped damage, and thought, ruefully, that the only house, which had escaped unscathed, was the little villa her beloved Bertram had built so long ago for Lucy.

# The Real Great Equaliser

By David Shaer

I sweep the streets, I feed the poor,
I nurse the old, I act the whore
I bake the bread, I drive the bus,
I fly the plane, the traffic cuss

I judge the crime, I count the cost,
I ring the bell, with that round lost.
I draw the plans, I teach the kids,
As veggies boil, I put on lids

I clean the house, I sweep the flue,
I sort the mail, I move the queue.
I run the show, the actors curse
I take the vow, for best or worse.

I heal the lame, I milk the cow,
It's not like then, it's different now.
I run the mile, I pass the ball,
It's busy here, I'll take that call.

I mend the shoe, the picture frame,
I drive the train, I'll just take aim.
Uphold the law or take a bung,
I climb the pole, up one more rung.

## Bedside Manner

It makes no difference what you do
Or whether I'm as good as you
To use the hands, or use the head
To be the leader or the led.

It matters not from where I come,
The things I face, my life humdrum.
When all is lost, or even won,
I'm overlooked by moon or sun.

At last, in me, I'm calm relaxed
My corpse lies still, its pressures axed
Whatever stress was there can go,
This is my world, both high and low.

Our common aim, the rest to beat,
My shell in which I can retreat
I don't care now, I'm nearly free
Just go away, there's only me.

My mind, my soul, my limbs are one
It's soothing now, my work is done.
I'm drifting from the daily toil
No longer coming to the boil.

That out of body sense is near,
I'm drifting far away from here
To rest, to sleep, outside my norm,
No longer in my normal form.

Just one step back, outside my skin,
I look down on my life within
I breathe a sigh and all release
At bedside now, I rest in peace.

# The Bed I Used To Sleep In

By Paul Bunn

## Chapter 1

The bed I used to sleep in .... was propped up against the wall ready for its final resting place - the dump.

I sat in the opposite corner and couldn't move, wanting the ground to swallow me up whole but there was Daniel to think of, my eight-year-old son. Chastising myself I absent-mindedly wiped a tear from my eye.

"Are you OK, Daddy?" Daniel had crept into the room, without my noticing. His soft blue eyes were fixed on mine, as he reached out to cuddle me.

"Yeah, fine." Was all I could manage in return. But it wasn't fine, not by a long way. We just sat there with our arms around each other, until the daylight had turned to darkness.

## Chapter 2

Night time was strangely comforting for Daniel and me. The road outside was quiet and the pain we were both feeling seemed to dissipate, as the last faint rays of the sun dipped over the horizon. The bed was still in the corner, not wanted and unloved. The rest of the room was in need of decoration, with no wallpaper and no carpet, something else I hadn't got around to doing.

"I wish we could move out of here." Daniel was scanning the room, as I was, the sadness in his voice evident.

"We will, Son, we will." I tried to sound confident. Would we? I sometimes felt we were trapped here, it seemed like a prison at times.

"Maybe Mummy will come back home soon."

Not for the first time, I felt a hot streak of anger coarse through me. "I don't want to ever see that woman again. She's evil."

Daniel's face crumpled into tears and he fled from the room, his wailing retreating down the hallway. I closed my eyes wishing I could take the words back. Although my harsh feelings for Carol were genuine, there was no need to inflict it onto Daniel. He still didn't understand what she had done, but, then again, neither did I at the time.

I knew where he would go anyway and followed the muffled sobs to his bedroom. He sat in the corner of his room, small fists pushed up and rubbing his eyes, stemming the flow of tears.

"I'm sorry. Dan, it was a horrible thing to say." I knelt in front of him, hands on knees, waiting for him to recover his composure. "Tell you what, let's play hide and seek."

Daniel loved that game, unlike many kids, he didn't sit on his PS2 or 3 all day, being turned into a zombie. He enjoyed the more interactive games that I used to play when I was young; board games like Ludo and Snakes and Ladders. However, he used to spend many a happy afternoon playing hide and seek, either with Carol and me or his friends, who soon came to understand the innocent fun of this type of game.

"OK," he said, visibly perking up. "You hide first and I'll count to one hundred." I smiled and ruffled his hair. "Make sure you do, otherwise it's cheating." He gave me his most radiant grin, before covering his eyes and beginning his count. "1…2…"

I slipped out of the room, unnoticed.

## Chapter 3

The noise that disturbed me sounded like a creaking floorboard but I couldn't be certain, even if it was very quiet in the house. I went to the bedroom door and peered out, the moonlight gave some silvery light to the landing but there were plenty of dark shadows.

"What is it, Dad?" Daniel stood behind me, his pale face turned up at me, questioningly.

"Nothing, Daniel, wait here." I crept outside, without another word, and made my way to the banisters. Already, I wasn't sure whether what I'd heard was genuine or a result of my imagination.

"Dad?" Turning to Daniel, who had followed me out, I put my index finger over my lips to indicate silence. He nodded and stepped back, frightened by my sudden movement. And by what I was implying.

The bottom of the stairs was hidden in a sea of inky blackness but I sensed someone was there, looking back up at me. A faint shiver ran down my spine and I felt a searing pain in my stomach. Grabbing Daniel, I ran back into the bedroom, pressing my back against the door and breathing heavily.

Lifting my shirt, I stared down at the source of the pain and saw nothing but pale, unbroken flesh. It felt like someone had prodded me with a hot poker, so excruciating was its intensity. Then, as suddenly as it had begun, the pain subsided to a dull ache, before dissipating completely.

I shrugged, passing it off as some sort of cramp, caused by my heightened tension. Had there been someone at the bottom of the stairs? Really? I went back to the landing again and looked down. This time, despite the fact I could not see anything; my senses told me no one was there. Relieved, I rejoined Daniel, annoyed at what I now perceived as an overactive imagination.

## Chapter 4

The following day was bright and sunny but my mood was not. Even going around the house ensuring everything was in place and tidy seemed like harder work than usual. I was restless, unable to focus my thoughts on anything for more than a few seconds. I had no idea why.

Daniel was keeping his distance, sensing my demeanour and saying nothing, although I could see he wanted to talk about something, possibly the previous night's events, which I had dismissed at the time. "Just ghosts," I had said jokingly.

Staring out of the window, I saw people walking up and down the road, minding their own business, and felt a pang of jealousy. It wasn't my world. Many of them were smiling and happy, despite the greyness of the day, and I wanted to be one of them. I had Daniel and loved him dearly, but there was still something missing, a deep longing, that I didn't understand. Forcing these thoughts away, I turned my mind to more mundane things like making lunch; I was suddenly ravenous.

We both sat in silence as we ate, concentrating on the food, rather than each other.

"Why do you hate Mummy?"

Such an innocent, straightforward question but it had me perplexed. Daniel stared at me with a steady gaze, expecting an immediate answer. He'd never asked me that before.

I smiled, trying to come up with something that wouldn't upset him, as I'd done earlier. I was confused myself; Carol had treated me badly when we were married, although Daniel was never involved with any of it. The string of affairs she'd had still left a bitter taste in my mouth. But there was more, much more, which my memory had hidden away, under lock and key, beyond my reach.

"It's complicated, Dan." I held his tiny hand in mine. "Just take it from me, that it's best we are no longer together."

"But it's not fair, I miss Mummy so much." His bottom lip dropped and fresh tears threatened to roll down his face.

At that moment, the dark coals of fury stirred again within me, raging at Carol for driving this huge wedge into the heart of our family. But it didn't last, she was long gone now, so I concentrated on trying to mend a boy's broken heart.

## Chapter 5

I noticed the marks on Daniel first: Thin red lines appeared across his stomach, chest and face, almost overnight. Studying them carefully I thought it might be some sort of rash, from either clothing or something he'd eaten. He didn't complain though, saying they didn't hurt at all and to stop fussing. I thought about taking him to the doctor but dismissed it, thinking I'd look a fool if it were only an allergic reaction.

As they didn't seem to be causing him any discomfort, I left it, just making a mental note to keep an eye on them, to ensure they didn't get worse.

A few days later, they appeared on me; crisscrossing over my chest and stomach, like a patchwork of tiny scratches. Studying them, I ran my finger along one of the marks, it felt rough, similar to a scab. Shivering, I hid them back under my shirt.

Reaching for the phone, I tried ringing the doctor's but the line was dead. Surprised, I hit the re-dial button but, again, nothing, no dial tone.

"Dan, come on, we're going to the doc's to sort this rash out." There was no response.

"Dan?" I searched, a wave of panic threatening to engulf me, he'd always replied before. He was in his bedroom, staring out of the window.

"Dan, didn't you hear me?" He didn't move, but I sensed something wrong. I approached him and gently rested my hands on his shoulders, they tensed and he spun round.

"I am not going to the doctor's, there is nothing wrong with me." Never had I heard him shout at me like that before – ever. He held his arms stiffly by his side, with hands balled into fist, eyes boring into me. I pulled away, as if hit by an electric shock.

"Leave me alone." He was shaking; such was the strength of his anger. "But Dan…" I couldn't say anymore, he had turned back to the window, ignoring me, as if I wasn't there.

## Chapter 6

Winter started early, snow was drifting lazily past the window and this was only mid November. The year had flown by, in the blink of an eye, and still a depression hung over the house, like a dark cloud.

I had to find out what Daniel's problem was. It was eating me up inside and I was becoming desperate, needing to know what had changed between us.

He had been reclusive and uncommunicative, shutting himself away in his room, for long hours at a time. I couldn't reach him. Sometimes I thought I could hear him speaking to someone in soft tones but, when I drew near his door, the talking stopped. I even entered the room on one occasion but saw no one except Daniel sitting in the corner, hands on knees. Was that suspicion I saw on his face? I didn't know. Ever since the confrontation, he'd hardly strung a single sentence together with me; we were like strangers in the same house.

The marks on both of us hadn't gone, in fact, if anything, they had gone an angrier shade of red although, from my viewpoint, there was no discomfort from them. Dan refused to talk about it, and anything else for that matter. I didn't want a confrontation with him, I was certain it would only make things worse. But what else could I do?

I was tired, tired and fed up with the situation and this house, with all its harsh memories, wanting nothing more than to leave, taking Daniel with me. But I couldn't, at least not without smoothing things over with Daniel first.

Going to his room, I said. "Dan, we need to talk."

I noticed a figure standing in the periphery of my vision.

At least, I thought I had. As soon as my full gaze fell upon it, there was nothing there, except light and shadows. I stood transfixed for a moment, blinking at the empty space, before shaking my head and turning back to Dan, who was now smiling.

"What is it, Daddy?" I went over to him and sat down. So many things came into my head that hadn't been said over the past few weeks that, for a few seconds, I didn't know where to start. We had always been close, and I needed to understand what had changed. The only thing I could think of was his mother; the problems seemed to have occurred after then.

Still, I felt sure that, whatever it was, we could get through it. The sound of the door, gently swinging on its hinges, interrupted my thoughts and I turned, to see Carol in the doorway.

In some respects, she was still as beautiful as I remembered her. Her long, flowing blonde hair hung loosely, in gentle curls around her head. She still wore the gold loop earrings I had bought her many Christmases ago. Her eyes were still of the deepest icy blue, one of the things that had attracted me to her in the first place.

There was something wrong with this picture though, that made me gasp and Dan scream. In her shaking hand, glinting viciously in the light, she held a 12 inch carving knife. It was one of a set of six kitchen knives we'd had for years; this particular one had hardly ever been used, so was not going to be blunted with age.

I felt Dan hugging me tightly. "Mummy, what are you doing?" His voice was barely a whisper. "You said you were going to talk to Daddy."

The thought of her having spoken to Dan almost sent me into a panic. Had she been here all the time? How could that be? This wasn't a big house, with hundreds of places to hide, the exact opposite in fact.

Carol appeared not to hear him, she made no acknowledgement, and her eyes were fixed, solely on me. I imagined the stare a snake makes, before striking its victim with a lethal blow, and tried to swallow, but my throat was dry. My only thought now was to get Dan out of there, as soon as possible.

"Mummy?" Finally her eyes drifted slowly from me to Dan. Her eyebrows furrowed for a moment in confusion. "Talk?" Then, her mind seemed to clear. "Yes, talk."

She was clearly disturbed, and I was unsure how best to get us out of this.

"What are you going to do with that knife, Carol?"

She was blocking the doorway, so I couldn't make a run for it, especially not with Dan in tow.

"I've been watching you, telling all those lies to poor Dan." She stretched out her arm, pointing at me, bringing the knife more keenly into focus. "I've been putting Dan straight on a few things."

So, that was the reason why Dan had been off with me. She had been feeding him with her version of events, while I wasn't around, turning him against me. But how had she got in? I didn't remember letting her keep a key, when she left.

I looked down at Dan, whose eyes were fixed on the knife; and saw the fear and confusion in his face. "Daddy, why has she got that?"

I pushed him behind me, as I confronted Carol; unsure of how to answer why his mother was threatening us. Thinking furiously, I felt the only hope was keeping her in conversation, at least until I could work out an escape from here. "What did you tell him?" My voice was barely a whisper, such was the terror I felt.

She smiled back at me, but it looked more like the grin of a skull in the half-light. "About how you used to beat me, amongst other things." I felt Dan's body shrink from me, for just the briefest moment, before hugging me fiercely again. "How you forced me away, saying I wasn't fit to be your wife or a mother." Carol's attention moved to Dan. "Come over to me, Dan, you know I won't hurt you." Her voice was velvety smooth, but her face was a mask of madness.

Again, I sensed hesitancy from him, torn between two parents he loved deeply. Tears filled his eyes, as he looked from Carol to me, and back again. Grabbing his shoulders, I knelt down in front of him, barely holding back tears myself. "Dan, what your mum is saying is a lie." He took a step back, glancing at both of us and trusting neither. How could a young boy understand what was going on here? Bitterness filled me, adding fuel to my fury, but I had to keep it under control. Standing slowly, I focused my attention on Carol.

"Why are you doing this? Can't you see, carrying a weapon frightens him?" Carol stared at the knife, as if she didn't know how it had got there, and then raised it higher in front of me. Dan let out a short scream.

"Put the knife down, Carol." I tried projecting a confidence I didn't feel. She lunged and everything went dark...

## Chapter 7

*...And light again.*

I didn't remember passing out but I was on the floor, lying next to a weeping Dan, who had covered his eyes in terror. Looking around, there was no sign of Carol. She was gone, at least for the time being. It was then I noticed the blood all over me, and, to my horror, Dan. Sitting up, I cried out, pulling him to me and lifting his shirt, trying to see where it was coming from.

It was the red scratches I had seen before, which were now bleeding copiously, gaping much wider now. They looked like knife wounds.

I had to get him to hospital, right now. Lifting him up, I rushed across the landing, stopping dead after glancing into my bedroom and…

## Chapter 8

*…Staring into the lifeless eyes of me.*

Everything stopped: like a freeze frame on a video, I was frozen to the spot, unable to move or breathe in shock at this incomprehensible sight. Had I finally flipped?

I was on the bed, the bed I used to sleep in, spread-eagled on my back, a look of total surprise on my face. Finally, and without realising it, I entered the room on leaden legs, feeling my whole world shatter into a million pieces. How could this be?

Moving closer, I noticed another body, on the far side of the bed and my heart sank. Daniel. Both of us were covered in blood, deep cuts in some places, slashes in others; it had been a frenzied attack.

But… I was here, still living and breathing, with Daniel in my arms. It must be my imagination running wild, surely. The gruesome scene in front of me didn't waver like a mirage, or disappear, though - it remained crystal clear. A rising urge to flee filled me and I began to turn, then thought better of it.

If I reached out and touched it, maybe it would go away; a childish thought but something I clung onto, like a lifeline to my own sanity. It couldn't be real. Shifting Daniel, who was resting his head on my shoulder, to make myself more comfortable, I tentatively reached down with my other hand and watched, with incredulity, as it passed through the (my) shoulder on the bed.

I opened my mouth to scream, but nothing came out. This time I did turn and run, running as if the devil himself was chasing me. At the bottom of the stairs, I pulled the front door hard, causing it to slam back against the wall. A man stood in front of me, blocking my path, his pale face and dark, sorrowful eyes, holding me at the threshold.

"You can't leave yet. Go back." He raised a gnarled hand and pointed, back the way I had come. Terrified and breathing hard, I ran back through the house, to the back door.

He was there again, pointing back behind me, saying nothing this time. A gust of wind blew up from somewhere behind me, wrenching the door from my hand and closing it, before I could even think about trying to get past him.

Stepping back in shock, I felt Daniel wriggling against me.

"Daddy."

I lifted him down and placed him on the floor, his cuts were no better. How could he lose so much blood and still be alive, never mind conscious? Then, like a light going on in a darkened room, I understood. The wounds were a mirror image of what I had seen in the carnage upstairs.

As I searched Dan's face for signs of pain or discomfort, for an instant it changed, to that of the man at the door. Again, his voice instructed me, "We can't leave yet, Daddy," then his image melted away, leaving the two of us, very much alone.

## Chapter 9

*He came to me that night.*

I sat on the stairs, staring into the darkness, trying to make sense of what had happened that day. Dan was in his room asleep, oblivious to what I had seen, but traumatised at seeing his mother threaten us with a knife. Every now and then, I heard him call out in his sleep, as his mind teased him with nightmares only children could have. His bleeding had eased to a trickle and I had washed him, as best I could.

I didn't hear him approach but sensed someone, just beyond my field of vision. Light didn't seem important at the moment. His face appeared first, the same waxy complexion I had noticed earlier. His eyes were deep brown pools, that shone with intelligence, but the sorrow I had seen before was still prominent. The hair was long and greasy grey, tied into a ponytail, exposing a fine, inch long scar along his temple line. He smiled, showing a row of small, but even, teeth.

"Who are you?"

I thought he hadn't heard me at first, but then he spoke in the same clear, concise manner that he had before.

"A friend." My back stiffened.

"That's not how it appeared, when I was trying to get out." I tried to keep my voice even, but the hint of anger was there.

"You can't leave yet, I told you."

"But why?" I couldn't help but shout, glaring at him. "It's my house, I can come and go as and when I please." He came closer and rested his hand lightly on my shoulder.

He was dressed in a dark blue pinstripe suit, with white shirt and red tie, not something you would associate with a jailer. The smile had gone and he seemed to be wrestling with something, his bushy eyebrows furrowed in thought.

"That's not strictly true." He sat down next to me on the stairs, being careful not to crease his jacket.

"What do you mean?"

"When was the last time you left the house?" He leant forward, fixing me with his gaze. "For any reason, whatsoever."

I opened my mouth to answer and then checked myself; now it was my turn to think carefully. I raided my memory for any such excursion but there were only blank spaces, where such things should be.

"What about food, going to work, anything." His prompts were gentle, but they fell into a black hole, sucked in, with nothing coming back out.

"I...don't...remember."

He stood suddenly, brushing himself down before grabbing my wrist in a vice like grip. This time, there was urgency in his tone.

"What you saw upstairs actually happened." He glanced at his watch. "A year ago tonight."

"But I don't understand it..."

"You're dead and so is your son." My mind whirled in a fog of confusion. "That can't be."

"It is, and your mind, as well as your son's, has wiped the memory out; just as well I think."

"Then, why am I still here." This was so ridiculous, I thought I was going to laugh out loud.

"Shut up and just listen to me." He looked behind him uncertainly. "I haven't got long."

"You and your son are dead, end of story." He cleared his throat. "From what you have seen, you can deduce it was Carol."

Again, he looked behind him and this time, when he turned back, I saw fear in his eyes. "She won't let you and Daniel move on. She keeps you here, to punish you for perceived injustices, and to keep Daniel around her. You know she went mad."

It still didn't make sense. "But I've seen her, how is that possible if we are dead."

He stared at me for a moment, as if I was the loopy one. "Because after killing, you she killed herself."

For a moment our eyes locked and I saw his desperation. He needed me to understand. "But what do I do?" He said no more; with a final furtive glance behind him, he turned tail and was gone, back into the darkness.

## Chapter 10

I ran up the stairs to where Daniel slept, to check on him. He hadn't moved; a crumpled bundle underneath the sheet. Sitting next to him, I felt exhausted. It certainly wasn't something I thought you would feel, if you were dead. I still couldn't remember going out though, to get anything. Then I saw the blood. Not from Dan this time, but from me, seeping out from my red scratches. As I watched, the wounds got larger and the blood flowed more freely. I felt nothing.

Putting my head in my hands, I wept silently.

## Chapter 11

A gentle breeze blew coolly over my face and I smiled. How wonderful it felt. I imagined the sun beating down on me on a sandy beach, palm trees swaying and the sound of children laughing, as they built their sandcastles. The cool breeze turned to an icy blast, and I opened my eyes.

Carol. She stood over me, as I lay on the bed next to Daniel. The smile she gave had no love in it for me. "You saw it then, my handiwork?" I didn't want to make any sudden movements, so lay perfectly still. Those beautiful, laughing eyes, I had known when we were first married, were no more, replaced by a wild, glassy stare. There was intelligence in them though, a certain slyness, that was driven by the demons within her.

"You see, I couldn't let you leave; you were going to take Dan with you and that just wouldn't do. Wouldn't do at all."

A ray of light within my mind, revealed memories, that had been submerged for such a long time: of hurriedly packed bags; of fear; of pain; of torture; of Carol's descent into the abyss. Now I knew.

Her behaviour had gradually got worse, starting with the affairs. We had blazing rows and stayed together only for the sake of Dan. After the affairs, she started getting violent, towards other people at first, then Dan and myself. That's why we had to get out, that's why...

*...She killed us.*

The realisation sunk in, and the helplessness washed over me again. My world was now this house and Dan, kept in place by the madness of a woman, who just wouldn't let go. Carol raised the knife that I had seen earlier, her eyes transfixed by its wicked blade, the one that had so cruelly taken our lives.

I closed my eyes, not wanting to see anymore, but then remembered Dan. Fury flooded through me like a raging torrent. No! There was going to be no more misery for us, it had to stop right now. Opening my eyes, I saw the man's face appear on the ceiling.

*The knife.*

I heard it as clear as if it was spoken but only in my mind. Grabbing Carol's wrist, I sat up, glaring into her hate filled eyes. She pulled sharply back, trying to yank it free, but there was no chance of that. I tried to prise her fingers from it but they wouldn't budge, I saw her glance down at Dan behind me and re-doubled my efforts.

"I can kill you as many times as I like," she snarled. "Once a year, every year, doesn't it sound great?" She threw her head back and laughed. I seized my chance. Concentrating on the hand with the knife, I released the other hand and, using the combined strength of both my hands, forced the knife into her chest.

For an instant, nothing happened, then Carol stopped laughing, and looked down at her chest, in surprise.

"What...?"

Then she looked at me. "Goodbye, Carol." There was a loud crack and the whole house shook. "Nooooo," she wailed.

An explosion followed another much louder crack, as Carol fragmented into thousands of tiny light pieces, which flared up, before going out completely and disappearing into thin air.

## Chapter 12

For some time, I just stood there, watching Daniel sleep. I could see the house as it now was, albeit only faintly. It was like watching something through a curtain, with many details quite blurred. A new family lived here now; they had no idea of our presence, just as I had no idea of theirs.

They were happy, that's what mattered. Dan stirred in the bed and turned to face me.

"Hello, Daddy." His smile lit up my day.

"Hello, Son."

"Is it time to go now?"

I saw his eyes turn from me, and focus behind me. "Who's that?"

"He's our friend." He was still in the same pin striped suit, but now he seemed much happier than before.

"You're right, Daniel, it is time to go." The man pointed towards the door, which had the bright light shining through it.

Grabbing Daniel's hand, I picked him up, hugging him tightly. As I made my way through the door, I saw the bed, where we had lost our lives, but felt nothing; after all it was only a bed. The bed I used to sleep in.

"Let's go," I whispered in his ear. And we were gone.

# The Forever Sleep

By Simon Woodward

It is my party,
the lights are turned down low.
The heavy curtains are pulled,
shutting out the cold.
Everyone is here.

Music is playing,
and those that know me show
their respect for my choice.
And everyone else is here.

Standing at the sofa,
which is a coffee coloured leather,
filled with my relatives,
close... and from afar.
Without a doubt, I'm sure,
everyone is here.

Talking amongst themselves,
they chat about me,
happy in a way.
I hear everything they say;
their comments please me.
And everybody's here!

The false smiles of some,
cover a misery,
brought about by the box,
weighs down on my shoulders — but,
the buffet's nearly gone and
everyone's still here.

I stand next to my brother.
He shudders while he talks with my wife.
And I hear the things he says.
His comments please me and,
everyone is near.

The lights turn down lower.
A dragging tugs me, pulls me away.
This wake of mine is finished,
and I go.
Leaving everybody there.

I'm now gone,
from the world I knew,
happy in a way.
It's no longer dark, but light,
This lifts me and...
Everyone is here!

# Affair of the Heart

By Colin Butler

## Chapter 1

I listened as the beep, beep, beep of the heart monitor became erratic, no longer rhythmical and, as I looked down at my wife, lying in the hospital bed, fighting for her life in the Intensive Care Unit, I felt that I was looking at her from some distance. Her face was wrinkled, in the agony of the heart attack, and I was praying that she would recover. I knew that I was to blame for her condition and was overcome with misery and guilt. What had brought me to this state? Let me try to explain.

It was a Wednesday morning, the 4th July to be precise, when I made the terrible decision to kill my wife! The 4th July - Independence Day - I suppose that Day was appropriate but, in fact, I had been considering this action for some time.

I had met Maureen, my wife, when I first joined the firm, where she was employed as a secretary in the office. We were almost immediately attracted to each other and, very soon, I asked her out on a date. From then onwards, we went out regularly and, after a courtship of some 18 months, we tied the knot and became Mr. and Mrs. John Harris.

We have now been married for some twenty-one years and, for most of these, we were in love and very happy together. We enjoyed going out in the evenings to the theatre, concerts and restaurants. Sadly, we were not blessed with children and, in consequence, slowly began to drift apart, as many couples do. She rapidly lost interest in going out in the evening and began to acquire annoying habits – to nag and to criticise virtually everything I did. To our friends, we still appeared to be a happy couple, but this was merely a front we adopted. If I was honest, I was equally to blame, — as I became more selfish and self-centred. We began to row over quite trivial matters. Nevertheless, several times, I suggested we went out to dinner or to a concert.

"I'm too tired, I'd rather stay in and watch my soap-operas and reality shows on television, John," she would reply.

Gradually, we began to lead our own separate lives - she went to clubs for ladies and went out with her female friends and I joined a camera club and a golf club. She liked her soap operas and women's magazines, whilst I liked good novels and sport. The gulf between us seemed to grow ever wider, like a river approaching the sea. We seemed to see less and less of each other and, I suppose, we could have carried on living our parallel lives, till we reached the Darby and Joan stage, if I hadn't met Marie. I had told Maureen that I wanted to join a computer class at the local tech, as I have always been fascinated by computers and felt I would like to increase my knowledge and get a CLAIT certificate.

"Would you like to come along with me to the course?" I asked.

"No, that sounds really boring. In any case, I would miss my soaps; you go along and play with your computers," she said, disinterestedly.

So the die was cast.

## Chapter 2

The fateful meeting with Marie took place, soon after the start of the computer course. The students sat at their own terminals and the teacher, a rather excitable middle-aged lady, of wiry build and with prematurely grey hair, no doubt accelerated by the computer class, would come around to assist any student that had a problem. Unfortunately, there always seemed to be more problems than she could deal with.

At the adjoining terminal, was a striking young lady, who was frequently exasperated at her inability to make the computer do what she wanted.

"Can I help you?" I said.

"Oh yes, please, the computer seems to be stuck," she replied and flashed a beautiful smile at me - one that made me go weak at the knees.

Over the next couple of weeks, I helped her on a number of occasions, and there was an instant chemistry between us.

Marie had been born in France, but her parents moved to England when she was about 10. She still retained a slight French accent and, as a result, her voice had a lovely seductive quality about it. She had jet-black hair, a very pretty face with a retroussé nose and a figure to die for. We began to sit together at the tea-breaks, and, after discussing the computer course, we talked about books, films and music and discovered that we had similar tastes. We laughed and joked - it was like a breath of fresh air for me, I felt young again. When half-term came, I asked her to come to the cinema with me, and, from then on, our relationship developed, but, as it did, so the atmosphere with my wife grew more and more tense.

I don't think she suspected anything, but we just seemed to drift even further apart. One Wednesday evening, I felt it was time to broach the subject that had been gnawing at me for weeks.

"We seem to be drifting further and further apart – we hardly ever do anything together," I said rather diffidently, trying to be gentle.

"Do you think that perhaps we should have a period apart – a trial separation," I added.

Immediately she flew into a rage.

"I suppose you have found someone else," she screamed.

"Well, I will never agree to let you go," she added and immediately began to swing her fists at me, before beginning to cry uncontrollably.

I had rather expected this reaction and quickly mumbled that I did not really mean it. I have always been a sucker for a woman's tears, especially when they really turn on the waterworks. I presumed that she was insecure and was worried how she would cope on her own.

It had been a very tense situation and, for the weeks afterwards, the atmosphere between us was arctic, to say the least, in spite of global warming!

I knew, in my heart, that Maureen, my wife, would not change her mind – she was naturally obstinate and contrary.

During this time, my relationship with Marie was beginning to suffer. I could not spend any real quality time with her – we just had brief meetings, when I could sneak out and, of course, the computer lessons. Marie wanted us to go away together for a week or at least a weekend, and she began issuing ultimatums.

"I really love you, but I am not prepared to play second fiddle to your wife," she said, with a distinct edge to her voice, her blue eyes flashing, in the reflected light of the restaurant.

"Either you leave her, or we continue our relationship on a purely platonic basis - just good friends," she threatened and I began to worry about her intensity. Her Gallic temperament was beginning to show through her normal soft demeanour.

"If you leave your wife, we would then become an item," she said, switching back to her soft and seductive voice.

What should I do? I was torn and struggled with my emotions – I couldn't sleep. My work began to be affected and I received several reprimands from the boss, for loss of concentration. After a lot of deliberating, I made up my mind to broach the subject of separation or divorce with Maureen, once again. When I finally summoned up the courage, I got the same reaction as before, an absolutely negative response, more temper and hysteria, washed down with tears. I wrestled with my conscience - the desire for Marie was so strong. I could not give her up. I went through all the possibilities and rejected each one. How could I resolve this?

Then one evening after dinner, I sat opposite Maureen and again broached the subject of a divorce.

"Over my dead body!" she said emphatically.

As I sat looking at her, I reminisced that I had once been deeply in love with her. Times and people change, however, and, as I looked at her, I only saw the image of Marie and could only see Maureen as a barrier to my happiness with Marie. I even began to wonder whether Maureen was seeing another man; perhaps I rather hoped she was.

'Over my dead body', she had said. My brain began to work sub-consciously in a way that disgusted me, at first. Gradually, however, my conscience was eroding away and, eventually, I began to think the unthinkable.

## Chapter 3

And so, reluctantly, I reached the decision that the only way out of my problem was to dispose of Maureen. But how was the deed to be accomplished? Obviously, it had to look like an accident, as I did not wish to spend the rest of my life residing at Her Majesty's pleasure.

The following week, after the computer lesson, whilst sitting in my car, I discussed the situation with Marie, who agreed that the only solution was to dispose of Maureen. But how was I to achieve this? We quickly rejected guns – they were too noisy, and in any event, I was a terrible shot, whilst knives were too messy. I could not face the thought of strangulation. After much deliberation, we decided on a car accident.

Over the next few days, I gradually formulated my plan; I would take Maureen on a surprise trip to Somerset and, there, the dreadful deed would be done.

"The weather forecast for this week-end is good, so I've booked us into a Travel Lodge near Minehead". I announced this surprise when I got home from work.

"Oh, I don't know John, I was planning to work in the garden, this week-end," she replied, rather uncharitably.

I was annoyed and somewhat surprised by this reaction, but after some persuasion, she agreed that it would do us both good. So we duly drove down to Somerset on Friday and she relaxed on the journey, as I tried to give the impression that we were on holiday. After we had booked into the hotel, I said that I would like to go to watch the cricket at Taunton the next day, as Essex were playing there. I suggested that she could visit her old school friend, Betty, who lived in Ilfracombe and I magnanimously said that she could have the car, as a coach was running to the Cricket from Minehead.

"So that's why you suggested a trip to Minehead – typically selfish of you, and I thought you wanted to give me a treat," she shouted.

After a few moments of reflection, she added, "Still I have been intending to visit Betty for some time. We can catch up on all our news and enjoy a girly day out," she said, her manner softening

Maureen duly phoned her friend and made the necessary arrangements. That evening, we had a really nice dinner, washed down with a fine bottle of red wine, a merlot, I think. As we ate, I kept thinking of the phrase – the condemned ate a hearty meal !

While she was dozing in the bedroom after the meal, I slipped out and carefully made a cut in the brake cable on our car. I reckoned that it would last until she reached Porlock or Countisbury Hill, before it severed completely.

In the morning, I gave her a long embrace, wished her a safe journey and kissed her goodbye.

I enjoyed an excellent day at the Cricket, for once the sun shone all day – there was plenty of beer and a good match, with

Essex scoring 328 for 6 wickets - Johnson 151 not out and Khan 62. At the match, I met an ex-colleague and we enjoyed a couple of beers together and talked about old times. He offered to drive me back, as he lived in Watchet. When we arrived back at the Travel Lodge, I asked him in for a nightcap, as this would help my alibi. I explained that my wife was visiting a friend in Ilfracombe, but should be home soon. We talked till quite late about our cricket memories and I repeatedly expressed my concern at my wife's non-appearance. Surprisingly, there were no messages on my mobile. As the evening wore on, I privately presumed that something dreadful must have occurred. I was puzzled, however, that the police had not contacted me. I kept looking at the door and the phone anxiously.

That night I went to bed still not knowing what had happened and my mind kept inventing various scenarios.

Early on Sunday morning, my mobile rang and my heart began to race. Was this the police or a hospital? I picked up the phone with a trembling hand and rather shakily said "Hello" – The voice at the other end was Maureen's. I sat back on the bed, my mind racing – what had happened?

"My car broke down on the way to Ilfracombe and the AA came along and diagnosed a faulty carburettor. As they were unable to fix it, they towed the car to a local garage and drove me to my friend's house," she blurted out.

"Oh, I'm so relieved that you are alright – I was so worried about you, when you didn't come home last night," I said, trying very hard to sound sincere.

"Why didn't you ring me?" she said with a distinct edge to her voice.

"Why didn't you ring me?" I quickly countered.

"I had left my mobile at the hotel and was unable to remember your new mobile number," she explained.

"But you still haven't said why you didn't ring me," she repeated.

"I met Bill Hawkins at the cricket, he lives in Watchet now and he drove me back. We got talking till quite late and I didn't want to wake you or Betty," I mumbled.

"That's no excuse," she growled.

"By the way, the car won't be ready till Monday evening, so you will have to hire a car and come and meet me."

"I'll stay at Betty's till then," she said rather pointedly.

I sighed and resigned myself to trying a different method. When we went to the garage, to collect the car, the manager said that my wife had been extremely lucky, as the mechanic had found that the brake cable was damaged and that it could have sheared through at any time, especially if the car had travelled down a steep hill. I intimated my utter surprise and shock at the news and thanked the manager and the mechanics for their diligence. As we left the garage, Maureen turned on me.

"Do you realise, I could have been killed, if I had driven down Porlock or Countisbury hills," she shrieked hysterically.

"I know dear, I can't tell you how really bad I feel about it – I really must get the car serviced more regularly," I replied, trying to express a genuine sense of guilt.

## Chapter 4

In my car after the next computer lesson, I reported the events of the week-end to Marie, and we discussed what to do next.

"You will have to find a different method," she concluded with just a trace of menace in her voice, her slight French accent showing through.

I began to plan my next attempt and went to the local library for a book about poisons. Naturally, I avoided asking the assistant for help, but searched the shelves myself. I found a book that was very informative and, in consequence, I chose arsenic. The next day, I visited my local Garden Centre and bought some fertilizer, together with a can of weed-killer. I was not happy with poisons –

they could be extremely painful and may leave traces, but they seemed the only solution. I thought that, if I waited till the next weekend, there would be more witnesses to the 'accident'. Our friends, Marjorie and Frank Webb were coming to dinner.

So, after a very nice meal, we settled in the lounge for some drinks. Naturally, I offered to act as barman and, in the kitchen, added that little extra something to Maureen's wine. She took one sip and immediately spat it out –

"That's revolting. She said and immediately poured the remainder into the pot of the rubber plant that was near her chair. The plant subsequently turned brown over the next couple of days and promptly died.

"I bought that wine on my last trip to France. I thought at the time it was too cheap. I'll get you a martini instead," I blurted out.

I went out to the kitchen and poured her martini and then tipped the rest of the wine down the sink.

"That wine really smelt bad - I certainly won't buy that type again," I announced to the waiting group. "Those bloody French getting their own back, for the defeat in the rugby world cup," I joked.

Our guests then recounted their own experience with a dodgy bottle of French wine, last year.

I met Marie at lunch-time on the following Tuesday and we tried to work out what to do next.

"You should have used a tasteless poison," she insisted, being wise after the event

I was now on Plan C and running out of ideas - back to the library and again I perused the book about poisons, I kept imagining that the library manager was looking at me suspiciously, and it made the hairs on the back of my neck stand on end. Surely, it was just my guilty conscience. She was a very slim lady with large heavy-framed glasses and a prim jacket and skirt. A typical career spinster, I thought. Anyway eventually, after much research, I found a poison that fitted the bill - tasteless and fairly fast-acting - I honestly did not want to cause Maureen any more suffering than was absolutely necessary. I left the library, after borrowing a book entitled "How to win friends and influence people." The manager, however, still gave me a funny look.

Once again, I waited till we had friends round. This time it was our old friends, Angie and Rob Henderson and, after another enjoyable dinner, we settled back in the lounge for a game of cards and a chat. Maureen said she would like a martini and I duly retreated to the kitchen, where I 'pepped up' her drink. Straightaway she took a tentative sip; I held my breath and her smile indicated that she thought that it was alright. She picked up her glass again to take a real drink and I was on tenterhooks.

Just at that moment, Angie said "Come on Mo – it's your turn – hurry up and play a card."

Maureen promptly put her glass down. Over the next half-hour she repeatedly picked up her glass, but each time, she was prevented from drinking by a request to concentrate on the game or by getting into gossip about members of the Ladies Club. She did manage a couple of quick sips and I wondered how much would be necessary to fulfil my purpose. Then she got quite animated when discussing the new chairman of the club, whom she described as a 'real interfering cow' - raised her arm and promptly knocked her drink over on to our new beige carpet.

"Oh damn!" she said, or some such expression, perhaps rather stronger, and I rushed out to get a cloth to clean the carpet.

Despite my efforts, the carpet went a strange colour after a couple of days and some of the fibres began to rot.

"Would you like the same drink again," I said.

"Yes, of course," said Maureen,

Unfortunately, before I could move, Rob, ever helpful, said that he would go - again frustration. Incidentally, Maureen did complain of stomach pains that night, but blamed the prawns she had eaten in the prawn cocktail and worried in case her guests suffered similar pains.

Next day, I sat and puzzled. What should I do? Marie was getting more and more insistent.

"I really can't wait any longer. You must leave Maureen or put her out of the way," she said irritably and with a veiled threat in her tone.

I had run out of ideas. I was completely discombobulated. I ran through all the other methods of disposing of Maureen, but none seemed to be appropriate.

## Chapter 5

That night I dreamt that I was chasing my wife down a very long dark corridor. I was wielding a very large axe and kept trying to swing it at her, but each time she was just out of reach. I woke up sweating, shivering and shouting. This woke my wife and she bent my ear with complaints.

"Don't you know that I need my beauty sleep?"

As I looked at her, I thought, boy, did she need her beauty sleep!

A couple of days later, Maureen complained that in the middle of the night I had begun attacking her in my sleep. Evidently I had repeatedly tried to punch her and she had restrained me with great difficulty.

She was crying. "You could have murdered me."

"I'm really sorry, my dear – I had a nightmare that I was being attacked," I mumbled apologetically.

Things were getting serious; she would soon begin to suspect something. One night, I even awoke, apparently calling out Marie's name and I really had a difficult job to explain this. I told her that Marie was the new temp, we had hired, who was causing me grief, with her stupidity.

The next week I had an appointment at the doctor's for my annual check-up.

The doctor, who was one of the 'old school', examined me and said

"You're patently unfit, and at your age, you should stop smoking, cut down on your drinking and watch your cholesterol level."

He emphasised that diet is more important for the over 50s as the risk of a heart attack or a stroke increases significantly.

"So cut out the rich food and the cream," he said as he poked a finger repeatedly in my chest.

I went home and began to realise that the answer to my problem had been given to me. Maureen was over-weight, smoked heavily, enjoyed drinking and did little exercise. She must be a prime candidate for a heart attack or a stroke. I was overjoyed, as I would not have to kill her – just help her on her way. I was so relieved as I had never relished the thought of actually killing her. You see, I am really a very gentle soul at heart. I mused that the various frustrations had actually been a blessing in disguise.

So I set about planning the new campaign. That evening, after dinner, I sat next to Maureen on the sofa,

"I realise I have been become very selfish. I have neglected you recently. We will go out together more often – in fact we will go out every Friday evening – either to a restaurant for dinner or to the theatre or the cinema," I announced.

She was somewhat surprised but, after some thought, jumped at this idea and started to become less aggressive.

"That sounds very nice, dear. It will be just like old times," she said with a strange rather school-girly, grin.

That Friday we went to a high-class French restaurant and I encouraged her to have the richest food on the menu. The following week, we went to the theatre and I treated her to a big box of chocolates. She had always had a weakness for chocolates and, once she started on a box, she couldn't relax until she had eaten them all. So, week after week, we indulged in good food and visits to the cinema or theatre accompanied by the – chocolates. In the restaurants, she would invariably choose a very rich dessert, encouraged by me, of course.

As a result, she even began to show me some affection, something that had been missing for a number of years. She complained, however, that she was putting on weight, and threatened to go on a diet.

"Don't do that, I like you being buxom - all the more for me to cuddle," I said with a mischievous grin and again she started to giggle like a schoolgirl. As a result of all the extra weight, she began to get out of breath, after even the gentlest exercise.

In October, I planned a few days in the Lake District at a guest-house in Keswick, just a few minutes walk from Derwentwater. It was a very nice clean establishment and the landlady, Mrs. Osborne, prided herself on the state of the house and her breakfasts. Each morning, she would stagger into the dining-room with a tray piled high with the full English - the works – two sausages, two rashers of bacon, two fried eggs, fried bread, hash browns and beans, on each plate. After each breakfast, we would vow to have a light or continental breakfast the next day, but that resolution soon melted away, even though we both felt decidedly overweight.

On the third morning, I suggested that we should climb a local hill.

"There is a marvellous view from the summit and the guide book says it's a very easy climb," I assured her.

She reluctantly agreed and we set off soon after breakfast. It was a lovely sunny morning, but the writer of the guide-book must have been some sort of sadist, for it was a steep climb

"Who wrote this bloody guide-book, Sherpa Tensing?" she remarked with a rare touch of irony.

When we eventually arrived at the top, the view was splendid, but I could hardly breathe. Maureen was nearly collapsing as she slumped on a bench and, to my eyes, resembled a beached whale!

"We are really getting out of condition. We will really have to change our diet and life-style in the future," she said, her breath coming in short pants, unlike the Bridget Jones underwear she habitually wore.

"Yes dear, when we get back, we will both join a gym and try to lose weight," I agreed.

The next day, after another full English breakfast, we did another walk – less steep this time, but longer and at the end, Maureen suddenly stopped and complained of pains in her chest. I advised her to sit down, but her face went a very peculiar grey colour and she did not look well at all. I was very concerned and decided to phone for an ambulance. After about twenty minutes, a paramedic eventually arrived and began to administer first aid.

The Ambulance took her off to the hospital, as soon as possible and they offered to take me with her. When I arrived, at the hospital, they had taken Maureen off to the Intensive Care Unit. I was left in the corridor, alone with my thoughts and, as time ticked slowly by, so my guilt grew. How could I have been so selfish? I closed my eyes and began to pray for her recovery and for forgiveness. I asked a nurse, as she dashed past, what was happening. All she would say was that Maureen was in a very serious condition.

After I begged them, they said that I could go into the room, just for a few moments. I entered very quietly and saw her lying on the bed with numerous wires and tubes attached to her. In the corner, the heart monitor was beeping away and the line on the screen was very uneven. I prayed that she would survive, as I crept silently from the room, at the doctor's suggestion. The authorities suggested that I might like to stay in the guest room overnight. The room was typical of a hospital room, all white, cold and definitely inhospitable. That night I tossed and turned, but sleep would not come. I kept thinking about my evil plans and resolved to contact Marie on my return to tell her that I had decided to stay with my wife and that our affair was over.

## Chapter 6

The next day, I awoke to a sunny day and there was good news, Maureen was responding to treatment. I was allowed to see her and she held her hand out for me to hold. The doctor said it would be a slow process, but assured me she would make a full recovery. I gave thanks that my prayers had been answered.

Some weeks later, as I lay in bed, I began to feel ill – there were pains in my chest and I began to find difficulty in breathing. I had severe palpitations and the more I worried about my condition, the faster my heart beat. Maureen woke up and asked me what was wrong.

"Just a touch of indigestion, my dear," I gasped. Then I began to feel worse, I was sweating profusely and the pain got more and more severe. Maureen realised that there was something wrong and immediately phoned the hospital. After about ten minutes, an ambulance arrived. The paramedics examined me and then put me on a stretcher.

As I lay in the ambulance, I heard the medic say to my wife.

"You should make him watch his diet and life style at his age. Try to make him eat simple food, do gentle exercise and cut out the smoking."

As I listened, the words seemed to go fuzzy, it seemed as if the voices were fading further and further away. Just then, I began to sweat more profusely and I really believed that my time was up. How ironic that I should be in the same position as my wife had been just a few weeks previously! Why had I been so stupid? I began to think that I was about to get my nemesis - justice was being wrought.

Suddenly everything went dark and I seemed to be travelling along a long tunnel with a strange white light at the end, which seemed to be drawing me towards it - and then it all went black......

The next morning I gradually came to and wondered where I was. Everywhere was white - was this heaven, surely not after what I had done, – or was this hell? As I looked around and tried to get my bearings, I saw a face looking down on me. It was my wife smiling at me. I smiled back and squeezed her hand very gently. As I looked at her, I began to wonder whether it was a genuine smile of affection, or was it a more sinister smile. Had she suspected that I had wanted to get rid of her?

The doctor said that I'd had a severe heart attack. Again he warned me to cut out rich food, stop smoking and to do regular exercise.

The following day, as I lay in the ward, the chest pains began again, I began to sweat profusely. I stared around, and again my wife was smiling at me. This time, I became convinced that she knew the truth and that it was a smile of revenge. I looked across at the heart monitor and the waves were very uneven – a bad sign and then I began to lapse into unconsciousness. My life began to flash before me, all the murder attempts, my affair with Marie. How stupid I had been, I was being repaid for my evil motives. As things began to fade, I heard a rhyme I recalled from my early childhood,

*"Just one step back, outside my skin,*
*I look down on my life within*
*I breathe a sigh and all release*
*At bedside now, I rest in peace".*

While I lay there, I heard the click-clack of my wife's heels going down the ward and out the door. Did she know that I had plotted to kill her? I would probably never know.

Then everything went black......

## Lying in My Bed

By Nicolette Coleman

Lying in my bed I think of you,
And all the lovely things we used to do,
And all the fun we had
Before things went so bad,
I love to lie in bed and think of you.

Like the time we went to Alton Towers,
And rode on all the rides for hours and hours,
And laughed about the cold
And the stories that you told,
And what about that time you bought me flowers?

Do you recall the day we hired a boat?
I shivered and you lent me your coat,
We drifted round the lake,
Ducks swimming in our wake,
And crumpled in your pocket was that note.

Lying in my bed I think of you,
And all the tender things we used to do,
And the way you said goodbye,
And how it made me cry.
I'm lying in my bed, just missing you.

# Death is Nature's Way of Giving you a Warning

By David Shaer

## Chapter 1 - Death is nature's way......

"Now there's absolutely no need for you to get worried or panic but one of your heart's arteries is completely blocked. A second one is severely blocked and a third one is partially blocked. You could possibly wait a year before this becomes critical but since you have adequate insurance, I would suggest that maybe we could bring you in next week for a triple heart by-pass."

Jesus – I've heard it said before that death is Nature's way of giving you a warning but, come on! I'm only fifty-one and I'm certainly not ready to die yet. To say that my day was not going well was somewhat of an understatement. I don't really remember hearing much else of what was said, as I slipped into a form, I suppose, of shock.

What does it all mean? Why me? I'm not ready. I have loads of things I want to do yet, I want to write. I still want to play more rugby – alright, I might consider refereeing. I want to play more cricket – I swim – I walk at least three miles every day – what caused this? I know I'm not the fittest person alive, in fact I'm the only person I know who sweats while he's swimming. But why me?

> *"......97% of these operations are successful and, as a consequence, we can basically give you up to about a ten year extension on life......."*

From when? Christ – what about the other 3%?

So many questions flying around inside my brain that I cannot organise them into any sort of sequence. I've never been in hospital, apart from the odd visit, a very occasional x-ray to confirm that my nose was broken once again – ten times so far, in fact. Oh! And a broken collar bone. But never anything serious. 'Stand clear, everyone' – I've seen it on television – getting a heart re-started. I can't do this. I've never been really ill – ever.

But ten years from when? Help me here. What do you mean – that depends on me? No – I stopped smoking over ten years ago. OK – I'll never drink bitter again if the yeast clogs my arteries. I really am not ready to pack up bags and go yet.

I shall remember it forever, that day. I have never experienced a shock like it. It is so vivid in my mind to this very day – that day when somebody told me that actually life is not eternal, especially my own. Sure I've had friends and relatives who have died, some of them very close, but to be told that my own days are numbered was something totally different.

Change of lifestyle. I remember those very words even now. As I lay there a week later, having been shaved from head to foot by a terribly nervous, gay nurse whose hand was trembling so much that he slashed me to ribbons. The surgeon nearly passed out when he saw so much dry blood and demanded to know who had done that. I couldn't or wouldn't remember. I just knew that I was being chastised for years of abusing my body. All the things I had enjoyed for decades were coming home to roost.

Worked hard, played hard. Even my current wife has said often that hard work never kills anybody but she is obviously wrong. For heaven's sake, how dangerous is being an accountant?

Sure, there were late nights working on system design, quarter or year end accounts, system migration, staff troubles, reconciliation differences, potential fraud audits, preparation of results and reports for nigh impossible deadlines but that was all part of life. Or possibly death.

Eating habits? Well rarely have I over indulged. OK – the odd grasped sandwich lunch in the outside lane of the M25 while driving to a meeting for which I was going to be late. Even getting home at ten in the evening and finding only just enough time to eat before going to bed was only two or three nights a week. I always had at least six hours sleep, apart from the odd touch of indigestion or getting up to make notes on things that occurred to me during the night. Out by seven each morning and launching into a black coffee at my desk, before the rest of the staff got in, was important. Sometimes I enjoyed a slice or two of toast with Marmite on it. It enabled me to see clearly the fifteen or sixteen things I needed to list as things to do that day (before the list got increased rather than reduced).

But I usually have weekends off from work. My secretary always rang all of my rugby team to make sure that they were all fit for Saturday and we had enough cars to get to our away fixtures. As long as I gave her the list on Tuesday morning after our selection meeting at the club on Monday night – I never missed that – OK sometimes I might not get there until about 9.30 – but since it was only the A XV I didn't need to be there for all the match reports and higher team selections. My secretary always sent across my match report to one of the other captains who read it out. Anyway it was my chance to have a bit of a night out with the boys. Selection always finished about 10.30, so at least I had a chance to have a few beers with some of the older lads (who always had more stamina than the younger ones, who had to go home to their sleep, their wives, their kids because they had to get up at seven to be in the local office by 9.00 the next morning). I always stayed on to relax and to discuss important things like the International Monetary Fund's policy on Third World investment or breasts until about one in the morning. By then the police had changed shifts and it was safe enough to drive home, even if we had had the odd beer or four.

So, come the weekend, I always got up fresh and early, albeit to go and get sausage, bacon, eggs, mushrooms and tomatoes for a good cooked breakfast. You needed that before a game of rugby because after the game, you needed a stomach lining for the usual four or five pints of bitter before people started to drift off home. Unless, of course, it was a game against some old buddies from Dartford over the river or local bloodbaths like Southend or Rochford where we knew most of the opposition and would stay for a few extra jars with the older adversaries. Then it would be about 9 p.m. before I left the club, thought up a good excuse for being that late and rolled in slightly the worse for wear to fall asleep in front of either the box or some dinner guests I had forgotten were coming. They always found it amusing and said it was just me getting rid of the week's pent up frustration of working in the City. They understood. Even if my wife didn't always. I suppose it probably was about eight or nine pints of bitter but who was counting? At least the red wine with dinner afterwards was good for me and the 'Digestif Calvados or Cognac' helped the meal go down and conversation flow, with cigars.

Sometimes, either at the beginning or the end of the season, I would go on tour for a weekend but the A XV never went to Oxford or Warwick or Bath like the 1st XV. I used to organise our matches against old friends in Dunkirk, Calais, Paris or Milan. OK so there was a bit more work involved but that was part of the fun. Whenever we reached our destination, those old friends always looked after us well and made sure we had a visit to remember. Superb food, excellent wines, night clubs that knew us and welcomed us back and stayed open until 6.00 in the morning when we would go back to the hotel, shower and prepare ourselves with croissants, strong coffee and cognac in preparation for the game later that morning. We would always play a tough game and afterwards were always ready for a good refreshment before we went off to sample the local beer and wine while supporting England's rugby team playing France or Italy, live in the afternoon.

That was always followed by a celebratory dinner with the local dignitaries, such as the Mayor and President of the EDF team or Kleinwort Bensons' Bank we had played earlier in the day. Usually this was followed by an evening in another series of clubs until we returned to our hotel rooms for breakfast prior to the departure for the homeward journey. We knew how to survive from Friday morning to Sunday evening without sleeping. It was a sort of macho thing that never did us any harm. Or was it?

And those Cricket weeks that I and my mate Nick used to organise to make money for the Rugby Club. We hired from Essex County Cricket Club a marquee at Southchurch Park for the Essex Cricket Week and had to make sufficient profit to cover the vast cost. Two of us did it for nearly twenty years. We would take 8 days' holiday and run a bar and food function for club members in this marquee. Real ale, superb three course lunches, fine wines and great fun. We were well known by the County for putting on a performance that put to shame the professional caterers who fed the players, other clubs, the Mayor and the public. The two of us plus a group of regular helpers would stock up every morning shortly after 6:00 a.m. (well you can't leave alcohol and food in a tent in a public park overnight and expect to find it there the next morning). A hired van acted as our overnight mobile stock room, office, security vault and, it seemed, sometimes other peoples' free taxi service. All stocks were checked out and transported down to the ground by 9.00 a.m. when we had to clear away any debris left from the day before's late revellers. Preparation for the advent of members, guests and other incoming wounded involved all sorts of things when running a proper bar, preparing dishes for lunch which always involved a choice of menus, cleaning up rubbish and cigarette butts that we had missed when clearing away in the dark the night before at about 10.00 p.m. Working in a field is hard and never appreciated by those who simply relaxed, wined, dined and eventually fell over while the volunteer helpers spent their week's holiday getting more tired and buying their own drinks all day to keep them going.

The effort that went into the week was always incredible and the few who worked eventually realised that it would have been cheaper to have stayed at work, put a couple of hundred quid into a bag and thrown it into the rugby club coffers and not had to stand the sleepless nights, sleepless days and stonking hangovers – but then it wouldn't have been that much fun. We even decided that by mid-afternoon too many people in our tent were getting bored with the cricket match and might wander aimlessly around the ground seeking other people and refreshment. So I started doing burgers on a barbeque and discovered a whole new way of cooking my beer gut medium rare. The burgers were special and had to be obtained each morning from a local butcher who was having problems keeping pace with demand. The pleasure of producing this new winner was soon countered by the stress of controls inflicted by the Essex County Cricket Club's secretary who started a personal vendetta against us for upsetting his franchised professional caterers. My goodness. Being summoned each morning to the Secretary's office with an exercise book down the seat of my pants became such a ritual that many of the ground staff for the County and the local Council used to wait in hiding near the mobile office to hear each day's rows, shouting, discussion and finally compromise and there used to be a standing ovation for the return journey to our marquee. Eventually we became too much of a challenge and were banned from using our barbeque completely. But even that caused a row because I wasn't prepared to lose the cost of that day's stock and insisted that our swansong would be that day, not the one before. Stressed? Moi?

I finally lost it completely when the County reduced the week's cricket to five days and the viability of the whole operation for the Rugby Club become questionable. I cancelled our marquee contract and within two years so had most of the other clubs and

Essex Cricket Week is no longer held at Southchurch Park. The relief for the two of us prime operators was immense as was the financial burden. But we miss the fun.

However, undeterred, Nick and I continued with another similar couple of functions we had also organised for our spare moments.

For just as many years, we had been running a couple of rugby related functions. We had taken a minibus to Twickenham to enjoy the surroundings of the famous West Car Park. For a very reasonable fixed price, we entertained friends and our Rugby Club members to all of the food and all of the drink they could consume during the day of the rugby Middlesex Sevens. Our bus would contain a few seats but was mostly occupied by fine wines, champagne, beer and spirits that I had gone across to France to purchase, as I had done for the cricket week, together with a splendid selection of food ranging from pink lamb, rare beef, the occasional spicy curry with freshly made, at the ground, salads and a cheeseboard to die for, prepared or provided by my learned colleague, an independent financial advisor. Pints of Bucks Fizz for breakfast, gin for afternoon tea, always accompanied by homebaked fruitcakes, with further supplies of cheese in perfect condition. The refrigeration system was second to none and we provided chilled beers, white wines, champagne and a constant supply of ice cubes for afternoon and evening gin and tonics after guests had become full of beer, selected Bordeaux of fine vintage, and some of the best Sauvignon Touraine blanc available outside the Loire Valley. There was always a drop of top quality Calvados available for those who knew how to cross the palms of us two organisers but not until the weather turned cold, wet or even dark. The fridges were, in fact, new, plastic dustbins filled with ice and some water – our trade secret.

Oh and then, for up to about forty people, the Varsity match between Oxford and Cambridge in early December, which requires great stamina and capacity for each of the guests. Not all seem to have that level of dedication, although it has become apparent over the twenty odd years that that has been part of my spare time pleasure, that it is not always the ladies who cannot last the pace. In fact, au contraire, it is always the ladies who are there at the bitter end – the men have become weak willed and ever mindful of domestic responsibilities or their livers. I just don't understand the way people can't last the full circuit.

And then there is the office annual wine tasting Master Class where I have invited over from France a viticulteur who owns a vineyard in Bordeaux but provides many fine wines, most of which have become the base for the cricket and rugby functions mentioned before. He and his family arrive each year in time for a decent lunch in the City, at which they have always insisted that I taste the wine, damn them, and then prepare for up to 120 people to attend a presentation of eleven different French wines starting with light, dry whites, poring through five or six Burgundy or Bordeaux, each improving on the quality of the previous, culminating in a really superb St Emilion or Medoc prior to an amazing champagne from a small producer. They describe each wine in detail, its source, blend, region, potential usage, such as "ideal for accompanying poultry, game or extremely rare meat" and build up a picture of each individual product. Sadly not one of them speaks English so throughout all this time I have been forced to enjoy the taste of each wine only after I have translated into English the poetry of their graphic descriptions. Initially this is a very trying experience, my command of French being reasonable for the first one or two items. By the third or forth, my French has become more confident to the extent where I just have to add in a few minor points they may have overlooked in their excitement about how best to enjoy each wine. By number 6 or 7 there is no holding me back and I am usually inviting questions from the floor. By number 8, I don't know whether I am speaking English or French and by number 9, it is now my show.

Fortunately, most of my work colleagues and friends ignore me, as they often do anyway, and they are interested only in either tasting the final product, the champagne, or Sophie, the viticulteur's daughter who has by this time always become chic and drop dead gorgeous.

By the end of the evening, orders have to be taken and debris cleared because the French have to shoot off to catch their late night ferry home to re-open for normal business the following day and, by the morning, our office would revert to the humdrum of normal life. Would that this were where it finished but each wine is priced advantageously at 'collect from the cellar' which is about an hour inland from Calais. So my final small task has always been to provide the tools to complete this, which involves persuading a group of friends and colleagues that they want to come to France with me to help bring back about 2,000 bottles of wine, the average volume sold. This easy task has usually been shared by 8 cars and 16 people with each car transporting a predesignated selection of about 250 bottles each of which has to be code marked in such a way that the logistics work and each car load is either delivered to customers in the area of the car owner's home or transferred into a central part of the office, clearly labelled and stored in such a way that each person who has ordered collects his/her delivery.

Getting 8 cars and 16 people to collect this is, in itself, another logistical nightmare, so I arrange for us all to travel together on a specific ferry to Calais, adjourn to a close by restaurant of some high repute for an aperitif and a good lunch whilst a truck is despatched from the cellar with 2,000 clearly, but discreetly, labelled bottles ordered to the same restaurant and a subterfuge rendezvous takes place to distribute into each of the appropriate car boots without arising the suspicion of local gendarmes, customs officers or even wine rustlers. As an accountant, I have always found the most difficult part of all of this is dividing the restaurant bill by 18 and getting the correct money in any sort of currency out of my friends and colleagues. The subsequent manhandling of stocks from car to car, car to office garage, office garage to specifically allocated secure space and subsequent distribution by physically carrying cases of wine to each recipient, is a doddle.

I cannot believe that stress would be deemed to be a contributory factor but, suddenly, needing a heart bypass brings it all home to roost.

And just when you thought that being an accountant was boring and repetitive.

And a couple of days ago, I even heard that my mate, the independent financial advisor, is now undergoing heart treatment for valve defibrillation issues, just like that Tony Blair chap.

Never before have I actually had the time to sit down and work all this out. It is only when death dealt me this slap in the face with a wet herring that I have had time to gather my thoughts. With the Grim Reaper sitting at my bedside, I think I might just have worked out that I really should be taking more water with it – life, I mean.

All I have to do now is to convince myself. Or maybe I should change my doctor?

## Chapter 2 – Jonathan's Morning After

Hey, how come nobody told me all about that? I thought we now lived in the world of keyhole surgery but what's all this stuff hanging out of me? Pipes, tubes, rubber bits, plastic bits and what's this? Oh my God! It's a bloody sack. I wonder where the tube for that comes from? Oh my...... I don't believe it. Who put that there and how? I wonder if I enjoyed it? Knowing my luck, I bet it was that gay nurse. I think I might just go back to sleep now. Ooh, hello. Who's this?

"Ah, Jonathan, we're awake at last. First things first. I'll just whip that tube out of your mouth – you do all that on your own now, Big Boy. And, by the way, I'm Christine. You've got me for the remaining twentytwo hours on a one to one basis. I've got two more tubes to pull out of your chest. They only allow any surpluses to flow out and you don't seem to have any surpluses of any sorts now. I'll get somebody else to remove your sack for you, I've got an urgent need to do something. Oh, yes; and to go and ask your visitor to come in".

Typical. Just when I was beginning to enjoy this. Maybe it's someone just as nice. Ooops! My wife!

"Hiya. I see you've started already!"

"Why – what have I done while I was under the influence? Usual, I suppose. Whatever it was, I reckon, I've got an excuse this time. Anyway, how come you're here this quick? I thought it was only last night I went down?"

"Actually the surgeon rang me at about 9.00 o'clock last night to say that all seemed to have gone well and according to plan and that you were now going into the one-to-one intensive care unit. He even suggested that I came up to town this morning to visit. So here I am. How do you feel?"

"I really don't know yet. I do know that I feel bruised and battered though. And all these pipes and things. Wow? Here comes that nurse again. She seems very nice."

"Oh, yes, Christine. Yes – when I arrived she sat and talked with me for about ten minutes and then the surgeon came in to see me as well – funny that, I thought you were the one getting intensive care."

Yes, I wondered about that too. But then, as if by design, the not unattractive Christine came to my rescue.

"Jonathan, are you alright for your injection now?" she asked.

"Should you be saying that in front of my wife?" I replied.

"I only asked if you were ready for your injection now."

"Bugger. I thought you'd asked if I was ready for my erection now?"

"He's obviously getting better," they replied in unison.

The trouble is that I really don't have a clue what she's talking about and I keep drifting off into a euphoric warm, sleepy glow. Except I do know that I seem to be one of the 97% and that is a bit of a relief. I wonder how many "went down" last night and how many came back. I think I need some more sleep.

I'm awake again and one of my colleagues is in trouble. It seems that three of us 'went down' and, after 24 hours intensive care, for which I seem to have been asleep most of the time, we three were transferred to another ward together, the recovery section.

Mike, to my right, seems to be OK in that he hasn't stopped talking since he woke up. Opposite, however, Mustafa has done nothing but moan. His throat is dry, his legs ache, he is thirsty, he wants a drink of water, he is hungry, then no, he is not hungry but he wants water. He is parched but can't wait until feeding/watering time. He must be dealt with now. Don't the staff know how important he is? They really should pay attention – the two English guys are not as ill as he has been – they don't warrant the attention they are getting, he is far more important. Don't they realise who he is? He is an extremely high and important Egyptian member of the Middle East peace talks and without him there will never be peace between Israel and anybody. He is also a pompous, arrogant, ignorant git who knows just how informing can make him a person to be dreaded by the hospital staff. Blackmail to get him examined seemed to be his natural forte but it wasn't holding any water with the hospital staff. He was just another stupid old bastard who wanted something for nothing. Water, in fact.

As the night progressed, his moaning became wailing. His wailing became long term; his silence was what we needed – all of us.

"I must have water. I am so parched."

"No water – you are not allowed any water for another 24 hours – it will react with your drugs and you will be dead immediately. Now just do as your surgeon told you. No water."

"Surgeon's a fool. I must have water. What does he know? I need water. You, stupid woman, get me water, now. I will not be treated like this. I know what I need so just give me water, stupid, disrespectful woman. I am a very important man. Get me water, now. Otherwise I shall report you and make sure you never work again. Water. Now."

Actually, don't worry about the water, nurse. Just leave him with us overnight, we'll make sure he's quiet – for ever. I am sure that we were both thinking the same thing. As the night dragged on, we both started to ignore him and turn off. The new gang of three were rapidly working on the next phase. Do you suppose that anyone would notice if the statistics went off the rails for one day? 3% failure when typed fast and with a stutter could appear on a report as 33% for one day and people would assume it was a typo.

By 6.00 am the moaning had grown weak, mainly through lack of interest or attention, so when lights started to come on and people began early morning activities, such as cleaning, electric sweeping machines and the whistling of slightly (tone) deaf porters, the relief was immense.

"Breakfast, boys" came the cheery greeting. "Two scrambled eggs, bacon, sausage, tomatoes and mushrooms." Goodness hadn't had a decent fry up for ages. "Just a joke, lads. Porridge or cereals. Dry wholemeal toast, no butter, fresh grapefruit and a tomato juice."

Oh, thanks.

"Only for today, though, boys. Tomorrow you get the real stuff. And if you're really good, there might even be black pudding! But enjoy it while you can because in a couple of days, you will be up and down the stairs and our lovely dietician will make you hate her. Healthy, fat free, good clean stuff. Not for you, though, Mr Mahmood. We've been a naughty boy all night, haven't we? You don't get anything until the surgeon comes round again. You've been taking silly stuff haven't you? As for telling your son to bring you in a fix, well you have been a bad boy all along. There will be no water for this morning either"

"Oh, it's academic, nurse. We got up and strangled him last night, noisy old sod. He won't need any water ever again."

"So you two are obviously going to be trouble this next few days, eh? Look, he's paid up, just like you. Actually his son has promised a new wing if his dad gets through this – but we're not counting our chickens yet."

Now that made us go quiet. Suddenly our thoughts of unplugging his support machine probably weren't such a good idea after all. Although we had both thought and talked about, it had been a bit of a joke. I mean, neither of us could actually sit up yet, let alone nip out and turn off his battery charger. But it made us realise that this was quite a serious operation we had been through and it was risky.

Breakfast was a new experience for both of us. Mike was a voice behind the screen next to me. Mr Mahmood was a wailing old sod opposite us both but none of us could actually move. To introduce myself to a voice I struggled to force my hand under the curtain around my bed and said, "Mike, I'm Jonathan. How do you feel?"

"Very weak and bruised," came the response, followed immediately by a complete projectile of vomit, straight into the breakfast dish that had just been placed on my bed. "Oh, my God, I'm sorry," came the rest of the sentence. "I always do that after anaesthetic, every time. It's so long ago, I had forgotten."

Not to feel neglected, I responded with a much noisier reciprocation.

"Oh my God, guys, the food's not that bad!"

"Don't know, we haven't started it yet," we answered in unison.

"Trouble with these bloody private patients, all this rich food they eat."

"Listen, I haven't eaten since Saturday."

"Well there you go then, it's Wednesday now."

"Give me water, stupid woman."

"Bugger off," came the twinned witty retort.

Needless to say, we all got wheeled away into the corridor while some poor orderly had to hose down the ward and then just the two of us were returned to restart the breakfast process, albeit just water, cereals and milk. Mr Mahmood didn't rejoin us, mainly because he was dead. It appeared that he had put off having his operation four times before and it was only after his second heart attack that he agreed to be operated on.

Well that sort of hoist a cloud over the day but it did strike up a sort of survival affinity between Mike and me; the only successful results (so far) of the Monday's bypass operations. In fact, the first to be released from the hospital would buy the first round, we agreed. There was a positive determination to escape the Grim Reaper standing at the bedside and be the first to be freed.

"Oh don't worry – you'll be out in about four or five days," advised the YTS student whom I felt sure I had seen fixing a leaky radiator earlier in the day. It turned out he was a surgeon, one of those people addressed as 'Mr.' rather than 'Dr.' He was certainly only about twelve.

The next movement was important. We were being wheeled off in our beds to separate rooms, our very own prison cells and there we would be wired for sound, or rather lack of sound as monitoring devices were attached to each available limb, and a few that I didn't think would be available for a long time to come.

"Now you press this button here for this, this one here for that and by tomorrow we shall get you into a shower. Nobody really wants to be that smelly, do they?"

Nothing to beat private medicine, eh?

"If you're a really good boy, we'll go in the shower together."

I don't think so, Big Lady, you're bigger than I am and I can't stand up yet, let alone show you what I'm made of. And I've got a large strip of sticking plaster running from my neck down to somewhere under my belly. That isn't going to be painless to remove.

## Chapter 3 – Jonathan's Pain and Anguish

The next morning, imagine my fear when the big lady decided I was ready for my shower.

"Are you going to take that bandaid off or am I? You won't feel much because your body is completely soft and relaxed."

Except I'm about to take off my three foot long plaster and everybody is going to know I'm a coward. Aaaargggh! You might have warned me, bitch. People on the river could have heard that. The River Nile.

And then I managed to do the really stupidest thing I have done for years. Having showered and patted myself dry, I was exhausted and lay down on my bed. I plugged myself into my mobile CD player and listened to one of those soothing empty numbers by Lionel Richie. No harm in that, I thought, until I had listened to most of one old CD and then, unannounced, I started to drift off. I was nearly gone when, finally, the music drove me back onto my deepest pillow and I thrust both arms up, down until, suddenly, there I was in severe pain, having tried to copy one of his tunes in my mind. The nurses from central control came running as my heart monitoring device stopped, just after I had been 'Dancing on the ceiling.'

"Can't believe it", they chorused. "Nobody has a heart bypass then tries shit like that – not even a stupid accountant."

I did.

Stupid boy.

## Chapter 4 – The Office Temp

Hi, everybody. I'm Fluff and I'm the office temp. OK, so my track record isn't brilliant but I have always started well. This job, however, is strange, very strange. Nobody seemed to know I was coming. Admittedly I joined as a temp and being a young, impressionable, blonde, single girl in the City, I didn't really know what to expect. The company was called Whelm, so we were all under Whelmed.

A small team of four ladies and our boss, a man who seemed nice but somehow always managed to get us to do whatever had to be done, whatever it took, including long hours, without shouting, demanding or bullying. He just commanded respect, especially in the pub when he looked after everybody. The girls were weird – Drama Queen Daisy, Eccentric Eleanor and Stroppy Sand, with me, of course, Claire. I was known by our boss as Fluffy – he said he thought I was nice and soft at the corners. I don't think he meant I was an air-head, although I am a natural blonde.

We had the weirdest job I have ever done. More than a billion dollars was being paid out of a receivership to people who didn't seem to want the money. My job, can you believe it, is to chase people who haven't banked cheques we have sent them, find out why and then make them pay in hundreds and thousands of dollars that are truly theirs. They are creditors of a group of failed insurance companies who would eventually recover to pay out most of the claims. There were two insurance brokers in the City in the 1980s that had fixed grillions of dollars of business in the North America Casualty market and then disappeared ignominiously owing millions, particularly to the insurance companies who had no option but to seek a Scheme of Arrangement with their creditors.

It was far more complicated than that but I am a blonde. All I know is that many of these people who are owed money, some of them lawyers, hospitals and insurance brokers are resident in North America so I have to wait until the afternoon before I can talk to them. (That's not because they're lazy but because they are more than five hours behind us in London). I love talking to a Southern drawl and hearing people say things like 'Y'all hev a real nice day now, d'ya hear?' I kept getting asked if I would be delivering the next cheque personally, like in Des Moines, Chicago, Philadelphia, Dade County, Bermuda and all over.

However, one of my first memories was being sat between Daisy and Ellie who were sometimes inseparable – but that was because they were either best friends or wanted to kill each other. Their moods were so unpredictable and Jonathan, our boss, was convinced that they were both mentally unstable. He said that he was too much of a gentlemen to deal with them – he would have 'either banged their bleedin' heads together or personally killed them jointly and severally if they couldn't grow up.' Some days I sew the seeds of discontent between them to see if they will take the bait, which invariably they do. It's far too easy. Daisy has been a ballerina but someone had dropped her one day – probably on her head. Ellie is always pretending her mistakes are somebody else's and she has made a lot. The trouble is that she believes she is an expert at reconciliations, which everybody has avoided through fear of having to listen to her explanations. She was also having a discreet affair with the Head of Human Resources – so discreet that we would lose her often and sometimes find her on the floor under her desk having heavy breathing telephone conversations with him.

Often the two girls would be the best of buddies and skip around arm in arm but more often they would roll around on the floor screaming and trying to pull each other's hair out. Each was in her late twenties.

Stroppy Sand, by comparison, was great. She knew how to wind everybody up and also knew how to get the boss to do some of those jobs that were nasty and nobody wanted to face. 'If I rub my tits on your arm, would you ring that bastard solicitor for the Californian Hospital Group for me, please, Dad? Oh, go on!' she would ask. 'Bog off,' came his response but eventually he always did it, if she promised NOT to rub her tits on his arm.

We were a great team until one day when the two hair tearers lost it big and Jonathan dragged them into his office and screamed at them. He never lost his temper but, if he did, he meant it and everybody knew. He never lost anything.

He offered them one chance – go forward together as a team or go out of the bloody door together, now. They cried and cried. He said that he was sick and tired of their childish behaviour and they 'can go home immediately and not come back until you can apologise to Fluff and Sandra for making their lives pure hell!' We didn't realise that they had but he was right. Neither came back and we got two new people, Ali Gee (another blonde girl who is brilliant but scatty) and Dev, another blonde girl who works very hard, or tells everybody she does. Ali's great and learned the job very quickly. Dev is good too, provided she has had less than three glasses of dry white wine, which isn't always the case, at lunchtime.

The new team is superb and we also have another two people working under the same boss. They work alongside us creating complicated database reports, using Crystal that enables us to keep control over the accounting for all this vast sum of money, particularly important because creditors have received only interim payments, never a full settlement. They also receive interest every time our distribution levels increase but we can't call it interest for tax reasons. No I don't know what any of that meant but I have to tell that to everybody whom I chase when they won't bank those cheques.

One very big hospital trust assumed the cheques were a scam, filed them first then, after one of my calls, handed them over to the police because they were convinced that nobody would just give them over $300,000 dollars! One of their directors had to resign over that when it hit the Los Angeles press. Ha!

I went through some traumas though and eventually decided that I needed to leave, mainly to get away from a bad relationship with one of the guys who joined us later. He was sexy and desirable but lots of other girls in the company found him the same and it screwed me up, since he couldn't say no to them. So I went, even though it meant I was leaving behind some really good friends. I spent almost a year travelling and even met up with some ex-colleagues from the same company who had always kept in touch, one from Australia and another from New Zealand. Secretly we all loved each other.

Almost a year later, having kept in touch constantly with the good people, I sent an email from Buenos Aires airport saying I was coming home to England and, bugger me, Jonathan had offered me my old job back before the plane took off.

But shortly after I got back into the job, Jonathan had an enormous row with his dickhead boss and was moved to a different section, the one that did all the reporting and had grown considerably. Since Jonathan was already in charge of that section, I suppose it was a sort of sideways movement but it was on the same floor.

The old team, however, stayed together socially and we all called Jonathan "Dad." He still arranged his wine tastings and rugby fixtures and we all went and got very happy and relaxed.

Well he is one of the long term servers (Whelm lifers, we used to call them) and Stroppy can still get her way with him, particularly since she has now transferred to his new team. She still knows how to threaten him with her tits.

Then, totally out of the blue, he came in one day and announced that he would not be in for some time as he had to go to hospital. He said he was going to be rebuilt and most people just joked and pulled his leg but I am squeamish, very, very squeamish and passed out before I even found out why.

When, of course, I found out why, I cried. In fact, we all did. The girls couldn't handle losing our "Dad" and we all went down the pub, our answer for just about everything. None of us came back that afternoon and by the time we came in the next morning, his desk was empty. I passed out.

Jonathan was due to go into a hospital just round the corner from the office and we all decided to visit him on the day after his operation. We stood in the reception of the London Bridge Hospital and discovered that we would all have to wait to see our "Dad" until after intensive care had taken place and, if all went well, we might be able to visit the following Sunday at about noon.

I passed out again.

However, three of us, Stroppy, Ali G and I were allowed to sneak in just before seven on the Wednesday evening only two days after his operation and, apart from Jonathan lying there looking very tired and weak, we managed to keep him occupied enough for eventually seven of us to sneak in without anybody noticing. Then, just as one of the nurses found us and was about to restrict our movements, or rather throw us out, Jonathan's bed jacket opened slightly and I saw the top of the scar going down his chest. Shit. It was over a foot long and very ugly. I had to get out and as I lunged for the door, somebody outside suddenly pulled it to, just as a Mr Mahmood was wheeled past in his coffin. Without ado, I passed out again.

I can wait until Sunday after all.

## Chapter 5 – Management

When I married him, Jonathan was the centre of my world. Well, perhaps not quite the centre because one or two little things were slightly off true. First, he drank too much, mostly beer though, so not a true drink problem. He had, however, wiped out my boss one Beajolais Nouveau day and he had taken our company director home at two in the morning when they had both been out on a serious bender, as only my director Ernest could manage. Jonathan had only driven him home to Surrey, even though he couldn't stand up or talk when he got home to me at six the next morning. All for the good of his career, he assured me.

Secondly, he spent too much time at the rugby club. OK, so he was an organiser, treasurer, bar secretary, a team captain and he sat on various committees. That all took up far too much time. I had to change that as well. So I joined in, because you do, if you are going to be subtle. There were many good guys there, and, of course, a few bad ones. But they all treated me well – they were nearly all gentlemen. I liked the good ones and their wives/girlfriends and loved ones, mostly.

The real trouble was that we also worked together. In fact, we met at work, albeit in different departments. Our first real encounter was a row. He said I got it all out of proportion. I said he was pompous and arrogant and he could stick his Financial Times up his arse. He said his offer to help was genuine. I said he was facetious and patronising but, yes, he could help me to stick his Financial Times up his arse.

Two weeks later, we had started our affair. He just metaphorically crept up on me when I wasn't paying attention. He said I was too busy talking to notice. I said that I was talking work and planning to get a new crew and water clerks down to a Portuguese ship that was arriving in dock that morning. He wondered what heated curlers and last night's Corry had to do with Portuguese ships. I said he should mind his own bloody business and get into his office and leave me alone. He said he thought his wife had left him. I said what did he mean thought she had left him? He said he hadn't seen her for two weeks. I said he was unobservant. He said he thought she was helping her mother recuperate from an operation but he had just found out the night before that his wife had gone out for the evening from her mother's house, which was quite interesting because her mother was going to leave for the States on holiday the next day – that's how unwell she was. Oh, and could he talk some sense into her stupid daughter?

So we went out for dinner that night and he wasn't that pompous and arrogant after all. We had both been looking for something different and this was different. We started our clandestine affair very gradually. It was so much of a secret that even I didn't know when I would see him. A bit like being married to him now, really.

It turned out that his wife confessed that she was having an affair. How dare she? He thought that he was supposed to be the philanderer. I didn't even know that he collected stamps. For six months we led an on/off existence of grabbed moments and occasional outbursts of controlled passion. Then I decided that he needed me and I appeared on his doorstep armed with six black plastic sacks. The next twelve took a few more days to smuggle out but finally we were together and I could start cleaning up his house. Any man who lives on his own for more than about three months and has a perfectly clean, tidy house, just has to be gay. I reckon he must have had about six months of Financial Times that 'needed reading'. And to think that that was what our first row was over. And our second.

For the next three years we worked in the same building, got transferred to different jobs, got moved to different offices, got moved into the same department, got moved onto the same project, with Jonathan as my daytime boss, got moved onto the biggest IT project the group had ever undertaken (with Jonathan still as the daytime boss) and only two people knew that we were having "a thing." Finally the project was due to come to fruition and full implementation, on the dot, six months late. We had booked a holiday together in the States for the month, unfortunately, after scheduled implementation. Obviously the project was at a climatic breaking point and there was no chance that we could go.

Rather than disclose that we had been living together for three years by now, and confess to pulling the wool over everybody's eyes, I decided that it would be easier simply to announce that I was going to get married. 'To whom?' came the instant response from virtually everybody (I had taught them good English). 'Him,' I said, pointing into the boss's office. 'What?' they all retorted. They all stood there with mouths gaping. Only one person of the 120 staff had the slightest idea, apart from the two confidantes. It was an amazing moment watching all of those people trying to think back quickly over the last three years for any indications. It had been great fun and kept us on our toes constantly.

At the point of getting married, most women have finally got what they have wanted. Then they try to change it to what they think they would like. Not I. What I had now was what I wanted. Well, apart from one or two minor blemishes – like time at the rugby club, tidiness, thoughtlessness, money, his 'girlies.' Oh, yes – his 'girlies.' Over the years he had worked with and enjoyed many of them. Not sexually, you understand, but as colleagues, friends, buddies. He just loved being a bloody smoothie. Inherited it from his father, I suppose, but he always stayed on the straight and narrow. I got to meet all of them and each assured me that they were just friends. Since I enjoy men's company, I could equate to that – apart from which, I would know the instant he strayed. And, if he did, he would be dead or, at least, Jonathan the Eunuch.

Shortly after the system was up and running and we had returned from our holiday, the company was sold and we were both referred to as key players and forced to stay. Jonathan had finished his project – I was now running the IT operation – and he recaptured his interest in the financial side of the new structure. He fought for months to take over the finance function and after an eternity of high profile squabbling with the new chairman, he eventually got his way.

Within two weeks, his hunches were proved correct and he demonstrated that the company would be trading insolvently if it continued without a capital restructure. He even proposed a new such structure but it would have required a new shareholders' investment programme. The new owners knew better, they thought, but within six weeks 117 employees were out of work and the Administrative Receivers were in. Despite an attempted 'Chapter 11' Scheme of Arrangement (an American term – there wasn't an English equivalent in UK law yet), there were no takers and only three of us remained to close the show down; Jonathan, the acting Finance Director, our head systems operator, Sharon, and I as the technical expert of the shipping operations and systems. Within six weeks, even we had finished and we turned out the lights and left.

As luck would have it, when we were in Florida a few months earlier, we met a Dutchman whom Jonathan knew. He was UK Managing Director of a competitor Dutch shipping line where Jonathan had worked some ten years earlier. Almost immediately after the lights went out, Jonathan started a new job as Head of Finance and IT for them, not only in the UK but in the building next door to the one we had just left. In the fullness of time, I joined a subsidiary company but the stuffing had been knocked out of me.

Jonathan did well but I was never happy and fell foul of an obnoxious Dutchman known by everybody, including his wife, as Tosspot, a shortened version of his proper name, Tissot van Hertzpot.

Jonathan and I never worked together after that and part of my life closed down. Jonathan, of course, carried on working as before and long hours and pressure were always part of his make up. I suppose that, at that stage, I began to retreat. I went through a couple of jobs but nothing like the old one I loved.

As part of our settlement from the original company (Jonathan had negotiated this before he had got seconded to the computer project), we walked away with a cheque for £10,000 and decided to invest it wisely by buying an old *fermette* in the Pas de Calais in Northern France. This would become a major source of pleasure, effort, heartache and grief over the years to come but it turned out to be one of those most sensible investment plans ever.

It was, however, a major financial drain and created a new stress. I suppose it was a material change of lifestyle, shortly before my younger daughter decided to have her two children. For three days a week, I became babysitter, grandmother, quasi mother and the doors opened on a whole new era. I wasn't really a 'mumsy' person before, but now that all changed. Little did I realise that for the next seven or eight years, I would become far 'mumsier' than I had ever been, although I knew that, theoretically, I could hand the children back each night. In practice, of course, instead they became a part of me. My "babies" became my protégées and, secretly, I am so proud that they understand and use expressions that went out in the 50s. What's that got to do with the price of fish? Not until the sun's over the yard arm! I can't walk home today, Nan, I've got bones in my leg. Well, nearly. Imagine my horror to hear 'Oh, gimme a break, Nan.' I respond with 'Ne touchez pas!' and 'that's a good idea – bonne idée' – so I always get the last word – well we have to, don't we?

However, the child minding is exacting, particularly when accompanied by a 50 mile round trip drive each day. These things all get stressful and trying until, one day, they have all crept up on you. And that was the day that Jonathan's heart blew it all out of the water. I would like to say that I can handle it all but sometimes even I get tired and this was all too much at once. Suddenly I had to sit down – metaphorically. I wanted to crawl under a shell and hide. If I'd had the energy, I would have thrown something.

Instead, I lit a cigarette and decided that the best thing was to go through the barrier where my two granddaughters go to school and no longer need my attention as they had done, take stock and find that place in the country where I can relax and enjoy the garden, sunshine and good company.

I don't know what the full effect of a triple heart by-pass is, but next Sunday at noon would be a good time to start finding out.

I don't want to work anymore, neither at a job nor at life. I have run my life, my children's lives, their children's lives, two husbands, six homes, waifs and strays and animals galore. Now it's my turn.

It's time to sit back and start afresh. I'm tired. Oh, so tired. They can all look after me now. Well from Sunday at noon, anyway.

## Chapter 6 – The Uphill Struggle

By now, I, Jonathan James, have worked out that whatever I am going to do after I get out of hospital I am going to look after myself better. Life in the fast lane was supposed to be the check out for less than 9 items in your supermarket trolley – not all this stuff.

So by day two, I had decided that I could go back to work after a few weeks and change. No more late nights, beers with the boys, rugby tours or cricket weeks. Debauchery was a thing of the past. Sod killing myself in the office. Training, delegation, relaxing and enjoying my next ten years while preparing myself for the following ten years and the ten after that. And the rest.

Then, on day three, I had to be weighed. Sounds easy enough, doesn't it? Actually it meant going up to the floor above. Someone would wheel me, surely. No, none of that – use the stairs – they're down the end of the corridor.

To say I leapt out of bed was a slight exaggeration – more of a 'roll over and start from the floor' exercise – similar to getting out of a Lotus Elan when you're obese. By the time I had advanced fifteen metres along the corridor, I was sitting on the floor, gasping for air. I had no more strength and I just wanted to be helped back into bed.

"Now, come on, Jonathan, we're not giving up already, are we?"

Well you might not be, Big Lady, I thought, but I bloody well am! At no time did anybody rush off to collect a trolley, chair or even stretcher, they just goaded me. So I forced myself another few metres further down the corridor and made it to the end. I turned the corner and saw my trolley, decorated, adorned and sort of floating. In my dreams.

"Well, you needn't think about that, decorated or otherwise. You're walking up the stairs," exhorted my big lady nurse. And she walked ahead to set the pace.

The next three days were full of that and by the time it came to the end of the week, I was raring to get out and head for 'them thar hills.' Or so I thought. First thing in the morning, my paper was always there but not today. Neither were breakfast nor fruit juices. In fact, I couldn't find anybody. Initially I thought of using the telephone but hadn't got a clue whom to ring. Press my emergency buttons seemed to be next. No buttons – they had all disappeared in my sleep. Disconnect my heart monitoring leads – already gone. Hey, come on, Guys – this is all being paid for – I'm supposed to be a valued client. Still nobody around. I even walked to a few of my neighbours' private rooms. All empty – beds changed – nobody there.

Suddenly this horrible fear came over me – I'm dead. Yes, that's it – I have slipped away during the night and there was nobody to find anything for me – I didn't need anything any more – ever again! How weird. Do I feel any different? Probably but I can't be sure. I'm not happy about this. I have too many things unfinished – too many things to do, to say, to convey. Too many goodbyes, words of encouragement, too much unfinished business. People, friends, loved-ones – too many things I need to tell them.

Bugger this, I'm going down to the heart monitoring room. They should know what has happened. They're watching me, from a distance, constantly. They're only down a floor at the far end of the floor. Yes, I'll go there. So, for about three steps, I stride with aim and grim determination. By the fourth step, this isn't one of my better ideas. By about the tenth, I realise that something was wrong. My knees feel like jelly, my heart, eyes, brain are all working – it is just the limbs. Co-ordination is not easy. But at least I can now see the door to the nurses' monitoring room. Only another ten or so steps. So long, oh, so long. Seems to get further and further away.

With merely three or four steps to go, I know that I'm not going to make it. The door handle is now in focus. It is one of those brass heavy things that I just know is going to be locked. One more pace, that's all. Even now I know I won't have the strength to open it and my only hope is that I can throw myself down onto it and force it open.

As I do, the door opens instantly and I all but fall into the room to be greeted by an enormous cheer, whistles, clapping and a complete group of friends and family who are obviously determined to give me an instant heart attack. They're all there – my wife, two step daughters, three sisters, my brother, that lovely, mad Irish lady, the beautiful Sophie, daughter of the wine family, Valerie, the very desirable daughter of the French builder, the gorgeous IT girl who can drink Guinness standing on her head, all my staff, beautiful every one of them – my goodness, everybody is here! Instantly all the lovely nurses appear with even more hugs and kisses and even a chair, into which I collapse immediately. Oh, yes – there are even some guys there too; Cider Jim with Alan, still looking like shit from the night before, Big Pete, desperate, as ever, for a cigarette. And then, the world's best secretary, who organised everything and everybody – thank goodness – the list seems never ending.

So typical of these lovely people, not a single champagne cork has popped – they've already done that and the drinks have been poured and are now being handed round. Everybody takes a glass that is charged with champagne from the wine cellar's own marque and a spooky silence has crept over us all. As though rehearsed, the two French ladies step forward and cross arms as they raise their glasses and say jointly, surprisingly in English, 'Welcome back, Jonathan, from all of us. Everyssing is ready for you.'

As I sit here, I can feel everybody desperate to talk at once, to explain, to contribute. 'You will 'eff to do nuzzink except approve ze plans, but we will not take no for ze answer. Tomorrow we 'eff arranged ze transport and everyssing will be eazee. All ees taken care off and your ssree months' rebuilding will start.'

I understand nothing but gradually others start to move forward to shake hands or kiss and I still don't have a clue what it is all about. As I sit here mesmerised, I begin to start guessing, to work out what it all means. The first clue revealed itself when number one step daughter explained that the St John's Ambulance Brigade, of which she is a member, is taking delivery of a brand new vehicle in a few days' time and we have permission to borrow it tomorrow for a couple of days before it gets handed over formally to take me home and to my convalescence in a much healthier climate.

France! That's it – they have decided. For my three month's recuperation, I shall go to the land where bitter doesn't exist (except when we beat them at rugby) and a couple of glasses of Bordeaux a day are mandatory. Salty Marmite is not available either and any cheese that would be bad in England for pregnant ladies is perfectly acceptable all across France (Brie and Camembert, for example). As the idea begins to formulate in my mind, I realise that I am supposed to spend three months building up my heart and the rest of my body in preparation for returning to work. It is beginning to appeal very highly.

I have always wanted to retreat to a commune in France to start writing and get away from accountancy. Of course, I have no plans to stop working yet but I have been severely tempted to extend my light, but prosperous, (for them) involvement in the family wine business. At my pace, I reckon that getting them up and running technologically, would take time but I have time now – three months, for example. Plenty of time to complete the website, together with a link to the British, to teach the French and the British the art of the internet hug.

Oh, dear, here we go again. Given that I have already had my life overrun with activity, can I face it again? This is different. Although it has already been said that Death is nature's way of giving you a warning, nothing like this will ever affect me — I am determined. So determined that I need to step back from everything before I jump to any conclusions, I need to be able to look at life from a different angle.

I'm not going to die – I am going to beat this and emerge from the other side with a whole new outlook on life. I don't need to know when the ten year count starts, I need to know that it hasn't yet and I'm not going to let it.

Just one step back, outside my skin,
I look down on my life within
I breathe a sigh and all release
At bedside now, I rest in peace.

## The Awakening

By Jessie Hobson

The ivy is growing
So thick round the tree
The cat cannot climb it
Nor the fox may not see
The nestlings close hidden
In bedding of hay.
The hen bird's a-brooding
While Father's away.

He's searching for insects
And grubs for their food.
He's swooping and diving
Through shades of the wood.
He soon will return
To the nest and his mate,
A beakful of goodies
For which they await.

Little mouths will be gaping
With eager request
For morsel or sop
In their throats to be pressed.
Now Mother is flying
Away on the wing.
It really has happened,
It truly is spring.

# About the Authors

## Paul Bunn

45 years old and works for a telecoms company. I became interested in writing about 10 years ago and then joined Writers Anonymous to help fulfil my dream of being published. I live in Rayleigh, Essex and am married with two children. To relax I like nothing better than a game of snooker with friends.

## Colin Butler

Born in Tottenham, but a fervent Arsenal supporter, he is married with 2 children and 6 grandchildren and currently lives in Thorpe Bay.

After retiring from a career in Local Government, he took a creative writing course and since then has had a number of poems published.

He rejoined Writers Anonymous in June 2007 and is also a member of Rocheway Writers Circle and is a keen photographer.

## Nicolette Coleman

It has always been my ambition to write a book as reading has been my favourite pastime since my childhood. I have had various articles published in church magazines, but "Shouting in a Vacuum" is my first novel, and I am hoping it will be in print very soon.

After two creative writing courses I decided to join the Writers Anonymous writing group which came into existence towards the end of the second course.

## Jessie Hobson

A retired widow; joined Writers Anonymous as an interest in the wake of her husband's death, together with knitting, crochet and dancing.

She has lived half her life in Barnet, Hertfordshire and half in Shoeburyness, Essex. Loves the Norfolk Broads, preferably afloat and has seldom travelled abroad, unlike her three adult offspring.

## David Shaer

A numerically challenged chartered accountant, my main ambition was to get past writing unpublishable letters to The Times. I played rugby during five decades but was only ever going to be the player most likely to be lent to the opposition if they were short. I also need a large atlas when driving, but only to see over the steering wheel. I was starting to get a complex about life when I was ejected from French evening classes, so I joined a creative writing course and now I shall let you judge whether I should go back and start again.

## Simon Woodward

After working consistently in I.T. for 18 years I decided it was time to forego the strictly logical world of computing and take up writing in my spare time. I don't think I'll ever truly get to grips with this literary world but I'm certainly having great fun finding out about it, though I think my wife, Yve, is not so enamoured by my frequent requests asking 'what do you think of this?'

That said, without her, I don't think my two children's books would have ever seen the light of day.

Printed in the United Kingdom
by Lightning Source UK Ltd.
129899UK00001B/91-132/P